"Look here, Phil.
This has to end."

Julian leaned across the table as he continued, "I'll take you to Lagos and put you on a liner, and you can leave the dissolution of that bogus ceremony in my hands."

"It is in your hands!" she cried furiously. "Go ahead with it, but don't expect to ship me around like a sack of meal. I'm sick of your insensitiveness—I can do without your protection—"

"Stop it, will you?" he said savagely. "The minute we get together sparks fly—your nerves must be cracking."

"My nerves were sound enough till you got to working on them," Phil choked. "Go for your holiday, Julian. Find a woman in Lagos and laugh with her about the kid down in Goanda who fancies herself in love with you...."

She got up quickly and ran to the bedroom.

Harlequin
Presents Collection

A new series... of old favorites!

Harlequin has been publishing its widely read
Presents series for more than eight years.
These beautiful romance novels, written by the
world's most popular authors of romantic fiction,
have become the No. 1 best-selling love stories
in more than eighty countries.

Now we are pleased to make available to you, our
more recent readers, a chance to enjoy many of the
early *Presents* favorites you may have missed.

We know you'll enjoy these carefully selected
volumes. They come from our not-too-distant
past—a past we are proud of, a past we are
sure you'll love!

ROSALIND BRETT

they came to valeira

Originally published as Harlequin Presents #43

Harlequin Books

TORONTO • LONDON • LOS ANGELES • AMSTERDAM
SYDNEY • HAMBURG • PARIS • STOCKHOLM • ATHENS • TOKYO

Harlequin Presents edition published May 1974
ISBN 0-373-15002-4

Second printing August 1974
Third printing February 1977
Fourth printing March 1977
Fifth printing May 1977
Sixth printing January 1979

This *Harlequin Presents Collection* edition
published September 1980

Original hardcover edition published in 1950
by Mills & Boon Limited

CHAPTER I

NOONTIDE heat seeped like treacle through the wire grid and the venetian blinds. The room sweltered, yet it was cooler than the palm-thatched veranda, where flies kept up a continuous humming and other, less tolerable, pests darted from between the floorboards, while lizards clung motionless to the outer walls, their pulsing visible to the naked eye.

Julian Caswell leaned both arms on his desk and surveyed in turn his two visitors. The mission doctor, grey-faced, grey-garbed, an apathetic dullness in his eyes; and Sister Harrington, poker-backed, her skin a tropic yellow and pitted with the legacy of some disease contracted and mastered in the course of her duties.

"I've been on this island just four days," he said, "and have met plenty of trouble on the plantation, without chasing more among the white population. Surely people of your experience can deal with this girl?"

"If she were the tough type we'd have no difficulty," the doctor answered. "But she isn't. From what I remember of her father—he died four years ago in a leopard hunt on the mainland—he was the typical, well-bred Englishman. I believe her mother came of good South African stock, but the tropics ruined her—morally. After only a few months here with her husband she left the island with another man. The children, this girl and her brother, were educated at boarding-schools in England and South Africa. When the father was killed the son arrived to carry on the shipping agency, and he managed very well right up to his first illness, a year or so ago. Then the girl came, to be with him and help him in the office."

"And now the young man has died of fever and this child is alone," Sister Harrington put in sharply. "She lives in a bungalow on the cliffs—with no other companion than a half-breed Portuguese woman servant. An impossible situation for a girl."

"She has no neighbours?"

"Several, of a type. Bryson, who owns the native store, a

5

forestry man and your own two overseers. No women."

"You've already asked her to live at the mission?"

"Entreated, Mr. Caswell," the woman corrected him, "and we've threatened to demand that the Portuguese authorities send her to British territory—Lagos or Freetown. Unfortunately, although this is a Portuguese island, we seldom see an official and, in any case, I doubt if these people would act. They would cast the onus on to an Englishman, like yourself."

"Has she any money?"

"More than enough for her needs. It is now two months since young Nigel Crane died, and the agency has been taken over by Burfords. She hasn't the smallest reason for staying on Valeira."

"Not what you and I would call a reason, maybe," said Julian. "How old is she?"

"Seventeen."

A precocious child who could doubtless do with a spanking. Julian had met the type in Kenya. Sophisticated youngsters, spoiled by a surfeit of men and unrationed drink. They matured into greedy sensualists, like Lilias. Hell, why think of her now?

"What do you want me to do?"

The doctor stirred from his lethargy. "Go and see her, Mr. Caswell. Explain to her the terrible dangers that surround a girl in her position. Both Sister Harrington and I have tried, but perhaps we have not spoken plainly enough, or have failed to emphasize the . . . er . . . appetites of men who are shut off from the diversions of the mainland."

"I offer her a choice between living at the mission and deportation . . . is that it? Her name is Crane?"

"Philippa Crane," said Sister Harrington, gathering a pair of stringy white gloves from her lap and planting her black laced shoes ready to support her small weight. "I sincerely hope you will succeed in persuading her to go home to England."

The doctor got up. "We have worried a great deal about the girl. Please get in touch with us after you have seen her."

Julian promised, and followed them out to the shabby

6

old bush car which, apparently, was driven by Sister Harrington, for the doctor sank into the left seat and assumed a comatose posture, his head dipped into his shoulders, his hands slack between his knees. Half doped, thought Julian, without emotion. At thirty-five, with ten years in the tropics behind him, a man does not hesitate to label symptoms and shrug off the victims. It was each for his own skin in this steaming Hades.

He came back to the living-room and poured whisky and water. For the next six months he needed labour, plenty of it. The cacao groves had to be cleared of fierce growths of weeds, the trees pruned and stripped of neglected pods. Then there were the oil palms to be exploited and increased numerically, and other markets to be opened.

Work. Months, years of it. Well, that was what he had come here for. Work and solitude. Freedom from clubs and polo-playing, from drink parties and scandals. Freedom from women like Lilias and their rank-tasting aftermath. You don't find such women in the West African islands, where the plantations are chiefly owned by Portuguese, and the daily dose of quinine is indispensable.

There was little on Valeira to attract the idle traveller, and much to deter him. At many points on the West African coast he could enjoy the same atmosphere of lush palms and prodigal vegetation against a background of perpetually roaring surf, with far less risk to health and mental balance.

He swallowed his drink and called the houseboy to dispose of the tumblers on the desk. Then he had lunch—a peppery soup, fish and the inevitable pawpaw salad—and soon afterwards drove straight through the estate to where Drew, the chief superintendent, was finishing his sandwiches and beer beneath the shadowy branches of a rubber tree.

Drew was small and sandy, a little younger than Julian and vague about everything but his job. Mr. Caswell measured perfectly to his idea of a boss. The height and width of shoulder, the lean dark features that sometimes appeared deceptively weary, the authoritative air and unsmiling mouth, combined to impress Drew profoundly. In four days he had fallen completely under the spell of Julian Caswell.

They talked of the new track and the division of labour over the tasks before them.

"Send Crawford to the mainland for more men," said Julian. "Three hundred men on a six months' contract, the usual wages, housing and medical service."

"Crawford's never done it before," Drew told him. "We've always got our labour through Matt Bryson."

"The trader? What's his standing on the plantation?"

"He hasn't any. Matt moved in years ago, built the store and has run it ever since. He has friends among the skippers of the freighters."

"All the same, I think we'll send Crawford this time. He strikes me as weakish, and the responsibility will stiffen him." Julian paused. "You and he live together, don't you?"

"We share one of the houses on the cliff."

"Get along all right?"

Drew nodded. "He has moods, but he's only twenty-six."

"What sort of moods?"

"Nerves. He doesn't drink much."

Nerves, in a fellow of twenty-six. Julian remembered something. "There's a girl living near you—Philippa Crane. D'you see much of her?"

"No, she stays home every night. Crawford likes her, but she's just a kid. Bryson's her closest neighbour; then Clin Dakers, the forestry man."

Julian said: "Tell Crawford to come and see me first thing in the morning. He'd better have a couple of weeks' leave in Lagos, and get it out of his system. He can recruit labour for us at the same time."

He left the car and mounted one of the hefty mules that were tethered near the track. The going was exasperatingly slow, through bamboo thickets, skirting young forests of tree ferns, sparing a glance now and then for the criminally neglected cacao.

It was late when he completed his tour of the plantation, which here was scarcely distinguishable from the primeval jungle that surrounded it. The early darkness had already fallen. His car stood where he had left it, and Drew had thoughtfully had a space hacked bare, so that he could reverse. At the house he took a bath and got into fresh shorts and shirt. The boy, one he had picked up at Cape Palmas and brought to the island, had braised a chicken and cooked rice and brown beans to go with it. The local coffee was good; it had a richer flavour than the stuff he'd grown in Kenya, or perhaps it was mellowed by the sense of isolation from his fellow-beings.

He knelt in front of the bookshelves and chose a novel. He had decided on two hours' relaxation every evening, and though reading fiction was not one of his vices, it would have to do till he was more established and able to follow more agreeable pursuits. Passing the desk, he saw the notepad scrawled with words and figures, and bent to read. Half-way down, between a reminder about supplies and a query on kola nuts, he saw the name "Philippa Crane."

Julian lit a cigarette and walked to the wire-screened doorway. Some time he would have to go and see this girl and make her realize the nuisance she had become. The mission people were right. You couldn't allow a girl to live alone among men in any climate, let alone that of Valeira. And Bryson next door. A middle-aged, pot-bellied trader who was reputed to have an apricot-skinned "wife" over on the Novada estate, the other side of the mountain. Oh yes, Julian had heard most of the gossip on his first day, from the voluble little Latin who had welcomed him: Rodrigo Astartes, owner of the Novada cacao plantation.

He thrust open the screen with his foot and went out to the veranda. The miraculous coolness drew him down on to the path, which widened at the storehouse into the plantation track. Tonight, he followed the narrow trail through the trees which led to the shore. Leaving the rough dip to the waterfront, he turned left up the slope towards the scattered houses which overlooked the beach from a long, low promontory. All showed lights, a couple brilliant, the others dim, as though the occupants were out card-playing or drinking with neighbours.

As Julian climbed it came to him that the nearest bunga-low, glowing brightly from every window, was the Crane girl's. A smart place, what he could make out of it between

9

the black fans of the palms in the garden. Why not call on her now and get it over?

He pushed open the gate, walked along a straight, weed-free path and up the veranda steps, gave two crisp knocks on the white wooden door, and waited. After a couple of minutes he tapped again, more peremptorily. Another minute ticked by and he slid back his cuff to see the time. A quarter to nine. Quite early yet.

The door swung in about eighteen inches, and a girl stood in the opening. A slim girl in a short yellow skirt and white blouse, her hair a tawny cloud around a small pale-gold face. Her eyes were large and fixed upon him, her red mouth had straightened determinedly.

"Good evening," he said pleasantly. "You may have heard of my arrival—Julian Caswell, the new manager of the plantation. . . ."

He had got so far before realizing that the girl was clasping a tiny little automatic, and had levelled it slightly left of the third button of his shirt.

CHAPTER II

PHIL spoke in a sweetly husky voice. "I'm sorry to greet you like this, but I never entertain after dark. I have nothing whatever to do with the plantation, but if you wish to see me about something, please call again tomorrow."

"Put up the weapon, child," he said curtly. "I've no designs on your virtue. If I ever have the urge again to kiss a woman—which is highly improbable—she won't be a seventeen-year-old. I want a chat with you."

"I'm sorry," she repeated. "If you come any nearer I shall shoot. So please go."

Julian, of course, had no intention of going. He ducked, swiped at her hand and caught the gun as it fell. The next second his foot was jammed between door and frame, and he entered the hall nonchalantly, his smile cool and appraising.

The girl took it well. With a slight shrug she indicated the door to the lounge and went in ahead of him. Julian crossed to the half-open drawer of a writing-table and dropped the automatic inside.

"This is where you keep it? I hope you lock the drawer during the day. Sit down and let's be friendly."

She inclined her head towards an easy chair but herself took a tapestry-seated ladderback and clasped her thin, capable hands in her lap. Julian sat on the arm of the easy chair, regarding her thoughtfully.

Phil Crane looked too intelligent to be treated as a recalcitrant child and too young to be accorded the status of a woman. Her wide, smooth forehead had an innocence about it which he had never before noticed in girls of her age, and the hazel eyes were startlingly clear and unwavering. She was entirely unselfconscious.

"Ever used that gun?" he asked abruptly.

"Only once, apart from practice. I heard a noise in the garden one night and fired. Next morning I found a dead monkey."

"Some shot," he commented.

She smiled, an unaffected curving of the mouth. "I told Matt Bryson about it and he didn't believe I'd killed the thing in the dark. He rigged up a target and we had a match. I scored eleven out of twelve, and he made ten. He gave me a length of silk as a prize."

"Bryson?" Julian frowned. "What sort of neighbour is he?"

"Grand." Her lids lowered. "He always helped during my brother's fevers, and he was here when Nigel died. I didn't have to do a thing, except . . . grieve." The crack in her voice mended swiftly. "Matt may be the rogue they say he is, but he's a marvellous friend."

"It's unwise to trust anyone in these places," said Julian sharply. "A man of Bryson's reputation doesn't dispense kindness without a motive. You should keep clear of him. What about the other men who live near?"

"They're all right," she said slowly, staring at him curiously. "I don't see much of Mr. Dakers . . . he's away a good deal. Mr. Drew sort of looks through me, but he doesn't mind my going up for a game of tennis on Sundays with Roger Crawford. They have quite a presentable court."

Julian inserted a cigarette between his lips and snapped shut the case.

"May I have one?" she murmured.

He offered them, and bent forward with his lighter. "Why do you remain on the island?"

She answered through a veil of smoke. "This is my home. Where else could I go?"

"You have a mother somewhere."

She leaned back. "So you've heard all about me. Now I know why you're here tonight. Someone from the mission has been to see you."

He admitted it with a nod, and persisted, "What about your mother?"

"She left my father when I was ten, but I haven't seen her since I was seven, when I started boarding-school in England. My parents were out East before they came here."

"You've no idea where she is?"

"None. Sometimes I wonder, but I'm not really anxious to meet her, though I don't hate her as Nigel did. He was eight years older than I," she explained, "and he remembered her. I'm afraid I don't."

"You came here from South Africa?"

"From Cape Town. Nigel and I both lived with a family there to begin with. Then he came to Valeira and I went to another boarding-school. I was horribly lonely, but he insisted that I must be much older before I could join him."

Julian took a deep pull at his cigarette and for want of an ashtray near by flicked ash into the cream carpet and ground his heel on it. She got up and fetched a tiny flat bowl, which she placed on the chair arm, close to his knee.

"You've never been married, have you, Mr. Caswell?"

He smiled briefly. "One loses some of the graces in the jungle. This house surprised me. Carved cabinets and tapestries are rare on the Equator."

"The materials are rotting," she said regretfully, "and the legs of the furniture have to be stood in tins of paraffin to keep it free from ants." She was in front of him, rather awkwardly pressing out her cigarette. "I keep a little whisky. Would you like some?"

"Do you drink it yourself?"

12

"No. To be candid, I seldom smoke, either, but I didn't care for the way you shut up your case right under my nose. I'm a person, not a tiresome infant."

"You could be a tiresome person," he suggested. "In fact you are. Why don't you go and live at the mission?"

"The doctor's a half-wit and Sister Harrington's haunted. I'd go nuts living with such people in a hospital atmosphere."

Julian sighed. "Look here," he said. "You can't go on living among men. You've got through so far because they've respected your feelings for your brother. You might be safe for a few more weeks, but sure as death there'll come a night when one of them will be cock-eyed enough to . . . well, forget himself. You're not a fool," he tacked on roughly. "You haven't lived on the island a year without learning that the men—white men —fight among each other over nothing. There are times when the heat and monotony rouse passions in them which are ungovernable—times when a girl wouldn't stand much chance." He paused and stubbed his cigarette. "I'm not *asking* you to go and stay at the mission. I'm *telling* you that if you don't I'll have you deported, if I have to carry you aboard ship myself."

Phil had backed away from the steely glint in the grey-blue eyes.

"D'you think I enjoy being alone?" she demanded, all the huskiness gone from her voice, leaving it hard and angry. "I'm not sub-human. This is the only home I've ever known. My father used to write me letters from this house —and then Nigel did the same. He and I were here together for a while. . . ."

"Cut out the sentiment and be sane. What's the good of four walls and a lot of memories in a place of this kind? A kid like you should be having harmless fun with boys and girls of your own age. You're not wanted here."

"It so happens," she replied without a tremor, "that I'm not wanted anywhere, but on Valeira I do at least possess a furnished house and a couple of friends. Perhaps you believe that being the boss of this part of the coast entitles you to dictate to us who happen to live here. It doesn't, though. My father paid cash for our land and the section of foreshore that goes with it."

"All right," he said. "I'll make you an offer on the company's behalf. A girl with money can soon find friends in London or Cape Town."

Phil's smile was shrewd. "What makes you think I'd be safer in a big city? Isn't it simply that you want me out of your way—off your conscience? For some reason you dislike women and you're trying to take it out on me. Well, you needn't bother, Mr. Caswell. I'll stay in this house as long as I please. I can take care of myself."

Irritably, Julian stood up. "You're just as precocious as I expected, which doesn't alter the fact that you're out of your setting and a menace to the peace of the men. You must either go to the mission or take the next British boat."

"I shall do neither," she returned quietly. "You've done your duty, Mr. Caswell, and now you can go back to your lone house in the cacao and forget all about me."

He twisted towards the door. "You have about a week to decide, there's a boat in at the week-end, and it's due out next Wednesday. Good night."

He left the lounge door ajar, but closed the main door with a thud. Phil heard his firm footsteps on the path, the creak and crack of the gate.

Supercilious beast. He needn't think his domineering tactics would scare her off the island before she was ready to leave. Tomorrow she would consult with Matt; he'd know how to deal with Mr. Almighty Caswell.

Smiling to herself—for she had come out of the encounter with her shield unmarked—Phil thrust home the bolts and doused the lamps. She peered through a back window and saw that the candle still burned in Manoela's room. Pity she'd forgotten to tell the he-man how good Manoela was with a knife. A scream would have brought the coloured woman running, the knife would have flashed through the air and sunk between the masculine shoulders. Manoela's was a comforting presence.

She kicked off her sandals, and unfastened her skirt. Some time soon she must make new clothes. The few school-girl garments she had brought from Cape Town had become tight across the chest and rode well above her

14

knees, and one couldn't go about in shorts all the time. It would be rather nice, she mused, as she slipped between cool sheets and adjusted the mosquito net, to wear the white silk she had won from Matt.

Phil was in her garden next morning padding with bare feet through the mist-sodden grass and pulling a weed here and there, when Matt Bryson hailed her from his veranda, a hundred yards away.

" 'Morning," she cried. "I need some paternal advice. Shall I come or will you call on your way down?"

"I was out last night," he bawled back, "and the hang-over's a beggar. You'd better come here, lovey."

She grinned and popped back to her room for shoes. About once every ten days Matt spent an evening on the waterfront; regularly the following morning his eyes were bloodshot and he confessed to burning needles under his ribs and a tongue like sheepskin; invariably he spent the early hours on the long wicker bench on his veranda, a glass of lime and soda-water at his side.

She found him stretched there now, in singlet and slacks, hardly a figure to admire, but to Phil his grossness was as natural as the moon and the stars. It was an indispensable adjunct to his generosity and good humour. Beneath a hairy chest and a superfluity of flesh Matt possessed an understanding heart.

"Have you had any breakfast?" she asked.

"Don't!" he groaned. "Last night I ate tinned pork and guinea-fowl and drowned them in rum."

"In that case you'd better fast today, and drink nothing stronger than coffee. If I were you, Matt, I'd be ashamed."

"So you should, lovey. I'm just a no-good hunk of food and liquor. Find me a cheroot, will you?"

"In your pocket?" She delved into the shapeless jacket which hung over the back of a grass chair, and waited till the cheroot had kindled to the flame of a match before enquiring: "Matt, have you met the new plantation manager?"

He nibbled and spat out a fragment of tobacco. "Not socially. He came to the store a day or two ago—said I'm to accept no chits signed by overseers unless they bear his initials. A flinty sort of chap, but I reckon the plantation

15

needs him after Mason. Caswell hasn't paid you a visit, has he?"

"Yes, at about nine last night."

"Didn't you shoot him?"

"No, but I wished afterwards that I had. He threatens to dump me on the next boat for England."

"Oh." Matt's head rolled back into the middle of the cushion and he lay staring through a grey haze at the sloping roof of the veranda. "How did he put it over?"

"A little more strongly than Sister Harrington. The lone girl among men—dangerous for me and I'm disturbing their peace. Rot, of course, but he'd got the idea into his head and there was no chasing it out."

"I don't know about rot," said Matt meditatively. "You don't upset my balance because I'm more than old enough to be your father and I could never regard you as anything but a good kid. Drew is out, too. Which leaves Dakers—who's thirty and an unknown quantity—and young Crawford."

"The great Julian named you as the arch-fiend."

"The devil he did!" he exclaimed, without rancour. "At that, he's not far out. Look at me."

"You're human," she said, "which is more than he is. I've a horrible suspicion he meant it, Matt."

"You bet he did. For one thing you're a jarring note in his community of men, and for another he has no time for women."

"How did you know that?"

"It gets around. A skipper from the Coast told me Caswell came from Kenya to Cape Palmas and began working there. An official's wife made a play for him—he's not bad-looking and I daresay he can be charming when he likes—anyway, he had to get out. He'd already had an affair with a woman in Kenya which left him despising the sex. He took the job on Valeira to be rid of them."

"I'm not one of his employees," she said stubbornly. "He's not going to boss me."

There was a long moment of silence. Matt smoked, gulped some lime and soda and made small noises. Phil stayed sitting on the veranda rail, her gaze moodily on the tangle of bougainvillea which Matt could never be induced to prune.

"It's tough," said Matt at last, "but I can see his point. The decentest men are apt to behave strangely when they have the heat to contend with as well as a lack of women. There is a way out, though. You're rather young, but Roger Crawford's keen on you. You could marry him."

Phil didn't answer. She liked Roger, and once, when she had hurt her wrist at tennis and he had kissed it, his touch had mildly excited her.

"That way you could keep your own house," Matt went on. "I believe Crawford has a five-year contract, so he should be going home in about two years. By that time you and he would have grown together, and he probably has a family in England who'd welcome you. It's worth considering."

"It might be if . . . well, I just don't fancy marriage, with Roger or anyone else. I want to stay as I am till I can make up my mind what to do with the future. Matt, I wish you were my father!"

"Well, I'm not, lovey. But when I've got my legs again I'll go and see Caswell for you. Don't expect too much."

CHAPTER III

JUST before lunch Phil slid down the cliff and made her way along the glaring beach to the lagoon for a bathe. There was never anyone about at that time, and she could step out of her shorts, take a swim and dry out all in the space of half an hour. Except on days when huge breakers splintered over the reef of rocks and washed right up to the foot of the cliff, the water was calm and languorous, the perfect cradle for an overheated body. Out there the sun could do its damnedest.

Lying in the lilting water, Phil remembered that the beach of the lagoon belonged to the plantation. If he wished to be officious, Julian Caswell could forbid her to bathe there, but she hardly thought he would. Apart from the lagoon, the whole of this stretch of ground was rock-bound; her own few yards of foreshore were worthless.

She turned on to her front, swam strongly for a while and then made her way back through the bush behind the beach towards home.

Phil had worn a path through this bush. As she emerged from it today she saw that a man sat on her veranda; a young man with square features and straight fair hair that flopped over his right brow.

"Hello, Roger," she called, as the gate swung back and he sprang up. "Why aren't you growing cocoa this morning?"

"Don't ever let our chief hear you call it cocoa. Till it's brown powder in a tin it's cacao. I've got some news for you, Phil. I'm going on short leave in Lagos."

"You lucky dog. How soon?"

"Tomorrow. The *Amirez* sails at dawn for Libreville. I'll get another freighter from there up the coast. He's given me the job of recruiting more labour."

"How long will you be gone?"

"About three weeks."

"Stay to lunch and tell me about it."

Roger looked at her quickly. Since Nigel's death she hadn't invited him in for a meal. "Lord, I wish I could, but he told me to go back to the sheds and supervise the last of the loading. I hopped across to tell you in case I mightn't see you again before I leave. Phil"—his voice dropped a tone—"you wouldn't change the invitation, would you . . . make it dinner tonight, or an hour together after dinner?"

She hesitated, conscious of his flush and a tiny spurt of exhilaration in her own veins.

"I don't see why not. Come early, about seven."

He gave her a strangled little smile, gripped her fingers and dropped them, said, "I'll be here!" and loped away down the path.

After lunch she rested on her bed with a book, but later, when Manoela had brought tea and the windows on the shaded side of the house admitted a grateful breath of cooler air, Phil let her thoughts dwell dispassionately on Roger Crawford.

He had told her a little about his family: his father a bank clerk in a small industrial town and his sister married to a back-street bookseller. Roger, like most agreeable young men, had a strong streak of sentimentality. He visualized the day when he would step ashore at Liverpool and hug his parents; the conventional wanderer's return. When his time on Valeira was ended he was going into partnership with his brother-in-law; and Phil could imagine no drearier fate than to be planted amid the broad-vowelled middle-class in a grey north-country town with a husband she had married for convenience.

However, by the time Roger presented himself, his hair sleek, his white jacket and slacks crisp from the laundry boy, Phil had forgotten her dismal meditations, and was faintly thrilled at the prospect of entertaining a clean-cut young overseer to dinner. In his honour she wore a green linen frock which reached the bend of her knees and allowed a fraction more breathing space in the bodice than her other dresses.

They ate a pot roast and sweet potatoes mashed with butter and seasoning, and followed it up with a tinned compôte of fruit and whipped tinned cream, and rye biscuits topped with soft cheese and served with tender green bamboo shoots. They took coffee on the veranda, which was a treat for Phil; it was a long time since she had smelt such a cool, night-scented breeze. The ceaseless roar of the sea was narcotic.

Roger broke into the calm silence. "This morning I was tickled pink at the thought of a holiday from the island. Tonight I'm less sure. Will you miss me, Phil?"

She smiled. "I shall miss the tennis. Clin Dakers is the only other player and he's gone off again today for a spell in the woods."

"I don't like Clin. I'm glad he'll be away while I'm here."

"What's wrong with him?"

"He's too smooth and cocksure. There's something queer about a chap who consistently wins at poker. And I loathe the way he talks."

"You mean what he talks about?"

He nodded. "If it isn't the lions he's killed in the Congo, it's the women he's floored."

"With his looks and physique both might be true," she reminded him. "Clin's single-track, but so are the other men here. Mr. Drew is only alive to his work, Matt exists chiefly for that round tummy of his, and you are devoured by the wondrous vision of a bookshop in small-town Lancashire."

"That isn't true," he protested. "I never think of home except when the mail comes in—and that's not often. God knows, I try hard enough to keep my keel even. It's not too easy, when you're tied to the same four walls with a man like Drew. He can sit for hours doing nothing."

"How frightful," she said soberly. "I should throttle him."

He laughed, but without pleasure, and let a full minute elapse before stating, "As soon as you're eighteen, Phil, I'm going to ask you to marry me."

Well, here it was. She had only to answer: "Don't let's wait till I'm eighteen, Roger. Let me go with you tomorrow to Lagos and we'll come back man and wife."

Instead, she looked out into the garden and said lightly, "Thanks for the warning," and moved from the chair at his side to take her favourite perch on the veranda rail. "You look after the shipping of the cacao, don't you, Roger?"

"It's part of my work—yes."

"What's the name of the British vessel due in at the week-end?"

"The *Bassington*."

"I believe it sails next Wednesday. Does it call at Lagos?"

"I think so—we're sending cinchona to a druggist there. She's a new boat." He paused. "Why the sudden interest in shipping?"

She shrugged. "One has to take an interest in something."

Roger was easily sidetracked. She led him to expand about his life in England and the impulse which had driven him to apply for the post on Valeira. Charmed by her sympathy and attention, he talked on and on, till Matt rollicked by in his dusty sedan and yelled an emphatic "Good night."

"Matt's right," said Roger ruefullly. "I've overstayed disgracefully."

"I've enjoyed it," she assured him as they walked the

path. "Usually I bolt myself within doors at sundown, and I miss these lovely hours of coolness."

He had halted and was gazing down at her. In the pale radiance of the stars she was slender and sweet and very feminine, and Roger felt a rush of need and tenderness that had to find outlet. He held her shoulders and kissed her mouth, became deliriously aware of her quickened breathing, and kissed her again, more thoroughly. Then he wrenched himself away, vanished through the gate and soon was again visible some way off, his white-clad figure racing back to his bungalow.

Pleasantly stirred, Phil went indoors and locked up. That night she slept as soundly as a child.

Next day Matt made his promised trip to the manager's house on the plantation. He chose twelve-thirty as the most likely time to catch Julian at home, and grousingly wore a white shirt and tie, and a pair of neat brown shoes which cramped his feet. When he came back about two hours later the tie waved a red tongue from his trousers pocket, his shoe-laces dangled and the shirt displayed the customary expense of hairy chest.

He sprawled in Phil's lounge, smoking one of the inevitable cheroots with annoying complacency.

"I had a genuine lunch," he said, "and Caswell opened a bottle of the best. I thought he'd be snooty—give me ten minutes and show me the door. After all, I do take good pickings from his natives, and quite often the wholesalers send trash that the poor blighters pay well for."

"You're as necessary to his workers as he is," she declared. "Do hurry up and explain what happened."

"All in good time, lovey. There's nothing exciting to report. You know, Phil, you handled him wrong. With his sort it doesn't do to be defiant—it puts his back up and made him determined to have his way."

"He hasn't any *right* to interfere with me. Anyone with a Portuguese visa can live here."

"True enough, but milk-and-water law doesn't operate in these parts. The plantation manager holds the key position, and if he decides to deport a lone young woman no one will dispute it, least of all the English and Portuguese authorities."

"He's a tyrant!"

Matt grinned. "He called you names, too. A pig-headed young idiot, a blind little fool, a damned nuisance, and one or two others. He also said that you were intelligent beyond your years, and you needed teaching a lesson, but he'd rather your education were furthered elsewhere. A complete analysis, and all for nothing."

"Did you sit back and let him say those things about me?"

"They slipped out during lunch. No vehemence—just statements of fact." Matt shifted and blew ash from his shirt.

"How did you leave it?" she demanded exasperated.

"On Sunday night the skipper of the *Bassington* will dine with Caswell. He's asked me along, too."

"Nice for you," she said witheringly. "Three tough men over a guinea-pig. You can save argument by letting them know at the start that when I decide to leave the island I'll book my own passage."

"It's no use getting hot," Matt yawned. "We've still an ace up our cuffs. You can marry Crawford."

"I can't. I'm not . . . I like him, but not enough."

"Oh, I thought you two seemed pretty snug together last night."

"We were saying goodbye. He's gone on leave this morning."

"The devil he has!" Matt raised his head, a sly smile on his heavy features. "Why not pretend to be engaged to him . . . just for Caswell's benefit? You can call it off when Roger returns, if you want to."

"That would only postpone the problem. Besides, I couldn't treat Roger so rottenly. You've no scruples, Matt."

He grunted himself upright. "Well, maybe not. I must agree with Caswell that you're a difficult wench. I've eaten too much. See you later."

Vexedly, Phil watched him go. Though she had not admitted as much to Matt, she was becoming really frightened. Supposing Julian Caswell succeeded and she was shipped to England. What could she do in a country that she knew more from Roger's descriptions than from her own memories? She was already aquainted with the cold-

ness and unfriendliness of large cities. The island had meant
home and security for so long; till she had definite ideas
for the future where else could she live?

During the whole of that stifling afternoon Phil rejected
one absurd plan after another. She saw herself aboard the
Bassington and leaving it at Lagos; searching for Roger
and seeking a judge's permission to marry; their joint
return to the island and Julian's discomfiture. But she had
a horrid feeling that Julian's reaction would sink into
unimportance when Roger came to share this house . . .
and her privacy. No, that was no good, either.

CHAPTER IV

THE *Bassington* docked just before sunset on Sunday evening. Phil viewed the arrival of the ship from the harbour
end of the promontory. The boat out there gave her a trap-
ped feeling. Somehow, since Matt had lunched with Julian
she seemed to have lost his allegiance. He had agreed with
Julian's verdict, had even accepted an invitation to dine
this evening with the captain of the *Bassington*. Presumably the three men would conclude arrangements for her
transport. It rather looked as if Matt were a traitor.

Yet when he called in on his way to the store the following morning Matt gave her the usual friendly wink.

"Thought you'd be itching to hear the decision of the
council of three," he said.

She was, but she answered coolly: "Too bad if it doesn't
coincide with mine. Did you have fun?"

"Not what you'd call fun. I learned that the *Bassington*
is equipped to carry eight passengers. She's picking up six
at Lagos, and you'll be the seventh—if you go. Caswell
reserved a cabin for you, and he's coming here this afternoon to see you about it."

"You told them what I said?"

"Yes, but they remained unimpressed. Don't worry,
Phil," he said airily. "There's time for a miracle between
now and noon on Wednesday."

"Matt!" Her tone changed, became eager and hopeful.
"Are you planning something?"

"Tut, tut," he adjured her sternly. "Would I hobnob with Julian Caswell and double-cross him at the same time? Be a good girl, keep your smile handy and let him believe you're giving in. And be sweet to the man when he shows up—it may pay dividends. So long."

Julian drove up at about three-thirty, and entered her hall with the same faintly mocking smile as before. He dropped his helmet on to a stool and, without invitation, reached for a cigarette from the crystal box on the table and set a match to it. The spurt of flame in the dim room illumined a strong, pleasantly bony face.

Today he sat well down in a corner of the chesterfield, one bare knee over the other. His gaze flickered over her small pointed face and straight shoulders against the flowered linen back of her chair, and it moved downwards, to her long, slim legs and white sandals.

"One of these days," he said conversationally, "you'll be grateful to me. You're far too pretty to waste your youth in the tropics."

"No time is wasted if one is happy."

"You haven't yet learned what happiness is, my child. It hasn't anything to do with keeping agreeable and occupied, or getting the better of a filthy climate. It depends more on people than on things and circumstances. This house is tastefully furnished and homely in atmosphere, but it could never take the place of the human relationships which are necessary to sane living."

"You rather harp on sanity, don't you?" she mentioned. "What do *you* use in the place of human relationships?"

He smiled. "I've had them and passed on. At my age one has ceased to expect happiness from the conventional sources. One no longer trusts them."

"How hateful. I shall never become jaded like that. I want to be loved . . . all my life."

His mouth thinned. "Of course you do. It's the chief symptom of adolescence. You won't find anyone on the island whose conception of love coincides with yours. They have an uglier word for it." He paused. "Did Bryson tell you your passage is fixed?"

Prickling from his contemptuous reference to her youth, she nodded.

24

"Then isn't it time," he asked, indicating the Chinese vase on a cabinet, "that this sort of thing was either disposed of to other residents here, or safely packed away for despatch? I'll lend you a boy, if you need one."

"I don't, thanks."

"What about the furniture?"

"It was made expressly for this house, and might as well stay."

"In that case I'll make you an offer for the lot. Have you any figure in mind?"

"If I'm compelled to leave the island," she shrugged, "you can have the house and the title deeds as a gift."

"Don't be childish," he took her up sharply. "I had in mind a sum of two thousand."

"Much too generous," she answered. "Discuss it with Matt after I'm gone. Can't we talk about something less harrowing? Will you have tea?"

"I will. But first I must make you understand that I'm deriving no pleasure at all from this situation." He leaned forward, ostensibly to get rid of his cigarette, but he stayed there, meeting her eyes across the room. "You've taken the attitude that I'm the bear in your garden, chasing you out of residence. I don't want you to think of me that way."

"Once I leave here," she told him lightly, "I shan't think of you at all, so your intentions will hardly matter. At the moment I confess to rather hating you, but—" she gave him a bright smile tinged with malice—"children always hate grown-ups who deliberately misconstrue their motives."

Ten minutes later he rose to go. "Thanks for seeing me," he said, with a trace of mockery. "Bryson tells me he will help you with your packing, but I myself will come for you at about ten on Wednesday morning."

"To ensure seeing the last of me?"

"Something like that. I shall feel easier when you're gone."

"That's awfully important," she conceded acidly.

"Don't worry. You'll do all right in England." He collected his helmet on the way out. "Choose a good hotel in London and make arrangements to continue learning. Go to a university if you can. You're bright enough to make a career at something unusual."

As he swung out into the sunshine Phil could cheerfully have killed him, and it was not till some time after he had gone that her temperature lowered and her fists unclenched. Of all the egotistic, domineering males, Julian Caswell must be the most maddening.

All the next day she waited for some sign from Matt. His house was locked up, his servant absent. Towards evening she made her way down to the store on the waterfront. She slipped round to the back and found Matt's houseboy, singing mournfully as he tipped chopped onions, tomatoes, pimento and peppers into a pot of stew.

"Is your master in the store?" she demanded.

"No, missus. Master on ship." He waved out to where a freighter lay at anchor.

"Who is in charge of the store?"

The boy gave the long, unintelligible name of Matt's coloured assistant.

"But you are preparing supper for the master?" she persisted.

"I do not know. Last night the master sleep in room here." He flung up an arm towards the little attic window above the store. "Tomorrow, I don't know."

Abruptly she turned away and climbed into the fringe of bush above the store.

Matt had forgotten her. One of his friends had steamed into Valeira Bay and he had neglected everything else in order to eat and gamble and work up a prime hangover for the morning. If he slept at the store last night it was likely that he would do the same again tonight. Shipboard parties broke up late.

Damn Matt! she told herself fiercely in the next breath. Her whole future couldn't be allowed to depend on the vagaries of a trader. Julian had to be taught that there was nothing she would not do to defend her right to remain in her own house. She had only to evade his threats once to establish herself as a person to be respected and allowed to live in peace wherever she chose.

British boats put in fortnightly or less often. Between the *Bassington* and its successor at the quay would stretch

26

at least two weeks in which to convince Julian that she could be as stubborn as he.

When she reached the house Phil went straight to the kitchen, where Manoela was preparing a meal.

"Manoela," she said, "would you like the big boat in the harbour to take me to England?"

When she had assimilated this the servant vigorously shook her head. "No, missus. Some man send you?"

Phil nodded. "We will go a journey till the ship has sailed. You see?"

A slow smile pulled wide the tan-coloured lips. "Yas, missus, we go a journey. How many nights?"

"Only one, I hope."

"We cross the mountain?"

"Lord, no! We hide, Manoela. They will search for us, but we must not be found. Do you understand?"

Yes, Manoela understood. "I fix blankets and food. They will not find us," she stated.

Phil said, "Good," and left the kitchen, her mouth compressed. The prospect of a night in the forest might hold its terrors, but there was a pleasurable excitement in defying Julian Caswell.

CHAPTER V

WHEN the sun had reached its zenith they rested. The spot Manoela had chosen was a bank of young ferns beside one of the little streams which rushed down from the mountainside and lost itself in a forest of hairy palms and buttressed kapoks.

"Here we are safe," she said. "I will cook food."

"How far are we from home?" Phil asked, gratefully sliding down on to the blanket.

"Eight miles, missus."

Only eight miles. Except for a break of half an hour, when they had emptied the flask of coffee, they had been walking for seven hours—since five o'clock. Not much more than a mile an hour. The going had been tortuous and wearying. They had not dared to use mules for fear of being traced. Manoela, a load on her head and another on her back, had gone ahead along the overgrown path used by natives for traversing the island, and wielded a lethal-looking knife whenever a branch or evil growth had barred the way. Wading through a swamp and then gradually climbing among tilted rubber trees, the hampering wild things for ever clutching at her bare legs or spattering them with a syrupy sap, Phil had wondered if the moist heat were affecting her brain.

Spend a night among these jungle giants? She shivered, and sudden new sweat joined the river which coursed down her spine. She took off her double felt, soaked a handkerchief in the surprisingly cool water of the stream, and bathed her face and neck.

Placidly, for she had a native's resistance to fatigue, Manoela placed a pot of water on the Primus and dropped into it a handful of kibbled maize, seasoning and a piece of cooked meat. For herself she mixed manioc meal and laid aside a few bananas. The usual camp fire was impossible here, where everything was sodden.

Phil ate without appetite. A little way away, with her back to her mistress, Manoela scooped her bowl dry and disposed of the bananas. Then she cleaned the pot with earth, rinsed and packed it, and glanced up at the filtered beams of the sun.

"We walk some more, missus?"

"They will not find us here, Manoela."

"How we know boat gone?"

How indeed? Dejectedly Phil shook her head. "We shan't know till you can venture near enough to find out."

"Maybe him gone already."

"Maybe."

"I go back some way, missus. Path good now. You sleep two three hours and I am here."

Phil let her go. Relieved of loads, Manoela loped off, and soon all sound of her was swallowed in a deep, uncanny hush. Phil was aware that no game lived on the island, but this place seemed to be shunned even by the monkeys. The heat and oppressive humidity opened every pore in her body and the blanket she lounged on was saturated from underneath.

If the captain of the *Bassington* had stuck rigidly to schedule by now he was riding the high seas, and she and Manoela might return home shortly after nightfall. She was rent by a shaft of horror. Supposing Manoela were caught! She knew the coloured woman would maintain a vacant silence, but Phil would be abandoned to spend the night in this macabre clearing with no noise but the dripping of mist from the leaves, no company but that of the creeping vines and age-old trees.

As often happens at times of intense fear, her mind went blank enough for sleep to steal over it. The dappled rays slanted, the sky paled with haze and a gentle wind whispered high up and brought the muted roar of the sea.

Phil awoke to stare unbelievingly at Manoela squatting beside her. She struggled up and looked a question.

"No," the servant said. "Him boat still tied."

"No one saw you?"

A triumphant smile. "Twice Manoela turn to tree . . . still, like this. Back there they are beating through the forest. Many natives with a white man . . . the little white boss chief"—this meant Drew. "When dark comes they must stop."

The nausea of fear surged into Phil's throat. The boat was waiting and the plantation workers spreading a network through the trees. Julian, thwarted, was a fiend with a purpose: to find Philippa Crane and heave her aboard.

Manoela said softly, "We walk now, missus, into the forest to more water. Then sleep till daybreak."

Phil's will seemed to have entirely evaporated. She got up and again followed the servant, her knees moving mechanically, her mind dazed beyond fright.

They camped. Manoela made coffee and they both lay down, the coloured woman happily muttering till she dozed and Phil in a nightmare of terror, the automatic hard against her side in her dress pocket.

Eventually a grey light percolated through the thick trees and revealed a hot heavy mist swathing the trunks. It clung in droplets to Phil's hair and drenched her to the skin.

Manoela prepared sweet black coffee and hard biscuits with meat paste. Phil drank, but she could not bear to look at the food. Her limbs ached and her throat was sore; her head felt as though it had received a blow from an axe.

As the hours passed Phil's eyelids grew heavy and, unaccountably, her chin trembled. It was all she could do to keep her teeth from chattering. She wished she had brought brandy and a waterproof groundsheet; she wished she had never conceived this fool escapade.

At about one o'clock Manoela decided to take another trip to the spot from which she could see the harbour, and Phil, after stumbling a little way along the trail with her, came back to slump down with her head in her hands and to weep a few tears of weakness.

By the end of that afternoon she knew each blade, each rubbery plant within sight. The dense green walls of ruthless vegetation no longer terrified her. She was too sick to be scared.

The light was lifting and leaving shadows when at last Manoela came in sight, riding one mule and leading another.

"Boat sailed!" she gleefully announced. "I wait and watch him go. When he small I run for mules."

Phil felt no flash of pleasure, no tingling of success. "Are they our mules?"

"No, missus. They feed in the bush. Belong plantation."

Phil asked no more questions. As soon as Manoela had secured her bundles, camel-fashion, over the back of one of the mules she accepted her help up on to the other. It needed concentration to stay astride an unsaddled mule with nothing to cling to but a sparse mane. Her brain swam and she was conscious of sharp pains like glass splinters in her chest and back. The intolerable ache persisted in her arms and legs, and, though the evening had gone shudderingly cool among the trees, her whole being was suffused with a dreadful wet heat. I'm going to die, she thought, and hardly cared.

Night washed in in a dark tide, but by now Manoela knew the track too well to make mistakes, and an hour later the mules emerged into the low bush from which the houses on the cliff could be distinguished as distant points of light. Where the bush petered out into long grass and occasional tufts of wild banana Phil slid to the ground, and Manoela did the same.

The servant took charge of the bundles and went ahead, quicker and quicker. Phil saw her scuttle past each of the houses bent like a monkey, and then she forgot Manoela in the effort of moving one foot in front of the other and trying to breathe. Past Drew's bungalow, past Dakers' untenanted dwelling, past Matt's, where a single window glowed.

Her own house was already lamplit at the back, but Phil was nearer the front gate. She hung on it for a second and closed her eyes. A sharp oath made her go rigid, a rough hand swung her round, and she was grasped by the shoulders and staring into the blazing eyes of Julian Caswell.

"So you've come back!" he bit out. "You deserve a damned good hiding."

His grip tightened cruelly and he shook her with such violence that a spear shot up from the base of her neck, and she cried out:

"Julian!"

For a moment longer he held her thus, his expression merciless, his fingers brutally clamped over her shoulders. Then the house door opened and Manoela stood there with a lamp whose radiance illuminated the girl's sweat-streaked temples, the white face with coins of feverish colour high on the cheekbones, and the bruised look under her eyes.

"My God!" he said, and slipped his arms under her and carried her into the house.

When Phil regained consciousness next morning Matt was seated on the other side of the mosquito net. Matt in freshly laundered shorts and a shirt decently buttoned, his entire appearance clean and chastened. Strange to see Matt just sitting, no glass near by, no cheroot, not even another chair upon which to cross his feet.

"Matt," she whispered.

He leaned forward and cautiously drew back the net a few inches. "Awake, lovey?" He, too, spoke softly, as if his usual rolling tones might be more than she could stand. "How do you feel?"

"Lightheaded, and there's a fearful taste in my mouth—

like one of your hangovers. I'll be better when I get up."

"You're staying right there for a few days. You've just missed a go of pneumonia—had us stiff with fright. Want a drink?"

"In a minute. Tell me what . . . what happened after I got here last night."

"All right—if you'll stay quiet." Matt sighed and shook his head. "We were in a hell of a fix, with darkness come again and no sign of you. Caswell was leaving my place when he saw you at your gate. I've never known a man move so fast. I couldn't leap any walls and by the time I got here he had you laid out in the lounge, and you were babbling. I drove up to his house for his drug-chest while he and Manoela sponged you down and got you to bed."

"*He* and Manoela?" she echoed, startled.

Matt cleared his throat. "I guess Manoela did most of it, but he carried you in here and stayed the night, forced crushed sulphonamide tablets down your throat every four hours and injected quinine in the intervals, to kill any malarial bug you might have picked up."

"No wonder I'm floating," she murmured. "Where's Julian now?"

"Gone home for a shave and breakfast. He waited till your temperature was down and you were breathing better. He'll be back."

Phil was silent, and Matt filled in by fussing with the carafe and lemon-squeezer.

When she had drunk she lay back. Dispiritedly she said, "You let me down, Matt."

"I didn't, you impulsive little fool!" Matt had got so far before recalling that she was ill and not to be bawled at. Less vehemently he went on, "I had it all arranged with the skipper of the freighter that was anchored in the bay. You were to go aboard and stay there—just there. I would have told Caswell you were in good hands and would remain hidden till the *Bassington* had sailed. He wouldn't have suspected the Novada freighter." Matt gave another of his gusty sighs. "I never felt so blasted sold in my life as when I came here in the morning at about six, with seaman's slacks and a jersey over my arm, to find the place locked and you and the half-breed flown."

"Oh, Matt!" she laughed weakly, "what a lovely idea! I'd have hopped aboard disguised as a seaman. If only I'd known!"

"No use telling you till I was sure the skipper agreed, and it was too late that night to call on you. In fact, I slept at the store."

"What did you do when you discovered I'd escaped?"

"Made another damfool error," he grunted. "I got it into my head that you'd paid someone to take you a few miles round the coast in a motor-boat so that you could hide snugly in one of the caves. I wish to God you had done that, Phil."

"It didn't occur to me. If it had, there was no one I could trust."

"I suppose not. Anyway, I laid into 'em down on the waterfront, and ran my own motor-boat right round as far as the Novada harbour. When I returned it was late and Julian Caswell was barking orders for work to cease and the search to commence. He was mad as the devil. 'That girl's this side of the mountain,' says he, 'and she's got to be found.' By sundown he was looking pretty haggard, and I was fairly rattled myself, but I had to rest."

"Poor Matt. I'm so sorry."

"If you'd seen us yesterday you'd be sorrier. When I decide to do away with a body I'll choose the jungle in preference to the sea. Several hundred of us, and we couldn't even smell a hair of you. Caswell had instructed the *Bassington* to leave in the early morning, hoping you'd crawl out of hiding, but she had some trouble and couldn't sail till the afternoon."

"Manoela watched for me."

"Caswell dragged the story out of her last night. Some girl, Manoela."

"He wasn't horrid to her, was he?"

"No, only abrupt. He'd been through a lot, but he certainly can take it. You should have seen him this morning after forty-eight hours without sleep."

Phil was glad she hadn't seen him; listening to Matt was tiring enough. She'd prefer to be stronger before inviting a scene with Julian Caswell.

Matt gave her another sip of the lemon-water, and pulled the mosquito net right back, as she requested.

"Now that we know you're going to survive to plague us," he said jovially, "I'll get along. Shall I send Manoela?"

"No, thanks. I may sleep again. I'll make up to you for the worry, Matt."

She lay on her side, looking through the oblong between the half-open shutters at the tall palm fronds torn one way by a hot wind, and round white clouds careering across the blue. A change from the usual breathless haze; one of those mornings, rare in Valeira, when colours were lucent and fresh, and the sea from pure joy smashed green and white over the rocks. After a while Phil dozed.

Manoela brought coffee.

"The white master is here," she said conspiratorially.

"Are you well, Manoela?"

"Yas, missus. You will see the white master?"

Not much point in refusing. You can't be high-hat with a man who has doctored you through a chill.

"Ask him to come in."

But Manoela hadn't reached the door before Julian pushed it wide open. After she had passed out he closed it from the inside and crossed to the foot of the white enamelled bed.

Hands in his pockets, the blue gaze critically roving her pale cheeks and tousled hair, he said, "Did Matt give you the couple of tablets?"

"Yes."

"At eight o'clock?"

"I think so. My watch has stopped."

"It's nearly twelve. Time for the next dose."

He came to the bedside-table and opened the drawer, extracted the white tablets and poured water. Obediently she swallowed.

"There are four more. You take two at four o'clock and two at eight. Don't deceive yourself that because you've no pain there's nothing wrong with you. No one can spend thirty-six hours in a swamp without paying for it. I'm putting you on your honour to stay in bed for three days and not to bathe in the sea for a fortnight." Giving her no time to reply, he added grimly, "You've chosen to remain

34

on the island and I shall make no further attempt to kick you out. But whether you like it or not, from now on you have a police boy on guard during the dark hours. Is that clear?"

She nodded, and drew in her lip. Matt was wrong; the two nights' vigil had marked Julian. There were tiny lines of strain at the corners of his eyes and his jaw was pulled so tight that a muscle twitched in his lean cheek.

"I thought you'd just be . . . angry, not upset," she said unevenly.

His voice was cold and bitter. "You didn't weigh up the spot you were putting me in. The men know of my decision to send you to England against your wish, and had anything happened to you I'd have been labelled a murderer."

"Was that why you . . . looked after me all night?"

"Explain it how you please." He half turned to the door. "Send your servant up to my house if you need anything."

He was going.

"I made a horrible mess of it, Julian," she said quickly.

His teeth clicked. "You're learning all the time," he returned curtly.

The door snicked shut. Phil sagged in the bed and pressed fists over her aching eyes.

CHAPTER VI

THE cacao and oil palm harvest had just ended. On the other side of the mountain where several small plantations existed beside the huge Novada estate, they were celebrating a heavy yield in Portuguese wine and song. Up at the mission, which was equally distant from both harbours, the natives got together for a thanksgiving service held by the old Catholic priest, and thereafter fights ensued between workers from the different plantations, which culminated in a gathering of Africans on the beach and the opening up of hidden "shebeens." The result, according to Roger Crawford, showed fewer casualties than last year: only five killed and forty injured. Not bad.

Since he had returned from his vacation and labour-recruiting trip a month ago Roger had renewed zest and energy. In Lagos he had met a friend from England who was cruising about in his own ketch. The fellow was just starting on a honeymoon trip—he had married the daughter of a Lagos official—and had promised to call at Valeira in a few weeks' time. The couple intended first to tour the Canary Islands.

When she heard this Phil exulted. A white woman, possibly little older than herself! Not a jaundiced skeleton like Sister Harrington, but someone pretty and youthful and well dressed. Straightway she ordered some lengths of material from Matt Bryson and began industriously to stitch. The dresses and new slacks were finished and hung away, and Phil came round to the cynical reflection that three parts of humanity were either fickle or liars.

Mostly she still wore brief shorts and a shirt, and tied her hair back with a ribbon. She fished from a canoe in the lagoon, and marvelled at the loveliness of the overhanging cliff and the palms which bent to examine their images in the rippling water. She bathed and lay on her back in the shade, regarding the sky and soliloquizing.

One day a shape materialized between her vision and the heavens. She blinked hard and took another look. A mouth, well cut and smiling, a clipped black moustache and dark, subtle eyes. She made a sudden sound of amusement.

"Clin! I thought it was the devil himself." She sat up and reached for her shirt. "When did you get back?"

"About an hour ago. There was no boy to prepare a bath, so I decided to take a dip." He dropped beside her. "No hurry, though."

"Where have you been this time?"

"Fernando Po: It was lousy." Clin Dakers leaned back on one elbow, watching her. "The job hung on, and I was sick to death of palm-olive cooking."

"Not much change from that on Valeira."

"There's poker . . . and you to watch and speculate about. You're going to be beautiful, Phil."

She laughed. "Going to be?"

"In about five years. If you were only pretty now, I wouldn't say that. But you have the features and intelligence for real beauty."

"How nice. I wonder where we'll all be in five years' time?"

"I'll be established in the South Seas. When my contract is up I shall travel south by stages, pick me a plump Tahitian girl who can cook, and settle beside a coral reef. I've seen enough of the primeval forest to last a lifetime. And you—" he span a pebble—"you'll be back among civilization, Phil, married to a handsome young man who'll blindly adore you, but will never come near understanding you."

"Poor thing. Why shouldn't he?"

He shrugged. "I don't know, but that's how it is when you've lived for any time in places like this. The tropics alter you fundamentally. There's no explaining how—it simply happens."

His eyes lingered on Phil's small, vital face. Vaguely he recalled spring in his native Gloucestershire and the pale green willows by the river. His blood quickened and his gaze lowered.

"May I cadge some food from you when I've had a bathe? Later on I'll send down an order to the store."

Lightly she jumped up, slipped a finger round the legs of her swim suit to loosen them and slung her shorts over her shoulder.

"I'll tell Manoela to take a tray to your house in an hour. Will that do?"

"Perfectly. I'll squat amid the mildew and eat."

His eyes pursued her till she had clambered out of sight. His mind followed still further, probed her knowledge and her innocence. In the seven weeks of his absence she had changed, was more serene and womanly. Grief over her brother's death no longer dominated her emotions. There was something else. Clin was intrigued; he was also weary of philandering with women in pidgin Portuguese.

With Clin and Roger both anxious for tennis in their spare time and neither one of them eager to play with the other, Phil was engaged as partner almost every day for the hour before sunset. She could beat Roger about once in every three games, but never had she had a clear victory over Clin.

The forestry man was exciting on the court, and away

37

from it he had a certain cheap glamour; the regular-featured film actor's face, the flashing smile, the dark, unstable eyes. Phil preferred his superficiality to Roger's increasing devotion; she could handle it more easily.

Since the episode of the *Bassington* she had had few contacts with Julian. Twice, after British boats had put in, he sent down fresh bacon and white flour, and on the second occasion she had reciprocated with a freshly baked chocolate sponge cake. A week later, after meeting him on a path through his own oil palms, he had helped her dismount, unsmilingly, but his expression agreeable. Drew was there, earnestly directing the boys who scaled the sixty-foot palms to sever the great pods. Julian had invited her to walk with him to where the nuts were being loaded into a mule wagon, and had expanded on the relative merits of palm oil and coconut oil, and the rising market for copra. Not once had he deviated from the subject of planting, but just before he lent a hand to get her back into the saddle he said she looked well, and flicked the brim of her hat with his forefinger. It really did seem that he might be recovering from the jolt she had given his ego.

The only man for whom Julian showed friendship was the trader, but when they knew him, everybody liked Matt. Two or three times a week he dined at the manager's house. Much less often, Julian came down for an evening at Matt's place on the cliffs.

Clin was taking a period of leave. All day, when it was too hot for tennis, he lazed on his veranda, and if he grew tired of the view of the jungle that grew up to his doors and sent sprouts through the plank wall, he sauntered down to pass some time with Phil.

Roger chafed. "Every day when I come home he's draped over your veranda wall chowing away as though you'd just met. I can't think what you two find to talk about all the time."

"Clin's had heaps of experiences. He's never dull."

"He sets himself out to fascinate you, and you seem to fall for it. Surely you don't believe everything he puts over?"

"No, about half," she said, smiling. "Clin aims to entertain, not to deceive."

"Do you bathe together?"

"Not by arrangement. We've overlapped occasionally."

"Does he ever eat with you?"

"Nothing more solid than a fairy cake with a cup of tea. Stop being an idiot, Roger, and I'll let you come in for a drink and some music."

For the moment he was mollified, though deep down he knew that his suspicions sprang only partly from jealousy of a colourful rival. It was her complacent acceptance of himself that irked. Phil was too high-spirited and sensitive to be casual to a man with whom she was falling in love. She wouldn't be able to help showing it in some way.

Clin, whose employers were Portuguese, suggested a trip over the mountain to the Novada estate. The Portuguese were known to be exceptionally hospitable, and he considered that Drew, Crawford and himself were sufficient bodyguard for Phil.

"Fat Rodrigo has two impressionable sons," he told her. "You'll knock 'em cold. We'll leave early morning by mule, and get there about six, in time for a scented bath and a large, well-spiced dinner."

It sounded fun. She nodded. "All right. Next week-end."

But the following day Matt said: "I wouldn't go if I were you, Phil. Astartes and his sons are great chaps, but you'll only unsettle 'em. His wife's in Lisbon now, flashing her diamonds and talking big, trying to attract wives for the boys, to keep them on the island."

"Oh, lord, I wish I were a man. I ought to be safe enough with three Englishmen. I'll act hard and unfeminine."

He grinned. "You couldn't keep it up, lovey. One smile and you'd sink 'em. Have you spoken to Julian about it?"

"No. Should I?"

"It might be as well to let him have the last word."

"But if you disagree, he's sure to."

"Not a bit. Astartes has asked him over. Perhaps he'll go along with you."

She laughed a little. "You think he'd keep me out of trouble? Got immense faith in him, haven't you?"

"Faith?" Matt rubbed his stubble. "I don't know that you'd call it faith. Seems to me he's the only one of us to be trusted with a woman, and that's because he's had more than enough of them. He doesn't regard you as a woman, though."

"Lately, he's treated me as a lanky boy."

"Leave it that way," advised Matt. "As soon as he notices you have eyes and hips he'll give you hell."

Phil put on her old wide-brimmed straw hat with the red felt lining and walked through the wild banana scrub to the plantation track. She had not visited the manager's house since, many months ago, she had gone there with Nigel to Sunday lunch with Mason, the former boss. She would like to make the trip again, to see Julian's ruthless improvements, but the chances of an invitation were slim.

Today, in fact, she did not even reach the spacious clearing in which the plantation buildings were set, for as she came to the bend where scrub ended and cacao began Julian's car came hurtling towards her. He stopped dead and poked out his head.

"Coming to see me?"

"Well, I was. But if you're tearingly busy it can stand over till tomorrow."

"The haste is temporary—I'm going down to the waterfront to make last-minute alterations to some shipping instructions. I shall be free after that. Hop in, and go with me."

She slipped into the seat beside him and hung her hat over her knees. Driving with Julian when he was in a hurry turned out to be a blood-freezing experience. When he swerved out to the shore road and braked, she let out a long, pent-up breath.

"Cut along to the market," he said. "I'll meet you there."

Phil always enjoyed strolling in the narrow lanes between the market folk. Most of them, both men and women, preferred to spread their wares on the bare earth and to sit beside them, gossiping in clicking syllables, and smoking some acrid weed in a variety of pipes. The men offered trophies and skins from the mainland, drinking-shells and clay bowls, jujus and vile medicines. The women specialized in food: cassava roots, kale, dried meat, manioc meal, peppers and yams. Natives with a few coins to spend bargained noisily, demanding their money's worth in pleasure as well as in kind.

Phil was interested in a native coaxing copper-wire anklets over a girl's heel when Julian joined her. The whole foot had been massaged with oil, and while the boy worked, the dusky young lady scooped fistfuls of oil from his tub and annointed every visible part of her body till she glistened.

Julian remarked sardonically. "She's out to snare a boy-friend or someone else's husband."

"It needn't be a married man," Phil protested. "She's good-looking enough to attract anyone."

"Women with looks don't care for easy meat—it's dry and uninteresting. They'd rather steal and experiment. Let's get out of this stench."

"But that's frightfully unjust," she argued, as they moved on. "According to you, every pretty face masks a snake."

"Let's say a potential snake. A good many don't hatch out, but those that do . . ." He let it tail off at that.

"You must have known some horrid women," she said soberly. "They've spoiled you for the right one, if she ever finds you."

He smiled paternally. "The chances are against it, little one, so you need have no concern on her account."

He shouldered between a mule and a mud wall, and dragged her after him. They skirted the usual bunch of ragged loafers rattling bones and calling numbers, passed a string of women and girls carrying driftwood on their heads, and eventually came out again to where the car stood on the shadeless road.

The interior was oven-hot, but less dangerous than sunshine. Julian leaned an arm on the wheel and turned her way.

"Let's have it, shall we?"

She tipped back her hat and told him of the proposed mule ride to the Novada estate.

"Matt's against it," she finished with a suggestion of mischief. "He's afraid Senhor Astartes will rope me in as a bride for one of the sons."

Julian's straight thick brows rose. "You could do worse.

41

They're an aristocratic and wealthy family. Are you expecting me to forbid you to go?"

Irritated by his tone, she answered, "I came to you for advice, not sarcasm."

"But after I'd tendered the advice you'd have pleased yourself," he said crisply. "You don't get me on that again. If you fancy the trip, take it."

"Had I guessed you'd be hateful about it I wouldn't have come to you. Matt thought you might accompany us."

"Accompany you! What do you think I am?"

"Since you ask," she was stung to retort, "I think you're a conceited beast. You live at the plantation in lordly splendour and treat the rest of us as if we were beneath contempt or morons. You could be charming if you cared to unbend. . . ."

"Thanks," he returned coolly, "but I don't. I wouldn't join this picnic even to keep you out of mischief."

She paused, then sighed. "You're awfully difficult to be nice to. Why didn't you state outright that you agreed with Matt? I won't go if you don't want me to."

"What's the matter?" he said. "Hooked a fever?"

She laughed, and they sat silent a few minutes, looking through Phil's window at the boats on the heaving waters and the combers splitting over the beach.

"I like to think the Cameroons are over there and Nigeria that way," she said, nodding seawards. "When I'm tired of Valeira I shall visit all the West African ports, as far as Dakar."

"That's an odd ambition for a girl. Don't you ache for a gold ring on your finger and a man under your thumb, like the rest of them?"

"Heavens, no!—not for years, anyway. And I'm afraid I shall never be the sort to *manage* a man. If I love anyone it's so absolutely whole-hog that they can trample on me."

"I seem to have heard that before," he said drily, "in more sophisticated language."

"You needn't believe it," she replied indifferently. "You're the last person I'd try to impress." She became alert, gazing intently out to sea. Her hand reached behind her and tugged his jacket. "Look, what's that out there?"

He bent forward, then snapped open the glove box and took out binoculars.

In a moment he said, "White sails. A boat heading this way—a private yacht, by the appearance. Want to look?"

"Of course." She grabbed the binoculars and adjusted them, gave an exclamation of delight. "The Fosters! How lovely! I'd given them up."

"Keep still. Who are the Fosters?"

"A young married couple—friends of Roger. Drive me home quick, will you? They're going to stay with me while they're here."

"Plenty of time. It'll take an hour to get in and quite a while to wade through the customs." He pressed the starter, before adding with exasperation: "I wish to heaven Crawford had had more sense than to invite them here. But there's one thing"—with a hard glance in her direction as the car slid along the road—"this woman may succeed where I failed. She'll make you long for smart clothes and parties, and everything else you don't get on Valeira."

"After which smug and vindictive pronouncement," she responded blithely, "he savagely swung the car inland. You deserve to break an axle."

CHAPTER VII

IN different circumstances Daphne Foster could have been termed extraordinarily pretty, for normally she owned a piquant face, a head of fair curls and nice curves. But when she arrived at Valeira poor Daphne sagged ashore like a thin bag of wet meal. Lagos, she moaned faintly, had been bad enough; since leaving the port the atmosphere had grown hotter and damper, and the sea, though comparatively smooth, had nevertheless produced an uncanny roll in the ketch.

Apart from concern on his wife's account, Gordon Foster turned out to be the cheerful, carefree sort that make excellent sailors and accommodating husbands. In England he and Roger Crawford had never advanced beyond acquaintanceship, but the meeting in Lagos two months ago Gordon had counted fortuitous. He had always wanted to visit one of the West African islands and here was a sound reason. At the time Daphne had concurred enthusiastically, for was she not on her way to the mellower air of the Canary Islands? Now, nine weeks a bride and longing frantically for the cosy flat which awaited them in London, she viewed Valeira with weary loathing.

"How do you *bear* it?" she lamented to Phil the first evening. "I was crazy about Gordon in England, and I'm hoping it will be the same when we go back, but this heat makes me feel I shall never be normal again. They tell you that heat excites the emotions, but it just flattens me out."

"You're tired," Phil said. "Wait till you've lived here a few days and you'll admit the island's fascinations. My father and brother were held here by them, and so am I."

"Men are different," Daphne shrugged. "As long as there are one or two other men on hand and the mainland near enough to get a woman now and then, they can make out. I suppose you're in love with one of them?"

Phil laughed. "I haven't even that excuse. I just like it."

After a day or two within the coolness of the thick-walled house Daphne revived, though she was still incapable of tennis and bathed only in the evening. Because she was a guest on the island the other cliff residents also turned out to bathe at that hour, and most evenings Phil provided salads and cold meats. Clin brought his guitar which, he boasted, had serenaded from Marseille to Singapore, and Gordon Foster carried down a portable gramophone.

It was Matt who electrified the party one night by announcing an invitation for them all to have dinner with Julian Caswell the following evening.

"Has he that much cutlery and china?" Phil wondered aloud. "What's come over the man?"

"It's a duty gesture," guessed Roger.

"Nothing of the sort," Drew reproved him. "He's the plantation boss, after all."

"That's what I said," murmured his junior. "Still, it's good of him."

"Are you sure he included the bad lad of the island?" enquired Clin. "Six men and two women. Some binge—for the ladies."

Daphne said: "Is he stuffy? Do we dress?"

44

And Gordon put in, "If only Daph could take to this climate I'd ask him for a job."

Matt searched his pockets for a cheroot.

"You go back to your desk in London, young man," he advised. "A couple of years in a place like this and you're a misfit anywhere else."

"You hear that, Phil?" said Daphne.

"Yes, but I don't believe it. Matt trots that out to new-comers in self-defence. He's afraid of someone starting up an opposition store."

Next evening Julian sent his car to pick up Phil and her house companions, and Matt undertook to drive the other men over. Phil's pulses hummed pleasantly. She wore a cream linen dress which enhanced the pale gold of her skin, and her hair, thick and curly, shone red on the crests of the brown waves. Under Daphne's guidance she had used a dusting of powder and an almost indiscernible rub of flame lipstick. She could taste perfume on her lips, and it made her feel strange and exotic.

Julian's house was without a garden; one could drive straight across the shorn grass to his veranda steps. He was waiting there in bright lamplight, suave and distinguished-looking in a white suit, his dark hair slicked close, his mouth amused and arrogant. Phil got the impression that he was digesting a private joke.

To Daphne, frail and attractive in pale green chiffon, he offered felicitations on her marriage and a couple of veiled compliments. He warmly shook Gordon's hand and spared a friendly smile for Phil. He was different: the faultless host and good companion.

They had coffee on the veranda while two boys cleared the living-room. Surveying the expanse of polished floor from the french window, Phil was puzzled, until she realized that one of the three bedrooms had been dispensed with in order to enlarge this, the main room of the house. Much of the furniture was new, too, though still of the service-able teak, and the cushions were uncompromisingly blue and grey.

Behind her, from his seat near the veranda rail, Julian was saying, "Is the trip to the Novada called off?"

"Postponed," Clin drawled, "unless the Fosters care to

go with us. Ever ridden a mule, Gordon?"

"Once, in Italy. What's the Novada?"

Clin explained: "The estate is worth a tour, and Astartes is one of those chaps who can talk for a week and never repeat himself. He knows the complete history of these islands."

Ever hungry for fresh experience, Gordon put a number of questions; but Daphne demurred.

"No mule ride for me, thanks. Sorry, but I'm just not the type."

"Why not use the boat?" suggested Julian.

"Yes, why not?" from Gordon. "You'd be all right in the boat, Daphne. The whole lot of us could go."

"Not me," grunted Matt. "I'm no seafaring man."

"Darling," said Daphne plaintively, "for me the best part of this honeymoon is when I'm on land. Next time I step aboard we head for home. You go to the Portuguese end of the island if you want to; I'll stay with Phil."

"But she's coming," said Clin. "Aren't you, Phil?"

She turned and met Julian's blue, enigmatic gaze before answering flippantly, "Maybe I ain't no seafaring man, either. I certainly don't intend to make the test in front of a lot of jeering hoboes like you. Count me out."

Julian grinned but withheld comment. Drew said that he'd seen the Novada plantation and that if Mr. Caswell was going, he himself had better stay here. Swiftly Phil again looked at Julian. His nostrils twitched at her as if he were aware of the names she was silently hurling at him.

In the morning Gordon ran an expert eye over the boat, ordered a few tons of ballast to be stowed and gave the native hands a couple of days ashore. It had been decided that he, Clin, Roger and Julian would set sail straight after lunch and spend a couple of nights at the Novada. The morning after tomorrow they would return, getting in about mid-day.

Phil and Daphne were on the waterfront to watch the line cast loose and the *Blue Ray* move slowly in a breeze that gently filled the sails as they were hoisted. The engine churned up a soapy wake as it pushed south-east, between Valeira and the mainland.

Daphne seemed relieved to be without men for a period.

46

She read and tinkled at the piano, showed interest in Phil's wardrobe and tried to fashion some of the little clay figures which to Phil's fingers came easy. They bathed twice a day and canoed round the lagoon. Daphne, who was highly superstitious, bought lucky shells and coins in the market and added a few pieces of palm-fibre basketwork to the heap of junk which she intended carrying away as mementoes of Valeira.

"I have a feeling," she said in thankful tones, "that once I get back to England I shall never leave there again. Of course, this holiday has been one I shall treasure—even apart from Gordon—but I'm so essentially a Londoner that I positively pine for cold nights and smelly fogs, the theatre and a cabaret once in a while. You're an awful fool to hang on, Phil. We'd fix you up in London and help you to make friends."

"Some day I'll happen along and surprise you."

"If one of these men doesn't chain you to the island. Roger's time is up first. As a husband he's the safest bet."

"Can you imagine me settling down in a small north-country town?"

"You wouldn't have to. He'd go wherever you wished. Look at Gordon and me."

Phil laughed. Young brides were notoriously matchmakers.

The time passed quickly. The second evening Matt and Drew were induced to dine with them and play whist.

In the middle of that night a wind freshened from the north-west and dry white lightning flashed through the slats of Phil's bedroom window. She got up and peered out at the walls of cloud which appeared static on the horizon. Overhead it was clear and starry, but the palms threshed and the waves roared ominously with an evil echo. Some time soon the calm weather would break, but this might be only a warning.

Back in her bed she listened, and breathed a generous sigh when the wind lowered to a whisper. Nothing to worry about after all.

But by daylight the sky was brassy and there was no mist. Low on the sealine a jagged wall of cloud seemed suspended, awaiting reinforcement.

Daphne was happy. "Let's make a snorting West African curry for the men," she said, "and work out something special in the way of a salad. We'll make them declare a half-holiday, and this afternoon we'll bathe and take a picnic tea. Won't it be great to have them back?"

Phil agreed. She felt absurdly lighthearted as she set out alone to bargain for a chicken at the market. She chose a pair of squawking cockerels and walked on to buy a basket of tiny tomatoes and some olives while they were killed and dressed.

The chickens were put to broil, onions, rice and seasoning prepared and half a dozen eggs hard-boiled ready for the casserole. A huge glass bowl of chopped pawpaw, precious oranges, bananas, raisins and nuts flavoured with sherry, was covered with butter muslin and stowed away in a dark corner of the larder.

At this stage Daphne wilted and Phil was left to mix the baking-powder bread and push the loaves into the oven of the paraffin stove. She was washing the flour from her hands at the iron pedestal under the kitchen window when a sudden roar rushed in from the sea; a tornado that rocked the walls and tore branches from the trees, and brought Daphne screaming into the kitchen.

It lasted twenty minutes, grim herald of the deafening storm that followed. Half-demented, Daphne pressed her face into her pillow and sweated and sobbed. Between her incoherent wailing Phil gathered that if Gordon got back alive it was ten chances to one against his finding his wife all in one piece.

"The men won't have left the Novada harbour," Phil told her. "They'll have seen the storm coming and waited."

"We didn't see it coming," wept Daphne. "The sudden wind would tip over the *Blue Ray*. We always heeled in a normal strong wind. Oh, God, I wish we'd never come to Valeira!"

In the early afternoon the thunder receded and ceased. Lightning still played about the mountain and rain continued to stream against the house. Daphne, weary and heavy-eyed, paced restlessly from window to window, but Phil, rasped by the hours of inaction, put on oilskins and waded down to the deserted waterfront.

Marooned in his store, Matt sat in his ancient swivel chair, his feet on a bag of maize and an accounts book across his knees. When Phil came in he tenderly scratched his chest.

"Have a good swim?" he asked conversationally.

She perched on an up-ended roll of cotton. "Deuce of a storm," she answered with gloom. "Daphne's frantic over Gordon being away in the boat."

"You're a bit white about the mouth yourself. Have a drink?"

"No, thanks. Matt, d'you think they'd have sailed this morning?"

"I don't. They're four grown men, lovey, with plenty of common sense between them."

"Couldn't we send a freighter round—just in case?"

"Julian would be mad as hell."

"I'd risk that—to be sure they're all right." She paused miserably. "The horrible part is not knowing."

"Now you understand how we felt when you disappeared into the jungle—only it was worse for us; you weren't four strong men. Stop fretting. They'll come tomorrow."

"Tomorrow! What am I going to do with Daphne?"

"Send her to bed early with sleeping tablets, and be thankful you're not a newly-wed."

When Phil reached home she was drenched in perspiration beneath the oilskin and her hair had gone as lank as Daphne's.

They drank tea and coffee, but neither could face a meal. In the early darkness they sent Manoela to the shore with a note to the harbour official, begging him to let them know by messenger as soon as the *Blue Ray* was sighted. Phil attempted to sew, but Daphne began to cry again.

"I should have gone with them," she declared through quivering lips. "They wouldn't have taken chances with a woman aboard."

"How do we know they've taken chances?" Phil argued. "Matt thinks they're still snug in harbour."

"Gordon would try to get back—he knows how I stew over storms. Phil, if anything has happened to him I shall die."

And much more in similar vein, till Phil went silent from nervous exhaustion.

It was towards eight-thirty when the messenger came. The *Blue Ray* was anchoring off-shore and a motor-boat had been sent out. Phil gulped hard and warm blood raced in her veins. She was first on the track, running as she had never run before, happiness welling up in her like an agony.

She saw them against a background of cascading black rollers. Four figures, the tallest Julian's. Shyness caught at her throat and she slowed.

"Darling!" Daphne was crying, and the next moment she had flung herself into Gordon's arms.

"Unclinch, there's a pet," he said. "We have an audience."

"I don't care," she said wildly. "I've been terrified."

The other three came on ahead, and Phil saw that they were half-clothed, wet and tired. But Clin Dakers, his hair rough and curly, looked into her face and winked.

"Here's another little girl who's been terrified. Which one of us are the tears for, Phil?"

She turned and walked between him and Julian. "Tell me what happened."

Again it was Clin who spoke. "Nothing much. We saw the storm coming and waited till it finished before casting-off. Big seas and the rain account for our dishevelment."

They took the rest of the slope without talking, and where the track divided Julian halted.

"It's me for a bath and a bottle of rum," said Clin. "Good night."

Sulkily, Roger added: "Me too. I need my bed."

Phil called after them: "Good night, Clin. Good night, Roger."

And then she was alone at Julian's side, looking up at him with a liquid brightness in her eyes and a tremulous smile on her lips.

"Well?" he said.

She made a funny sound and pressed her eyes against his khaki sleeve, leaving two little smudges. The hard lines of his face relaxed and she felt a second's pressure on her shoulder.

"Shame on you," he said softly, derisively.

Then he twisted and strode through the bush path which led up to the plantation.

CHAPTER VIII

ON a fair morning, with a light south-easter billowing the sails and a pennant flying, the *Blue Ray* arrowed away from Valeira. The Fosters had spent three weeks and four days on the island, and left behind them pleasant associations and, in the breast of Roger Crawford, a nostalgia for England.

At first Roger's yearning was so acute that he sought an interview with Julian and asked if it were possible to break his contract.

"Is it worth it?" remarked Julian. "Twenty-two months will soon pass. You've a good salary piling up and the bonus percentage is improving every half-year. In any case, your contract calls for three months' notice, in which to replace you, and in that time you'll have settled again. Foster himself would have given a good deal to remain here in a job like yours."

Roger's tongue edged along his lips and he averted his head. "He wouldn't give up his wife for it, though."

"He hasn't had her long enough for that," returned Julian coolly. "You attach too much importance to women. I thought you had more sense than to harp on the impossible."

"You don't understand how I feel."

"I understand perfectly," Julian sharply took him up. "You're tired of living with Drew, and Philippa Crane is too young to be made love to."

"She's eighteen."

Julian paused. "Is she? Then what's stopping you?"

"It takes two. She likes me, but not that way." His fair skin flushed and his jaw was crooked as he went on: "My nerve isn't as good as yours, sir. I sleep badly and get depressed. I . . . I'm afraid of going under."

51

Julian let a minute pass before answering dispassionately: "Look here, Crawford, your position is no more extraordinary than that of any other white man here. You convince yourself that the reason you sleep badly is because you need a woman to share your bed, but the fact is the temperature keeps you awake and you're not strong enough to control your mind. As for depression—we all get it. That's another of the taxes you have to pay for living here. I'm not belittling what you're enduring, but I did believe you had the guts to get on top of it. It's not so long since you had special leave in Lagos."

"I know. I'm sorry."

Roger came away no happier and wishing to heaven that he had tendered his resignation without explanation. It was all very well for Caswell to hand out censure. He was the cold, merciless sort, as intolerant of weakness in himself as in others. Seeing Gordon and Daphne together would cause him no pangs; neither was he torn in two by the mere silhouette of Phil framed in her lamplit window.

Clin Dakers hung on and on. Matt Bryson hinted that the forestry man had been sacked and he was planning a trip south, but Clin's behaviour did not support the hint, and he mentioned next month and the month after as if he might still be at Valeira, lazing within his rotting bungalow and monopolizing Phil. That was the part that hurt—monopolizing Phil.

She, of course, ridiculed his notions. The trouble with Phil was that you could never get close to her, never know what she was thinking, or whether what she said came from the heart. For one so honest and sensitive she could be exasperatingly reticent.

When he told her that Julian had dissuaded him from rescinding his contract, she smiled rather gravely.

"Julian's concern is with the plantation, not with individuals. Naturally he doesn't want a new man on his hands just as his work is beginning to show results. His attitude is that if you crack up now it will be just too bad—for him. Your side of it doesn't bother him."

"What makes you say that? I thought you liked him."

"I do, but not blindly. Julian has cut personal feelings out of his life—we just happen to be the handful of people

52

he has to get along with. So if it goes deep with you—this wish to return to England—don't let him put you off."

Roger shrugged his dissatisfaction. "The way he spoke, I'd feel a rat if I got out now."

"That's his cleverness. No one else would blame you," said Phil.

Two days later she heard from Clin that he was leaving Valeira for good. He had followed her down to the lagoon and bathed with her, raced her back to the beach and slipped full length beside her to regain his breath.

Presently he lit a cigarette and looked her way. "This would be an ideal mode of existence in a better climate," he said. "Only fools work away the best years of their lives."

She laughed. "Aren't you tired of holiday-making yet?"

"I thrive on it. But I'm fed up with Valeira and the men here. I'm leaving, Phil."

"Oh. Permanently?"

He nodded. "I'm making south. Will you hate to see me go?"

"A little. With you and the Fosters gone it'll be dull."

"Don't you envy me the South Sea Islands?"

"Naturally. Everyone hankers to visit them, but I shouldn't care to go alone."

His voice changed, went low and thick. "I'm not asking you to go alone."

Phil lay very still. Through half-closed lids she saw Clin's dark eyes watching her, and was suddenly conscious that the blue swim suit left her rather exposed. She felt deceived by him—let down.

"What *are* you asking?" she enquired unevenly.

"You know well enough. We're not conventional people, Phil, but I'll marry you, if you like. We'll get a boat to the Cape, and then on to Australia and the islands—kick around for as long as it takes to find a good spot to settle. We'll make a go of it, Phil."

"I'm afraid we won't." Her tones were steady again; she had made them so. "Maybe you consider the useful part of your life over, Clin, but mine hasn't begun yet."

"It's no mean task to keep a man happy, and I guarantee you plenty of excitement. I've been in love a dozen

53

times before, but not this way. I've never touched you, have I?"

"You knew it would have spoiled everything if you had."

"Quite true." He spoke reasonably, confidently. "I could see you weren't to be rushed, so I waited. But I mean to take you with me, Phil. I'll wear you down within the next week."

"So you sail in a week?" she managed airily. "We'll all turn out to wish you luck."

His eyes narrowed down at her, and his mouth, which had never before drawn her attention, compressed in a faintly unpleasant smile.

"You shelter behind the other men here. You think that I won't dare to kiss you against your will because of them. Typically a woman's get-out, but a dirty one, Phil."

"I don't agree. Why should I tolerate distasteful kisses?"

"You haven't found my friendship distasteful."

"No. I've enjoyed it—till today. Let's leave it like that, Clin."

"Which means," he said through closed teeth, "that emotionally I've made no inroads. Well, I suppose it's my own fault for using the time so foolishly. I was stupid enough to believe it more important that you should trust me. It doesn't matter any more."

He twisted and pinned down her shoulders, bent and sought roughly for her evading mouth. Phil struggled. She brought up her knee hard into his stomach, wrenched herself to her feet and ran.

Clin did not follow her. When, gasping and weak in the limbs, she looked back from the top of the hill, he was still lying on his side where she had left him.

She was not so much disgusted as sickened and disappointed by the episode. Later, when Manoela set out to retrieve the couple of garments Phil had left on the beach, she was back within a minute. The shorts and blouse, folded and weighted by a stone, hung over Phil's front gate, and from between them fell a scrap of paper which read:

Forgive me, Phil. Don't blame a chap for trying his luck.

She stood wondering. It was Clin's writing, but hardly,

she thought, Clin's sentiment. She hadn't forgotten the viciously tight teeth and the animal dilation of his nostrils as she fought to avoid his lips. He was offering a swift apology to prevent her from confiding in one of the men. He needn't have worried. She had had pleasure from Clin's companionship and wasn't likely to cause unnecessary trouble for him before his departure.

During the following days she saw him only from her veranda when he passed on his way to and from the waterfront. He smiled at her, tipped his helmet and jauntily continued along the track. She asked Matt if a farewell drink party had been arranged, but the trader shook his head.

"Clin's a deep one. Keeps saying he isn't ready to leave, but his cabin trunk has been locked and labelled for days. No use saying goodbye yet."

The week Clin had mentioned slipped by and another began. There were several freighters in the harbour, mainly the cacao fleet, a tanker and a couple of small coasters. Clin would have to make for the mainland and take his chance on a boat to the Cape.

She was designing one of her clay figures one evening, a woman with a negroid mouth and nose and a thick, weight-carrying neck curving into square shoulders, when there was a brief tattoo on the main door. While she was hesitating the knock came again and she stood up, smiling a little. Whoever it was had passed unchallenged by the police-boy. That meant Julian; he had come at this hour that first evening when she had met him at the door with a gun.

She went into the hall and shot back the bolt. The door opened and her smile became fixed and enquiring.

"Hello, Phil," said Clin. "I've come to say goodbye."

He looked stiff and respectable in a grey lounge suit, and his manner appeared subdued.

"Do I have to stay here or will you let me in?" he asked.

Disarmed, Phil moved aside and indicated the hall seat. "So you really are leaving this time. Tomorrow?"

"At daybreak. I'm going aboard tonight."

"Do Matt and the others know?"

He shook his head and let it rest against the wall. "They

won't care, except that I've done them out of a binge. It's strange, I've never made friends anywhere."

"Travelling too much, I expect. People come to recognize you as the flitting type and won't bother to get to know you properly."

"You did," he said casually.

"No. I accepted you, that's all."

"Up to a point," he commented. "You gave my pride a smack the other day—not to mention the knee in my middle. No one would have guessed I'd just paid you the compliment of proposing to you."

She laughed and looked out through the open door. "You'll come across someone more to your taste."

"No hope of a last-minute switch-over?"

"Afraid not, Clin."

He shrugged. "So be it. Got a drink to spare?" As she turned uncertainly towards the lounge door he added, "It's all right, Phil. I won't shanghai you."

She said, "What about inviting the men in to wish you *bon voyage*?"

"Matt's soaking his hide at the waterfront and the other two hate my guts."

She got out a bottle of whisky and a tumbler, and as he reached for them she was assailed by a hot gust of liquor-smelling breath.

"I'll get you some water," she murmured quickly.

"Don't bother. I prefer it neat." He raised his glass and his eyes burned at her over the rim. "Here's to chastity," he said, and swallowed.

She fought down a rising tide of panic. "You must go now, Clin."

"No hurry, sweetheart. Let's put out the light for an hour."

"Don't be absurd."

"What's absurd about it? I've told you I love you." He shifted closer. "Come on, Phil. Be matey."

"You're drunk, Clin!"

In a frightening flash she recalled Julian's earliest warning: "Sure as death there'll come a night when one of them will be cockeyed enough to forget himself." She stepped

56

back, but before she could twitch aside the curtain he had thrust down her hand.

Clin was very near, between Phil and the door. The automatic was in the writing-table drawer, to her left. As she edged towards it she tried to soften her lips into a smile.

"You'll loathe yourself tomorrow, Clin . . ."

"Not so much as I've loathed you since that day on the beach," he grated. "I promised myself this, you maddening little prude."

Phil had contrived to put a yard between them. She whirled, snatched open the drawer, swung back and pointed the gun.

"I know how to use it, Clin!"

His teeth bared. "D'you think I can't see that you're half dead with terror? Give me that!"

She was prepared for him to duck as he struck at her hand; this time the automatic stayed tight in her grasp. But Clin had pushed her arm high and held it there, while his other hand gripped her neck. He was straining her back over the writing-table. Her head hit wood and she could see the lamp, a few inches above her forehead. His breath was heavy and foul upon her face. She went limp, his hold slackened, and she brought down the gun.

Phil heard the report and knew herself free of him a moment before the tearing agony started in her arm. She caught at the edge of the table and dragged herself upright. The lamp toppled. Clin was gone and she was alone with a gushing groove in her arm and the weight of his pressure at the side of her throat.

She stumbled outside to shout for Manoela, but only a croak came and, dazed with pain, she lurched to the gate and on to the track. She didn't know that she turned right instead of left; nor did she feel the cool tug of wild banana leaves as she floundered through the bush. Right arm across her breast, the palm cupped over the long sticky wound in her left upper arm, her chin sunk to ease the dreadful rasp as she breathed, Phil staggered on in the cool, moist darkness.

She came to the clearing and attempted to run. Somehow she mounted the steps and reached the veranda.

A man leapt from his chair within the room and crashed wide the mesh door. She gave a dry, racking sob.

"Julian! Oh, Julian!"

CHAPTER IX

WHILE he cleaned the wound and dressed it she lay white and still on the couch, scarcely breathing. But as he was washing the blood from her forearm and hands the drug he had made her gulp down with whisky began to wear off, and fiery waves of pain engulfed her. She trembled and sweated, a defenceless collection of nerves and agonies.

Julian held her and wiped her brow with a damp cloth. He spoke quietly, only his eyes revealing a cold and deadly violence.

"It's the antiseptic that's giving you gyp, but I had to use plenty to prevent infection. It's a brute of a gash, but the worst should be over soon. Talk a bit, if you can." He was pale at the nostrils as he measured his thumb over the purpling mark at her throat. "Who was it?"

"I . . . I did it myself . . . fired the automatic. He was . . . drunk."

"Who?"

"Clin. The gun went off and he . . . ran away."

"I'll deal with Clin Dakers tonight."

"No . . . let him go. He's sailing at dawn."

"By God he is! Maybe before." He put a glass to her lips. "You're to sleep now. I'll find you a capsule and leave some boys on guard."

He went out and came back wearing a jacket. As he bent to give her a clean handkerchief his pocket swung forward and she clutched it, feeling the hard shape it contained.

"No more shooting, Julian. Please!"

"I always carry it. Get some sleep."

Outside he called the boys, instructed them in curt dialect, and slid into the car. As the trees thinned on either side of the road he noticed the orange glow between and above them, and from where the plantation ended the blaze was clearly visible. One of the houses on the cliff was afire.

Half-way along the bush track his beams picked out the gesticulating outline of a man, and he pulled up beside the coughing, choking figure of Roger Crawford.

"It's Phil's house," he panted. "Practically gutted, and we can't find her."

"Get in," ordered Julian. "She's at my place."

Roger slumped into the seat, made a strangled sound and dropped his face into his hands. Farther on they picked up Drew, and Julian drove past the flaming building, past Matt's dark dwelling to the equally blank-looking house that belonged to Clin Dakers.

He told them what had happened. "So now we find the devil," he said without emotion. "A quick glance over the house and then we'll go down to the waterfront to search the vessel that's getting ready to leave."

Clin's trunk still stood in his bare, musty living-room. His bed was stripped of everything save the disintegrating mattress. As they came out again Julian made a swift dive after a cotton-clad woman who was sidling, bent low, along the path towards the track. He yanked her to her feet.

"So it's you, you——I'll"

"Missus Pheel," she whimpered. "She dead."

Julian had flung her down again, but Roger stayed to say, Missus has been hurt, Manoela, by the white master who lives in here. You tell us if you see him."

She wailed something and grovelled away.

Phil slept, unaware that at intervals the houseboy came in with the insect spray or to examine the lamp. He was there when she awoke, and the lamp was out. Pencils of grey light invaded the room through the venetian blinds, and somewhere in the building a native was singing as he started his chores for the day.

She said, "Has your master come?"

"No, missus."

"Oh. Pass my wrist-watch, will you?"

It was caked with blood and she bade him clean the face. A quarter to six. Julian had been gone nearly eight hours.

"Have you heard nothing from your master?"

"Little master come two-three hours ago. Him go 'way again."

Drew or Roger, she supposed.

"I'd like some coffee," she said.

Waiting, Phil cautiously raised her left wrist, but the knife-twist up near her shoulder brought her hand back to its former position at her side. Her neck was stiff, her throat parched and hurting. She had never known such a concentration of pain.

The coffee was long in coming, and when at last the boy placed the tray on a small table and pushed it near to the wicker couch Phil could not budge to pour it out.

"All right, Sam," came from the doorway. "Bring another cup and leave it for me."

She had heard neither the car nor his footsteps. When Julian came near and pulled up a chair she saw grime on his face and clothes, and sweat in the armpits of his drill jacket.

"Did you find him?" she whispered.

He nodded. "Black or white coffee?"

"A dash of milk, please." Her eyes pleaded. "You must be very tired, Julian, but . . . I have to ask."

"Sugar?" He dropped in a spoonful and stirred. Intent upon filling the second cup, he said abruptly, "Yes, we found him hiding below the cliff, about half an hour ago."

"You'd searched all night?"

"Climbed and watched. He'd made friends with the skipper of the freighter, and though I'd forbidden the man to sail I didn't trust him. I guessed Clin had decided to swim out before it was light. We shook some life into Matt Bryson and the four of us spread out from the harbour to the lagoon."

He dragged the handkerchief from his top pocket and dried inside the open collar of his shirt.

"Which one of you . . . captured him?"

"He wasn't captured. I was crouching in the ferns above the beach when I caught sight of him flat on his front and drawing himself along one of the paths to the lagoon. He heard me and got up to run, and I let him have it in the leg." In a voice like steel he added, "I meant to take him alive."

"But, Julian, what good . . ."

"I crippled him, but the woman—your servant—sprang

up from nowhere and stuck a knife in his back."

"Manoela," she breathed, her eyes wide and dark. "How . . . frightful!"

"He was lucky," he said in clipped tones. "Here, drink your coffee."

He questioned her about the sensations in the injured arm, and spread a brown ointment over the bruise.

Presently she had the courage to say, "What did you do to Manoela?"

"Nothing. We let her escape."

"I'm so glad. I hope she's gone back to her room in my garden to wait for me."

There was a silence. Then Julian said: "You won't be going back to the house on the cliff. It's burnt out."

She pushed up on her right hand, staring. "Burnt . . . out?"

"The heat was too fierce to trace a cause. At first it looked as if Dakers might have thought he'd killed you and returned to destroy the evidence, but it must have blazed up as soon as you left. It was an inferno when I got down there."

"I remember," she said dully. "The lamp fell."

"That was my conclusion. No use fretting about it."

"My piano," she reminded him bleakly, "and the books and tapestries. My clothes . . ."

"What about them?" he demanded roughly. "You might have fainted and perished with them. Can't you be grateful you didn't?" He sat down again and inclined her way. "Later on, Matt's coming up for a talk. Meanwhile I'll have one of the sheds cleared and a wooden floor and ceiling put in. It'll be primitive, but we'll do our masculine best to contrive a decent, all-purpose room for you by this evening."

"Thanks."

She lay back and managed to turn her head away, to face the wall. He went through for a bath and a shave, and in a few minutes Sam came to set the table. Despairingly, she wished Manoela were here with warm water, a towel and a clean dress.

Teeth clamped, she swung down her legs, used a chairback for support and stood up. After a moment's vertigo she got out to the veranda and leaned against one of the posts. Sam must have called his master, for Julian strode out, mopping off traces of his shave with a face towel, which he threw down on to a chair. He sat on the rail and looked up at her, squeezed her fingers and let them drop.

"Hell, isn't it, being a lone woman . . . but you chose it, Phil, and you've no option but to take what comes. I'd drive you up to the mission if it weren't so full of disease."

"I shall be all right," she muttered. "It's odd, but losing the house—and everything, is much harder to bear than this," indicating her swathed arm. "I've no home, no clothes, and for the next six months, till my yearly allowance comes from the lawyer in Cape Town, I shall be penniless."

"None of which is important," he said crisply. "I'll provide you with food and shelter, and Matt will order you some clothes. What worries me," teasingly, "is how to get you washed and slicked up now. The best way would be for you to have a shot at it in my bedroom, and to call me if you're stuck."

His demeanour, though considerate and helpful, dared her to give in. The time for collapse was past and from now on she had to build. His attitude was: "We'll help you, but don't forget that you brought it on yourself." Like everything else at the moment, it hurt.

Matt's mien, when he strolled in mid-morning, was more sentimentally sympathetic. He patted her head and clucked with distress, and his jaw literally slipped when he noticed the discolouration at her throat.

He stayed to lunch, and afterwards the two men conferred over her temporary quarters and left Phil to rest. At about four Sam brought tea, and when Julian came home at dusk she was sitting on the veranda, the small capable hands locked together in her lap, her face colourless and resigned.

He brought her gin in a lime and soda and had something similar himself, but he made no effort at conversation till the glasses were empty and Phil had returned to moody contemplation of the black outlines of the trees.

Then he said: "Crawford's peeved that you should have fought your way out here last night when he and Drew were only two hundred-odd yards from your house. I told him you were probably driven by an instinctive dread of passing Daker's place."

"I suppose that was it," she agreed dispiritedly.

"You're sorry you came to me?"

"You've been very kind, and it's wonderfully generous of you to arrange living space for me, but . . ."

She halted, and Julian, apparently, had no intention of helping her out. He finished his cigarette and stubbed it.

"Would you like to go to your quarters now?" he asked offhandedly, "or will you stay to dinner?"

"I'll go now," she chose.

He brought a flashlight and took a firm, impersonal grip of her right arm, just at the back of her elbow. They passed the fermenting sheds and the garage, a large storehouse and some smaller sheds. The last but one had three new white wooden steps leading up to a door. Julian went ahead to open up; he scraped a match and set it to the wick of a lamp.

Light grew in the room, illumining a whitewashed wood ceiling and log walls, an iron bed covered by a large blue blanket, and a vaguely familiar Belgian rug on the new floor. The lamp stood on a lowboy, its plain cream shade reflected in a square mirror. Away in the shadows lurked an armchair, a dining chair and a small table. As she surveyed one article after another, Phil's chest went harsh with emotion.

"It's crude," he said, "but you can superintend improvements. We've fixed you up with an outhouse which you can use as a bathroom, and so on."

He'd thought of everything. Phil tugged in her lip between her teeth.

"I'll send Sam over with an extra lamp and a meal." He paused. "I doubt if we'll be able to hire you another woman servant. Manoela must care a lot for you. Could you stand having her around again?"

"Yes. Oh, yes."

"I'll chase her up tomorrow. She can prepare your food in my kitchen and sleep next door. You needn't worry at night. A couple of boys always patrol the buildings in case of attempted theft." He laid his box of matches beside the lamp and cast a final glance around the room. "Whatever you want, tell Sam. Shoot the bolt when I'm gone and he'll knock. Good night."

Mechanically she answered and obeyed his instructions. Restlessly, she drifted back to the lowboy and pulled open the top drawer, expecting it to be empty. But inside there were a pile of printed handkerchiefs such as Matt sold in his store, and a few large white ones with a J in one corner; a new military hairbrush and a black comb, a card of hair grips, a canister of talcum, a toothbrush, toothpaste, sponge and soap.

Heartstrings unbearably stretched, Phil examined the next drawer. Towels, sheets, pillow-cases, check tablecloths and napkins. The bottom drawer held lengths of material from Matt's bales, and . . . a cellular shirt and a pair of shorts!

Phil sat on the side of the bed, cradling her wounded arm, her whole being heavy with useless longings. She ate a little of the dinner Sam brought, and got ready for bed. Slowly and painfully she sloughed her clothes. Then she put out one lamp and dimmed the other, and turned down the blankets.

On the crisp white pillow lay the final push to the floodgates: a folded suit of men's blue pyjamas. Phil laid her cheek against them and cried.

CHAPTER X

AS soon as she could use her arm Phil's buoyancy returned. It needed courage to visit the blackened area where her house had stood, but already the pale green of new growth speared from the ashes, and it would not be long before all traces of the fire were overlaid by a young jungle. So she looked on it as dispassionately as she could, and passed on. Clin Dakers' house, too, was demolished, leaving only Matt's solid structure and the cream-washed building shared by Roger and Drew.

In her own log cabin, kept sweet and polished by Manoela, and in the small garden which had been fenced off in front, she found plenty to fill her time. Apart from replenishing her wardrobe, there were curtains and bed-cover to stitch, and mats to embroider. As a change from sewing and gardening she made a couple of sketches of the waterfront, and knocked up frames to contain them. Impossible, of course, to get hold of any glass, but one benefit of creating one's own pictures was that when flies had ruined them new ones cost nothing.

Yes, there was plenty to do and see, and when night had swept in and noises ceased Phil could, if she wished, loop back a curtain and enjoy the sense of companionship offered by the lights at the house. Entertaining was beyond her hut's capacity, but occasionally Matt or Roger came over at sundowner time, the trader bringing his own bottle of whisky and Roger more than willing to absorb the lime or grenadilla she served.

Phil had written to the lawyer in Cape Town stating her plight and begging him to send part of next year's allow-ance. At the rate mails moved in equatorial regions she would be lucky to receive a reply within six weeks, but it would be good to be independent again. Even here, where she could run a stores account with Matt and tot up Man-oela's wages against the day when her cheque would arrive, it irked to possess no ready cash. A trip through the market was no fun at all if you couldn't purchase a few yams or a pair of beadwork slippers that caught the eye.

It was astonishing, when one was forced to begin again at scratch and accumulate fresh property, what a vast number of goods make up the normal person's quota. Phil's most difficult acquisition was a swim suit. Matt stocked only woolen trunks, most of which turned out to be moth-chewed or mouldy. She selected the best she could find and made a flowered top which shrank lamentably and had to be discarded in favour of another cut from a pair of interlock pants.

Some time she would have to visit the mainland, to buy underclothes which matched and felt sleek to the skin and one or two tailored dresses, and to search around for a gramophone and records. She missed music more than books.

A few weeks after Clin's death Rodrigo Astartes came to the plantation. Astride a well-groomed mule, his generous torso and limbs clad in a pale grey flannel suit, Rodrigo made his way down the mountain-side to where the road widened, and sent a man ahead to announce his coming and to entreat the loan of a car for the last three miles of his journey.

An hour later, after Rodrigo had bathed away his sweat and taken a double whisky in cold soda, Phil was summoned to pour tea for Julian and his guest. When she entered the living-room, blinking a little till her pupils became accustomed to the dimness, Rodrigo's small eyes scintillated, and he bowed and clicked his stubby heels in the way she remembered from their single brief meeting eighteen months ago.

"But how charming," he exclaimed. "Do not ask me to believe that you are the child who abandoned her education in order to nurse the poor brother! You were so young and big-eyed."

"So different," murmured Julian drily. "Believe it or not, senhor, the child is as rooted in the island as our trees. One day, of course, she will go wrong in the head, commit suicide and become a legend."

"You joke, Mr. Caswell. She is as sane as you are. Look at the wide, smooth forehead, the clearness and depth of iris in her eyes, the humorous mouth." Rodrigo closed his lids for an ecstatic moment. "Senhorita, you are everything I thought never to meet on Valeira. You have beauty, simplicity, courage."

Apparently Julian deemed it time to curtail the flattery. To Phil he said: "Senhor Astartes likes mint tea, the way you prepare it. Do you mind?"

She gave him a demure, half-mocking glance, to which he returned a tolerant smile. Unspoken between them lay her challenge that since she had lived in the plantation buildings he had never invited her into his house unless a second man were present.

Over tea, which Rodrigo praised with locked fingers, he gave reasons for his visit.

"Only this week, senhorita, have I heard of your misfortune—the burning of your house. It grieved me profoundly. Mr. Caswell will tell you that the Novada casa has many rooms, all of them furnished. It is my desire that you will accept whatever furniture you need."

"How extraordinarily kind," said Phil warmly. "Mr. Caswell and Mr. Bryson have provided me with a home and all that goes with it—everyone has been overwhelmingly helpful. . . ."

"Pardon, senhorita . . . these gentlemen must have denuded their own homes to fill yours. We exiles in the wilderness prize certain possessions—if you have lost something you valued may I not be permitted to replace it?"

"I loved the house for its associations," she said simply.

He spread his hands. "Will you not relieve my crowded rooms of a single article? A cabinet, a desk . . . something? Surely there is one thing you miss as though you had lost a dear friend?"

"Two things," she admitted, spearing a slice of lemon and setting it afloat on a second glass of tea for Julian. "My piano and gramophone."

"Ha! That is good. We have two pianos, and my sons no longer use their little gramophone since my wife brought back from Lisbon a large one. It will make me very happy to provide you with music."

"But, Senhor Astartes——"

Sharply, Julian broke in: "I didn't know you'd lost a gramophone. You can have mine."

Rodrigo, his round face puckered with hurt, looked from one to the other. "I have intruded? You are perhaps . . . fiancés?"

"Not at all," said Julian. "Till she leaves the island I am Miss Crane's unofficial guardian."

"I should have understood that," Rodrigo answered with humility. "Later I will ask your permission to send the senhorita a gift."

An awkward moment expanded and held the room. It was Rodrigo, the exquisitely polite Latin, who ended it with a delighted laugh.

"Now for my news. My elder son is to be married! You remember him, senhor . . . Amino? My wife spent two exhausting months in Lisbon and has now made a contract with a girl of good, but impoverished, connections. Amino will meet her at Libreville and be married there. We think it wise that they should be united before the young lady experiences life on Valeira."

"Supposing she dislikes the island," suggested Phil.

"Exactly," the Portuguese returned blandly. "We cannot risk it, especially as our younger son, Tomé, has declared that he will choose his own wife. Tomé is wild and daring; he means what he says. Amino is the solid, the stable one." He turned to Phil, and added with animation: "You would make friends with Tomé . . . he has the nature of the explorers you admire. I would like you to be among my guests at Navada for my elder son's wedding festa."

Julian did not ask Phil to dinner that evening, nor did he call her to say goodbye to the Portuguese next morning. It was Rodrigo who waddled over and cried a farewell through her window.

After lunch Julian brought over the portable gramophone and a pile of records.

"I haven't used it since the Fosters were here," was his reply to her protest. "In any case, we can't have people we hardly know loading us with expensive gifts. I turned down the piano on your behalf."

"Did you? I'm sorry."

His brow met in a straight line. "Sorry? Both his pianos are baby grands and cost at least four hundred each. Would you care to be that much in his debt?"

"I didn't mean I wanted his piano. I was thinking of his feelings. You injured them pretty badly yesterday."

"Rodrigo is a continental," he said with a trace of contempt, "and born to intrigue, especially for his own ends. A piano is rich bait, but he thinks you worth it."

She jeered. "Not so long ago you advised me to consider entering the family. Tomé sounds interesting."

"He's little different from an English boy of twenty-three, except that he smells of garlic and perfume." Julian shrugged offhandedly, and leaned in a familiar posture against the doorframe. "I'd sooner see you married to young Crawford."

The smile faded. Her glance on his hard, averted jaw, she said, "If I were to marry without love I'd marry for money. That makes sense, doesn't it?"

"There are Englishmen with money on the coast."

Phil's tongue damped her lips. "Are you back on the old theme of how to get rid of me, or repenting your kindness in letting me live here on the plantation?"

"Neither." His tone was cynical. "I'm merely warning you that now Rodrigo has seen you he won't relax his pursuit of you for his son unless you leave Valeira or become another man's property."

"You invited me to meet him!"

"Only because you interested him at a range of a hundred yards or so and he insisted on closer acquaintance. It was bound to happen some time." He shifted and quizzed down at her coolly. "How much longer are you going to kid yourself you're having fun?"

Her chin rose, the hazel eyes glinted. "This is a fine time to ask that, when all I own is my skin. You needn't make it so obvious that it irritates you to have me near. Till my money comes there's not much I can do about it —except move in with Matt."

"And what," he queried deliberately, "will you do when your money comes?"

"I shall pay my debts," she flashed, "and take the first boat for the coast. I'm sick of your domineering and intolerance, your perpetual stony moods. I hate your inflexibility and grudging kindness. . . ."

"Shut up," he said brusquely, "you're ranting like a schoolgirl. God knows you're welcome to anything I've been able to do for you. If you hadn't been such a stubborn little fool . . ." he stopped, and then said "It's a bargain? When your cheque arrives you'll move out?"

Phil hadn't meant anything so final as that. It made her tremble inside to hear him state it, unequivocally. She moved to the table and took one of the records between her fingers, twisting and examining it.

"In a bargain *two* people gain in some way," she said. "I don't have to make any promises to you, Julian, except that I'll leave your property as soon as I can."

"Don't be an idiot. I wouldn't let you live anywhere else on the island."

"No?" She faced him, curious. "Why?"

"You're going to stay where you're least trouble." His

lean jaw twitched. "If it helps at all, I've disliked you less since you've camped here."

Her mouth quivered into a sudden smile. "Thanks. I've tried not to be a pest."

"You haven't succeeded—but don't bother, little one. I'm getting used to having a husky-voiced girl around. I'll miss you."

Now she laughed up at him. "Maybe! I made no promises."

But he was no longer smiling. His eyes glittered and his mouth thinned as he straightened and answered: "This position can last for a certain time, but the day will come when you'll have to get out or get married. Think it over. So long."

Five minutes later Phil still stood by the table, the tip of her forefinger tracing the tiny groove in a black disc. She was recalling a remark of Matt's: "As soon as he notices you have eyes and hips he'll give you hell."

It sounded . . . exciting.

CHAPTER XI

PERHAPS the person most unsettled by Rodrigo Astartes' visit was Roger Crawford. Quite by chance he had been the one to drive the stout little Portuguese to the end of the road, where his boys and mules were camped. Rodrigo, stinging from Julian's high-handed behaviour the previous evening, had basked in the deference accorded him by the young overseer. Expansively, he had issued another invitation to Amino's wedding feast and, his small black eyes shrewd, he had guided the conversation round to Roger's duties and the plantation.

"Besides supervising the copra and cinchona, you also arrange all shipping?" Rodrigo had gasped expressively. "That is very responsible work for a man so young. Doubtless you are well paid?"

"A thousand a year," Roger admitted.

"In pounds sterling? But how scandalous!"

"With bonus added I top twelve hundred—not too bad. There's nothing to spend it on."

"But you have an ambition?" Rodrigo suggested. "The money you save on Valeira is accumulating for a purpose, is it not?"

Warmed by the wealthy man's interest, Roger nodded. "I suppose most white men in the tropics have an object or they'd soon degenerate. Mine's a bookshop."

With a little sigh Rodrigo leaned back and waved short, thick fingers. "Me, I would pay good money to a man of your type. Already you have much experience of the cacao, and you have the Englishman's aplomb for handling natives. If some time you should need a change of wind, a different view of the mountain and a house that is comfortable and all your own, come to the Novada. I will give you two thousand a year."

To Roger's credit he was not dazzled. His pulses drummed, but simultaneously with a swift succession of rosy pictures he saw himself ostracized by both English and Portuguese on the island. Besides, Phil lived this side of the mountain.

"You are kind, senhor," he said. "Unfortunately, I am under contract."

"Contracts can be ended."

"Mine would cost me three months' salary."

"So? If you came to me I would be willing to put that right and allow you an extra sum for expenses." He smiled, his plump, swarthy cheeks ballooning each side of well-shaped teeth. "I do not ask for a prompt decision. In three years you can earn three thousand pounds. Consider it well, my son."

"Thank you, sir."

Rodrigo watched the passing trees, nodding appreciatively at a clean, wide cross-path. The Portuguese planters were less meticulous, but capable of great admiration for what they deemed unnecessary labour.

"Mr. Caswell is a fine manager. He gets things done. You find him a hard master?"

"Occasionally, but he generally turns out to be right."

"There is no . . . trouble between you white men?" The enquiry was suave, unpointed, except for the hesitation.

"Trouble? No, why should there be?"

A shrug. "One woman, four suitors. She is refreshingly

unsubtle, that girl, and too young for a man like Caswell."

The car shuddered over an exposed root. Sweat gathered in the palms of Roger's hands and under the open revers of his collar. For the first time in his adult life he knew a murderous impulse; he wasn't quite sure against whom.

Two full minutes passed before he was able to say: "Mr. Caswell dislikes women. He's tried all ways to get Phil to leave the island."

"I believe that," Rodrigo assured him. "However the girl attracted him, his duty would come first. But once the duty is done, once the girl has chosen to stay . . ." He snapped his fingers. "Tell me, my boy, have you heard him coaxing the young lady to go since she is installed close to him? No? I thought not. Is it your opinion that he still dislikes women?"

"He speaks to her as if she were a child!"

"You are deceived? I am not." He gave a throaty laugh. "No man could dwell within yards of an appealing young woman in this climate and these conditions without being aware and desirous. Not even cold-blooded Mr. Caswell. There was an incident yesterday afternoon when this girl . . . but never mind." Rodrigo laughed magnanimously. "She is able to take her pick. Who will blame her if she prefers the manager to his employees?"

Further comment from Roger was unnecessary. Astartes hummed an airy tune which nicely filled in till they reached the abrupt termination of the road, and when they parted he held out a moist hand and reiterated his earlier invitation. Roger returned thanks and a blank smile, and politely waited till the mule procession was out of sight.

He was half-way back to the waterfront before he could think clearly, and by that time the guttural insinuations had grown a thin skin of unreality.

Still, like the worm that curls at the heart of a peach without apparently damaging the fruit, during the following days the talk with Rodrigo sometimes made itself felt and caused him restlessness and dissatisfaction.

Roger slid back into his groove, but derived less and less pleasure from contemplation of the future. When Phil taxed him with being morose he blamed the appalling heat, yet he still asked her up for tennis.

One Saturday, when she appeared with her racquet, looking sweet in crisp white shorts and a silk shirt, he linked an arm in hers and persuaded her to walk through the bush to the rocks that overhung the beach. He dropped down in the shade of a tree, tugging her hand and patting the springy turf beside him.

"It's too soon after lunch to play. Talk to me, Phil." He touched the racquet which lay across her knees. "Did Caswell give you this?"

"No. Julian's spare was too heavy. Matt got this for me from Lagos. It's warping already."

"Aren't we all?" Quickly, he amended, "Not you, Phil, because for the time being you've got all you want." His fair skin darkened, but whatever he had been about to add remained unsaid. Instead he pulled his mouth into a grin and raked through his lank, wheaten hair. "Lord, I need a haircut! Don't you long for shops and hairdressers and parties?"

She nodded. "About once a week I go through all the yearnings just to remind myself of what I'm missing. After that I thank heaven I'm still on the island among people I know."

Meeting her candid hazel stare, his own eyes hot with sudden emotion, he muttered: "Phil . . . if you knew how hard it is! I can't help loving you and wanting you. We're the youngest here—it's normal for us to be together. I know you don't love me yet, but you do like me, and the other will come. Phil . . . darling . . ."

His cheek burned into her shoulder, and against her chin she felt his forehead, cold and clammy. Involuntarily—for his need tugged at her heart and he was too decent to hurt —she held him and turned her mouth to his temple as if he were a small boy seeking comfort.

"You see!" came his stifled exclamation. "It wouldn't be so difficult to love me. I'd promise not to take you back to England, Phil. We'd settle at the Cape, anywhere. We might even stay on Valeira. I could stick it if we were married."

His nearness disturbed her. Tiny fires leapt in her blood and a strange weight of love burdened her heart. Through half-closed lids she saw eyes like blue stones and a straight

73

ironic mouth. With a sound of distress she pushed Roger from her.

"Don't. I can't stand it. I don't love you, Roger. I don't love anyone."

She scrambled to her feet and avoided the hand that strove to detain her. In the white sunshine she sped between wild banana and tree ferns till he caught her up and clung to her elbow.

"Don't run away," he whispered. "Anything rather than that."

She answered him with a strained smile. "It's all right, Roger. No harm done. Could you find me a long drink?"

For the rest of the afternoon Phil was quiet, and when it was time to go she mentioned that the walk up to the plantation had tonic properties which might be of benefit to Mr. Drew. She went home between the two men and bade them goodbye where the track met the clearing.

To Julian, who was taking a sundowner on his veranda, Phil called an abrupt "Good night," to which he replied as briefly. She spent the evening paging through the dozen novels which Rodrigo had sent round by a Novada freighter.

In the middle of the night a squall roared in from the sea, heralding ten days of torrential storms. The storms mostly came up in daylight and spent themselves before dusk, so that the evenings were cool and freer from pests than usual. Some friends of Matt's from Cotonou had sheltered in the Bay, and for a week he gave a series of drink and gambling parties. Phil went to them, in Julian's car, and enjoyed the gossip which circulated round the wicker table in Matt's veranda. The chairs were low and comfortable, made either of woven grass or canvas with footrests and padded arms. The drinking was leisurely, pipes and cigarettes created a grey haze.

The rains ended, or rather they shifted a few miles south to shed unwanted moisture on the emerald montain slopes. The plantation was enveloped in a hot, enervating mist which kept the sweat glands perpetually working and tried the nerves. Phil's books became glued together with mildew and shoes unworn for a day or two grew blotches of fungus. The atmosphere was more drenching and debilitating than at any time during her stay on the island, and she felt mentally sick besides. How she longed for a letter from the lawyer in Cape Town.

CHAPTER XII

SHE was in the back room of Matt's store when the Portuguese official came up with the mail. He handed over Matt's batch of envelopes and newspapers and shook his head in response to Phil's enquiry. No, there was nothing for the senhora. See, the plantation packet was secured separately with string, and there were just these few for the Senhores Drew and Crawford. He was sorry, but in a fortnight there might be more letters.

Matt said, "What d'you want money for . . . a new dress for the Astartes' party? It's a month away. I'll get you some silk."

"Damn the party," she answered. "I just want to be independent—not tied to that log cabin and Julian's bounty. You'll let me pay a little of what I owe, but he never will. I hate him."

"Your perspective's all wrong. He's the big boss and you happen to be one of his minor responsibilities," Matt told her, brutally casual. "Count yourself lucky that he's treated you so well. Here, take this bundle of magazines and let me have them back when you've finished with them. And stop wanting to alter Julian. He's set too hard."

Phil climbed the steep rut from the waterfront. Reaching the shade of the trees, she dragged the wrapper from the roll of papers and opened one. Dawdling, she arrived at the clearing as the post official in his bush car was leaving. His head bobbed through the window-space.

"Pardon, senhora. There is one letter for you, but one —a small envelope among Senhor Caswell's mail. He will give it to you. Many apologies!"

Phil nodded to him and ran across the grass and up the steps to Julian's veranda. He was perusing a note in the living-room when she burst in, and he looked up to indicate her letter, which lay apart from his own.

"There's your cheque," he remarked with a half-smile.

"If you like I'll change it for you. I've plenty of currency in the safe."

She used his paper-knife. "I hope the old boy has been generous. I framed my request in a way to wring his heart."

But no pink slip was attached to the letter, nor did her panicky tearing of the envelope dislodge a cheque. So she flattened the paper and read most of the closely typed wording before raising her head to encounter Julian's questioning gaze.

"What's wrong?" he demanded.

Bewildered and fearful, she said: "Maybe I'm dense. Read it, and tell me what he's getting at."

He came and looked over her shoulder, and in a minute he took the letter from her and went through it again.

"God, what a let-down!" he said. "Your mother must be a bitch."

"Looks like it, doesn't it?" she managed thinly. "He says she was never divorced from my father and has only recently married again. The money is legally hers, not mine. It's . . . horrible, Julian."

"You can't get away from the law."

"Apart from that . . . how could she, after breaking his heart! She was the reason he stayed in the tropics. He worshipped her—Nigel told me so."

"Any man who idolises a woman is begging for trouble," he commented tersely. "I suppose she and her new husband are hard up, so she tried this—and succeeded. You notice she wishes you to write to her at the lawyer's office?"

"Convention," she said bitterly. "She never cared for anyone but herself. I'd rather die than take anything from her."

"Melodramatic, but doubtless true," he allowed. "Well, it could be worse. For three years you'll be broke, but at twenty-one you'll get three hundred a year. . . ."

"I didn't see that."

"Here it is in the last paragraph. 'In case this information has come as a shock to you, may I remind you of the clause in your late father's will which provides for a sum of three hundred pounds to be paid to you on your twenty-first birthday, or on the date of your marriage, whichever comes first, and annually thereafter.' "

She scarcely heard. Her eyes, large and dark, mirrored a sick despair. "I'm untrained. I shall have to go to Cape Town and find some piffling job."

"What would you *like* to do?"

"I don't know, except that I'm . . . scared of loneliness. Julian," she came closer and touched the shirt-cuff rolled above his elbow, "think of something for me—some way I can remain on Valeira and earn my keep."

"If you weren't a girl," he said with unwonted softness, "I could put you to work—make a planter of you. But you're as well aware as I am that there's nothing here for a woman."

"Except marriage," she said.

"Not that, either, unless you decide on Crawford, whose time is up in a little over a year."

"Perhaps Matt will have some ideas. I'll go down and see him."

"No, don't!" He grasped her wrist and she twisted back, surprised at his force and peremptoriness. "Keep it between the two of us for the present. Give me time to think it over."

Breathlessly, as though she had been hurrying, she murmured: "All right. I'm in your hands, Julian."

His short laugh was unmirthful. "The mission people implied as much eight months ago. I'm making no claims. Let's shelve this business till the week-end. Come to dinner on Saturday."

"Don't you mean lunch?"

"I mean dinner. Discussions are best conducted after sundown."

What Julian intended for her future she could only conjecture, but desperately, with every nerve and fibre of her being, she relied on his calm, merciless brain to conceive a miracle.

By Saturday, encouraged by his agreeable nod whenever they happened to meet, she was happy and excited with anticipation. She put on the tan linen dress which heightened the flames in her hair, and used a touch of the make-up left behind by Daphne Foster, after which she stood back to approve her reflection.

Julian paid her the compliment of wearing a white lounge suit and offering a cocktail without mocking her lack of years. For dinner they had roast pigeons, potatoes, tinned beans and asparagus, and a steamed fruit pudding which so delighted Phil that she ate a second helping. Sam brought coffee and cognac to the veranda.

Presently Julian lit a second cigarette from his first and leaned back, regarding her keenly.

"A while ago, you said you'd leave the island when your money turned up. Supposing you had three hundred a year from now on—would you go?"

"I'm . . . not sure." He was eyeing her with a ruthless intensity which froze her heart. Her head bent. "Yes, if you wanted it so badly."

"Good. Now we're getting somewhere." He stubbed the half-cigarette, slung one knee over the other and rested his arm on it. "This lawyer will be satisfied with a marriage certificate, but he's bound to verify the details. It'll have to be watertight. Someone must go through the ceremony with you."

"No!" she cried. "That would be vile. I couldn't do it."

"Listen to me," he said grimly. "We're going to settle this once and for all. Any preference as to the partner?"

She sprang up, trembling. "I won't hear any more. It's ghastly, discussing marriage as you would a tennis match. I'll stay on the island for the next three years. I'll work for the shippers and pay you back—"

"You won't." He was head and shoulders above her, clipped violence in his voice. "If there were any way of forcing you to accept money from me I'd take it. There isn't, so I'll marry you in Lagos, and make you legally entitled to your own."

For a frightened, frantic moment she was unable to drag her gaze from the taut brown throat. Then she put her hands to her face, pressing them to her forehead as if in pain.

His savage tones continued: "We'll send the lawyer the certificate and you can return here till the first cheque arrives. After that you go to the mainland and start annulment proceedings. Nothing complicated about it."

Her hands dropped. Pale and strained, she asked, "Why should you do this?"

"Why not? The name is mine to bestow as I please. It's one you needn't be ashamed of, and later you could revert to your own."

"What would the other men think?"

"They wouldn't know. We'd travel separately both ways and carry on as we are now till the lawyer parts up. The whole arrangement would be between you and me."

She paused. Then, "If I agreed you'd demand a promise from me?"

"Naturally. Valeira's no good for you, and never will be. Besides missing a lot of fun you're playing hell with your health. In addition, you're upsetting the men—"

"You'd get rid of me for Roger's sake?"

"For all our sakes," he corrected irritably. "In time there'll come a successor to Roger."

"And the promise?"

"That once your cheque is here you'll sail on the first boat for Cape Town or England. To cover eventualities, I want your word that, whatever happens, you'll leave within three months and accept financial help from me till you're straightened out."

Her knuckles gleamed pale on the veranda rail. "I see. You seem to have thought of everything. But as a plan it's not quite up to your standard, Julian."

"Of course it isn't. Your blasted independence is in the way."

"Eight months ago you'd have shipped me to England without compunction."

"Not penniless. Anyway, time has made changes. You can do things with a precocious kid that are out of the question with a woman."

"You're sure we'd have grounds for an annulment?" she enquired in a low voice.

"The best in the world."

"Wouldn't you hate to be connected with a case of that sort?"

"I might, if I intended ever returning to England. Out

here one can commit murder and remain a good fellow. The climate is a wonderful get-out."

He moved and called for drinks. No more was said till they came, and he was pouring lime juice and topping it with gin.

"Forget the fantastic angle. You need the cash, and a few words before a registrar will procure it for you. Simple, isn't it?"

So simple as to be almost funny, if she could have gone into it with a wink and a cocked thumb. She took the glass and sipped at it, looked up into sardonic blue eyes and contrived a faint smile.

"I'll sleep on it," she said. "You're in no haste to take on a wife?"

"I can hardly wait." He grinned and drained his tumbler. "It's clear-cut enough. You may borrow without hope of repaying any part of the debt for three years, or seize the chance of immediate independence. Either way I'm with you."

"I don't understand why. You've always resented me."

"One can resent and still have compassion."

"Compassion? You?" She had an impulse to laugh out her pain into his ironical face. Where one craved love, pity seared the soul. Unsteadily, feeling raw and naked, she set down her drink and dabbed her lips. "You won't mind if I go now? Thank you for the dinner. I . . . I'd prefer to give you the answer tomorrow."

His shoulders lifted. "I've disappointed you. You'd have liked me to be sentimental. Mind the step—it's just behind you."

He accompanied her to her door, held the flashlight till the lamp glowed and said a casual good night.

Phil lingered near the table, her fingers locked tight with uncertainty and dread. In the back of her consciousness lay a conviction that her future, as she had seen it this evening, was inescapable; a magnet compelled her on to fulfilment, perhaps destruction.

Strange and terrible to be in love with a man like Julian. If only she had the pluck to take a loan from Matt and clear out. But such sacrifice was beyond human courage. For some reason clear only to himself, Julian had proposed a sort of marriage; that he had also set its limit she must ignore. He cared enough to risk a scandal; was it outside the bounds of possibility that he could be persuaded to care more? Supposing she failed?

But when she walked over to Julian's house next morning, wearing her usual shorts and shirt this time and bearing a freshly made vanilla cake, her chin was well up and her eyes smiling.

Instantly he caught her mood. Brows lifted, he bowed over the cake and flipped a thumbnail at her fingers.

"Here we go, little one," he jibed gently. "Into marriage and out of it within six months. When it's all over I'll write a book about it."

"I'll help you," she said, and joined in his grunt of laughter.

CHAPTER XIII

DELIBERATELY, Phil buttoned up her doubts and existed in the present, carefully observing all the precautions upon which Julian had insisted. When he went off to Lagos "to see a dentist and do some business," she did not go down to the waterfront to speed him. A couple of days later Matt was surprised at her anxiety to board a boat bound for one of the ports at the mouth of the Niger.

"You can't spend more than a couple of hours on land at a dump like that," he protested. "Those ports are pestholes."

"I shall stay aboard and go down to Libreville. I've heard you can buy French fashions there."

"Make the round journey?"

"If it's possible."

"What will you use for money?"

"I have several pounds," she said carefully. "Julian made me an advance till my allowance comes. He knew I was keen to take the trip."

"If he agreed to it . . ." Matt shrugged. "Take care of yourself, lovey, and keep near the boat."

Early next morning, followed by a husky Negro carrying her soft-topped hatbox from which a thorough scouring and polishing could not remove the traces of blue mould, Phil stepped on the deck of a clean little coaster.

Late in the afternoon the ship nosed between thickening mangroves whose roots clawed the silt bars in the delta. For a while they moved through calm waters between mangrove swamps and forested headlands, and by the time the white houses of the port were visible a blood-coloured sky was painting them red-gold, and dusk hazed the ramparts of trees on either side.

Phil opened her case for the inevitable customs man, and proceeded through the shed to where, in the darkness of a huge-girthed tree, Julian awaited her in a borrowed car to drive her on to Batu, a tiny trading station dependent on the precious and plentiful palm oil. The schooner they boarded reeked of the stuff; the decks were saffron and slippery with it, the holds chockful of drums.

That night they anchored off Lagos, and Phil slept in a hammock beneath the stars while Julian played cards in the cabin forward. She awoke in an enveloping wet fog with a crick in the spine and a headache. This morning her consuming desire was to be done with the beastly affair and return to the island.

Fortunately, everything moved smoothly. Mid-morning she and Julian were canoed ashore and he hired a taxi to convey them to one of the dazzling buildings. In a cool room he introduced the two English witnesses, and went through the ceremony and its aftermath of handshakes and good wishes as if marriage were a form of diversion in which he indulged every month or so. But for the thin gold circle on her finger Phil wouldn't have believed that brief words and a few signatures had tied so solemn a knot.

Back on the boat they had a late lunch and soon afterwards again put to sea. Another night in the hammock, a sunrise full of golden glory, and a morning on deck with an uncommunicative Julian. Flying-fish and exotic sea birds, boatloads of chocolate-skinned fishermen who shouted and gesticulated, the ocean a molten reflection of the sky. At noon they approached Libreville, and Phil recognized the smart coaster which had carried her away from Valeira.

"There's your bus home," said Julian. "Tell the skipper that friends brought you down from Nigeria. I hadn't better come ashore."

"Will I have time to buy clothes?"

He hesitated. "The customs people might be awkward as you've no visa, and there's always the danger of other unpleasantness."

"I thought the French were famous for their chivalry."

"Chivalry's a novel way of putting it," he said drily. "Transfer straight to the other ship and I'll try to get a couple of dresses for you in Lagos. What size?"

"Thirty-four hip."

The boat had stopped and a dinghy was being lowered. Phil straightened from the deck rail.

"It's all gone like clockwork. Thank you, Julian."

Paternally, he patted her head. "I'll be back in three days. Be careful what you say to Matt and don't think too much. So long, little one."

Back on the island her short absence assumed a shroud of unreality. Her resolve to make Julian love her now seemed the uttermost edge of childishness and absurdity. He was thirty-five, and so mercilessly uninterested in women that the marriage had left little imprint on his ego. Except when the mails came in he would be able to forget it, whereas she could not help but be palpitatingly aware of it day and night. Especially at night, when a tropical hush pressed up around the clearing and she lay perspiring inside her net.

She admitted to herself that for some time her last waking thought had been of Julian; not so much a thought as a vain, heartshaking need whose meaning was only now becoming plain. What wouldn't she give to own a few more years and a corresponding degree of experience!

When Matt came up to see how she was faring he told her that Drew was having the devil of a time with the shipping. The other day he had discovered that one of the holds leaked, and had ordered the usual cementing up.

"The skipper replied that he wasn't taking orders from

a so-and-so whippet and caulked with tar. He loaded and got out. This morning the *Bassington* put in. She was handled by the shore boys like a vessel half her size and poked a chunk out of the jetty. Drew's blathering about sabotage."

"Oh, Matt! Could it be?"

"Could be and probably is. Since Caswell took over, the ships have been searched on arrival . . . he's even gone over them himself in his zeal to put an end to smuggling."

"What sort of smuggling?"

"Drugs and liquor for the natives. The skippers used to make a packet out of it, so of course they're sore, and the Africans are not too happy, either." He sighed and added, "I'm out of pocket myself since the smuggling stopped."

"Matt! Were you in it?"

"They had to have a middleman, lovey," he said reasonably. "But I'm not grousing. The trouble is, Julian's making a white man out of me, and I can't say I take to it."

Late the following day Julian came back. Phil stood at her window hoping his head would turn her way, that he would spare her at least a nod. But doubtless even in the dark he had detected renovations to the jetty, and shot a few enquiries. For his brows were ominously straight, his whole expression stern. He strode into his house and she guessed he had demanded explanations, for later Drew and Roger came over on mules, and there was no free-and-easy drinking on the veranda.

Towards noon next morning a boy brought Phil a box containing two dresses, one apple green and the other white. His master was away all day at the plantation boundary, but perhaps the missus would come for drinks tonight?

All day her chest had a painful hollow, and Manoela's curry and rice dinner was wasted. Phil wore the new green dress and pressed a fist hard over her pounding heart as she made her way to the house. But she could have economized on the qualms.

At a table in Julian's veranda sat three men: Matt Bryson, the captain of the *Bassington* and Drew. From the doorway Julian gave her an appraising but impersonal smile.

"Sit down, Phil." Her name on his lips filled her with a

strange bitterness. "I thought you might like to meet Captain Fawcett. It's not improbable that you'll be making a journey with him some time."

Conventionally, she smiled back and took a low canvas chair near the rail. Julian shoved another one forward and sank into it, stretching his legs so that his shoe rested close to her sandal; his bare brown knees were near enough to be reached, had she dared to extend a hand.

After the others had contributed anecdotes, Julian glanced at Phil.

"They tell me you've been sailing. How did it feel to set foot on the mainland?"

Wishing it were possible to dislodge his steely composure, she answered: "Nightmarish. I was far happier at sea."

"The mainland does that to me, too," Matt submitted. "Last time I visited Lagos the women were wearing skirts above their knees and frying-pan hats. They fell in and out of marriage quicker than a fly in and out of a bowl of sugar."

"The kind *you* mixed with, Matt," she told him.

A mocking glint in his eyes, Julian said: "Today they consider marriage superfluous except as a meal ticket. Another drink, Captain?"

CHAPTER   XIV

AMINO ASTARTES brought his bride to Valeira in style. Their ship, a sleek white yacht belonging to one of Rodrigo's influential friends in Lisbon, flew bunting and an assortment of flags. She came in close to the British plantation, so that from the cliff and the waterfront the young Portuguese and his pretty olive-skinned wife could be seen smiling and waving from beneath a giant multi-coloured umbrella.

The young senhora was to be allowed a week in which to accustom herself to the heat and her in-laws before the wedding celebrations, which were scheduled to last three days. Rumour whispered that already the Novada harbour was jammed with the private craft of guests from Spain and Portugal, and that a genuine bullfight was being arranged.

All five of the English were invited, but Julian intended to send his apologies. Someone must stay on the plantation and at present he preferred it to be himself. Though Matt distrusted the sea, he had decided to make the run in his own little motor vessel, and Phil could go along if she liked.

Drew and Roger were still dourly discussing modes of travel when the white yacht steamed back into the bay, and a lithe young man in a tussore suit and beige sombrero, his magenta tie floating in the breeze, came ashore in a rowing-boat. He was met by a Portuguese official and saluted by a hastily summoned handful of the militia. A car carried him through the bush to the plantation.

Phil had just risen from an after-lunch siesta when she saw the arrival of the car from her convenient window, and guessed at once that the dark-complexioned visitor was Tomé, the younger son of the owner of the Novada.

"Manoela," she called.

The servant appeared from the outhouse where she had been rinsing the zinc bath.

"Manoela, there is a guest at the house. Tell Sam to offer him a drink and to send for the master. Explain that I will come shortly."

She found Tomé Astartes in Julian's living-room, his head critically on one side as he surveyed the bare surfaces of the furniture. His glass was already empty.

Tomé gazed at her. He gazed and gazed. Then: "Pardon, senhorita," he exclaimed. "I heard from my father that you are beautiful, but not how beautiful! I am Tomé Astartes."

"So I guessed. We were not expecting you."

"No. It is still three days to the festa, but my father sent me to assure his English guests how welcome they are, and to offer them the yacht as transport."

"Senhor Astartes is always thoughtful and kind."

Tomé had come forward. His eyes dark and devouring, he looked down at her; not far down, for his height was but average, yet it was sufficiently above hers to admit a sense of masculine superiority.

"My father admires you very much, and I, senhorita, have longed to make your acquaintance. To think that you

86

are on the island so long and we have never met!"

"There is a mountain between us. Won't you sit down? Mr. Caswell will not be long."

But Julian was in no apparent hurry. For an hour Tomé talked in the agreeable manner of the educated Latin.

Julian surprised them in the middle of a gust of laughter. Underneath his suave greeting Phil detected displeasure, and she remembered his dislike of Rodrigo.

She said, "Now Mr. Caswell has come I'll go back to my wooden house."

"But you do not remain always in the cabin? I shall see you again this evening and tomorrow?" Tomé demanded anxiously.

"You are staying till we all go back in the yacht?"

"If Senhor Caswell can accommodate me."

"Of course." Julian's acquiescence was firm but without cordiality. "I will arrange a little party for tonight."

"Oh, but I was hoping you would consent to have dinner on the ship," Tomé implored. "She is equipped and staffed. It would be very informal, but quite delightful. Senhorita, I command it!"

Julian shrugged. "Dine with us tomorrow, then."

Phil moved to the door and Tomé followed and bowed, displaying a crown of brilliantined black curls.

"Till seven, senhorita. Ha?"

Dinner on the yacht yielded its excitements. The captain brought his pet chimpanzee to the table and fed him with bananas and ground nuts. Phil, seated between Tomé and Matt, fascinatedly watched the thing hug his master and mouth the bristly cheek before he was led back to his chain.

Toast followed toast. Amino and Carlotta; Rodrigo; the English guests and Portugal. When an adjournment to the deck was suggested Matt and the captain stayed below to tap a fresh bottle of Scotch.

Tomé took Phil to the rail. Lights glimmered on the waterfront. The sea washed in crystal sheets over the beach, and along there past the houses a camp fire cast a triangle of flame over the waters. In the darkness one could always locate the natives by their fires. By night, Phil loved this hot, oppressive island for itself. While the cruel sun blazed and blanketed everything with steam, she tolerated it to be near Julian.

Tomé was saying: "The young overseer, Crawford, has been glaring at me. Is he annoyed that I should show more daring than he? Senhor Caswell also has a disagreeable look. I must not cross him, for is he not your guardian? Is it not of him that I must request permission to court you?"

Phil smiled. "It is, but it's not necessary to approach him. I would like to be your friend, senhor, but nothing closer."

He gave a pleased and comprehending laugh. "You are shy, and I adore shyness. I adore all of you, senhorita . . . your fair skin, your hair as rich and soft as silk, your smoky voice. Believe me—"

"I certainly shan't. If you continue now you will have nothing left to say tomorrow and the day after."

"I shall repeat it all in different words, for the rest of my life!"

This impassioned utterance seemed to echo along the deck. As, with studious casualness, the three Englishmen closed in upon them, Phil grinned to herself. Poor Tomé had no weapon against this bastion of British impassiveness. The rest of the evening had a flavour all its own, and Phil travelled home in the back of Julian's car feeling sleepy but exhilarated. It was good to be liked and protected, and to have fun.

Overnight, Tomé recovered his enthusiasm for the chase, and soon after breakfast he knocked politely on Phil's door and begged her to show him the lagoon and—dare he ask it?—to bathe with him. He swam well and he showed off. With what he deemed the *blasé* manner peculiar to the English, he offered her a cigarette and lit it for her, and produced a flask of brandy from his robe pocket.

In contrast to the highly flavoured dinner on the yacht, the meal which Julian ordered his boys to prepare was more nourishing than tasty. Stewed chickens of the scrawny West African type, tinned vegetables, a mixture of raw and tinned fruits, soft cheese and salt biscuits. Phil enjoyed it, for was she not placed opposite Julian so that occasionally they exchanged glances?

The constraint in the atmosphere did not entirely pass

her by. She knew that Roger still prickled from a one-sided argument with Julian over the mishandling of the *Bassington,* and that Tomé's composure rocked with the effort of eating food he loathed in the company of men he abhorred. Even Matt's mien was sober, as though he had promised his liver an easy passage this evening. But these things were external to the bitter-sweetness of the secret she shared with Julian . . . to which neither ever referred.

"My father is hoping that I, too, will soon have a wife," Tomé said, adding artlessly: "When his first grandson arrives he will divide the plantation and retire to Lisbon. Amino will live in the casa, and I"—he almost peacocked —"will build a new villa for my own family."

No one commented, but Matt gulped his coffee and took a cheroot from his case. The others lit cigarettes, and Tomé was asked what time tomorrow he wished to leave.

"We will go early, if it is convenient," the young man answered eagerly. "I am unwilling that we should miss the canoe races in the afternoon. I myself wish to compete." Politely he looked at Julian. "My father will greatly regret, senhor, that you are unable to be of our party, though he will comprehend your difficulties. It is not as if you *owned* this plantation and could afford to take chances."

"Exactly," said Julian coolly. "That is why I extracted a promise from you that a boat would bring back my overseers at the end of four days."

"Of course, senhor. But I hope the time limit will not also restrict the senhorita? She will be well looked after and amply chaperoned. My mother herself will watch over her as if she were a daughter."

"Your mother," returned Julian deliberately, "will not be put to the trouble. Phil isn't going with you tomorrow."

This announcement fell into a silence. Tomé's eyes, burning with angry dismay, flashed from Julian's cold expressionlessness to Phil's momentary smile of bewilderment. The other men appeared surprised and interested, though Roger scowled.

Matt said smoothly: "You see, Tomé, our friend Caswell takes his duties hard. He doesn't much care for the idea of Phil being exposed to the attentions of so many handsome

Spaniards and Portuguese. Maybe her visit would be best left over till later, when your father's guests have departed. See?"

"Yes, I see. I see very plainly," came the rapid reply. "We are Portuguese — not good enough, in Senhor Caswell's opinion, to have contact with the English girl whom he has annexed as a ward." Blazing with humiliation, he sprang up. "This island is Portuguese, senhor. You do not mind earning your miserable salary from our soil. I will get my father to write to your company and tell them of the contempt you have for us—"

"I have no difference with the Novada," Julian cut in. "Phil will tell you herself that, owing to a clause in her father's will, marriage will be out of the question for a very long time. She is planning to leave the island within a couple of months."

Violently Tomé twisted towards her. "Is this true, senhorita?"

"Yes," she said, low-voiced. "Quite true."

Tomé pulled himself upright, shoulders erect. His throat worked. "If you were of my race I would challenge you, senhor, but you are English and afraid to fight except with your tongue!"

Without haste Julian stood up, dwarfing the excitable creature. "You have not yet acquired the polish of your father, Tomé. He dislikes me, but he is a gentleman about it. Perhaps you had better sleep in the yacht tonight. I will send a boy down with your things."

Tomé had flushed darkly. Jerkily he bowed to Phil and then again in Matt's direction.

"Tomorrow early, senhors. Good night!"

While his footsteps still echoed, Julian poured a whisky and pushed it towards Matt.

"Hot-headed young cub," remarked the trader, accepting the glass and peering through it. "He needed the lesson, but I don't know that it's wise to make enemies of the Astartes. Phil could have managed him."

"Perhaps, but it's safer for her to do as she's told. She's becoming a hell of a pest."

Phil swallowed. She got to her feet and forced a tremulous smile. "I've no defence to offer. Good night, everyone." And she turned and ran out into a cloud of scissor-winged flies which plagued the clearing.

In her room she ignored the tears that sped down her cheeks and lit a cigarette. Pacing between the curtained window and the door, she felt the wounded thud of her heart beneath her folded arms and a weight of grief behind her eyes.

She heard Matt's car start up and told herself it was late, but shrank from the thought of a wide-eyed night within the mosquito net. There was no getting away from Julian's cruelty and in bed she would be alone with it, whereas here in the dimly lit room she had the company of insects and the somnolent lizard in the corner.

A tap at the door swung her round. Something leapt convulsively against her ribs. As he came in and closed the door, Julian's face was set. For a moment he paused, his hands dug into his pockets, and then his jaw loosened and took on a hint of gentleness.

"I saw your light," he said. "Why aren't you in bed?"

"Sleep doesn't come easily here at the best of times," she replied. "After a scene like this evening, it's more elusive than ever."

"I know. That was a filthy crack I made."

"I'm used to your filthy cracks, but not in front of others. It . . . rankled."

"The young Romeo annoyed me—his father can make plenty of trouble if he likes." His voice dropped. "I get no pleasure from hurting you, but the way we are, it's inevitable."

To evade his baffling stare she reached to increase the lamplight. Her head inclined in agreement.

"Yes, I don't believe I realized that till tonight. I . . . I've decided to leave Valeira as soon as possible, Julian."

His answer was so long in coming that she was impelled to look at him. His eyes had darkened and a hand came up to rasp his chin.

"All right," he said. "I'll make the arrangements. You can go to some people I know in Lagos till your lawyer writes. We'll go into details tomorrow. You won't have a thing to worry about." He spoke with unaccustomed thickness. "It'll take courage to start a new life, but you have plenty, and I'll always help you in any way I can."

She murmured a husky, "Thanks."

Julian should have gone then, snapping the door and striding home with his habitual decisiveness. But he hesitated and Phil could strangle the pain no longer. It brimmed in her eyes and forced a gasp from her lungs. Swept on an irresistible wave, she groped towards him. She was shaking as she leaned close to him, yet nerved for the rebuff that would shatter the intimate quality of this moment with the tearing speed of a bayonet thrust.

She was scarcely aware that his whole body had stiffened before she felt his hands slide up to her shoulders and pull her tight into his arms. She saw glittering eyes and flaring nostrils, felt his heart pounding deeply and angrily against her, and then the brutal pressure of his mouth upon her own.

A minute later he was pushing her away from him, his face drained white with fury.

"Blast you!" he breathed. "You're like the rest of women —without conscience or loyalty. Isn't it enough to have Crawford and the Portuguese wanting to sleep with you?"

"That's . . . horrible."

"No more horrible than the rest of torrid nature. Get away from the door."

Mechanically she obeyed.

He kicked the door wide, admitting a burst of primitive scents. And then he was gone, and Phil was left standing with closed eyes and fingers laid over lips which still throbbed from the savage contact with Julian's.

CHAPTER XV

MATT returned after only two days at the Novada. His excuse was a surfeit of pimento and Portuguese wine, but Phil suspected a last-minute suggestion from Julian.

In his store near the waterfront, Matt sat back and smoked while he described to her the wedding feast and the bride.

"A nice little thing, but no spirit," he said. "Not like the old senhora, which, perhaps, is as well. No room for two viragos under one roof."

Phil smiled faintly and said: "Did you see the bullfight?"

"I did. It wasn't so much a fight as a scramble for the flowers that the ladies threw. Very weak." He paused, inspected the tip of his cheroot and shifted his feet from a bag of meal to a pile of sacks. The old chair creaked and split a reed. Matt frowned. "Julian was right again, lovey. You were best off here. Even Drew got tight each evening."

"Oh, dear. And Roger?"

"He was merry, too. Roger's popular with Rodrigo and it wasn't pleasant to see them leaning tipsy heads together. Can't think what's come over the fellow."

"It's the heat and monotony," said Phil. "Anything for a change. I feel that way myself."

"I reckon there'll be a change soon for a few of us," Matt remarked moodily. "A couple of seamen were in the shop early this morning offering to pass me some drugs. I kicked 'em out, but they'll unload the stuff through someone else."

"They're smuggling again? Does Julian know?"

"Probably, but he's too tied up to interfere. You can bet he'll stamp on it as soon as the others are back in the shafts. He ought to engage more overseers, but he won't, because it would entail an increase in overheads and a drop in bonus. He's a maniac."

Which was not a word Phil would have used to describe Julian.

During the last three days she had avoided him. She knew his habits; that he went down to the lagoon for his bathe before breakfast and set out for the plantation soon after seven, returning at twelve-thirty for lunch; at two he drove off again or spent some time in the sheds. The sky had shadowed when he garaged the car for the night. Whereas previously she might have made a purposely accidental appearance in her garden and hailed him, she now kept to the cabin, hourly expecting a note to the effect that her passage had been arranged. She had a conviction that however his work pressed, Julian would not forget that detail.

Yet the days passed without word from him. Drew

ambled down the mountainside on a donkey and stiffly dismounted at the gate of his cement house. His complexion was yellow, his gait unsteady with internal disquiet. Roger, Phil heard, was stretching his holiday to a full week. She could only guess at Julian's battened rage and hope that Roger would be suitably abject when he did come back.

As it happened, she was on the jetty when a yacht bound for Lisbon anchored in the bay and lowered a boat to take off a passenger. Full of admiration for the blue and silver vessel, she watched the manoeuvre and the approach of the dinghy to the quay. Immediately after Roger and his valise were disembarked the boat sped back across the water. Roger let a boy take his case, and he joined Phil.

"How nice to be met," he said with the trace of a sneer, "if only by chance. Do I look as bad as that?"

"As what?"

"Your shrug of distaste. If I carry signs of dissipation and smell of scent and cigars, you're to blame."

"You sound in poisonous mood," she said lightly. "I suspect contrition."

"You're way out. My better self doesn't work any more. You killed it."

"Don't be ridiculous." She laughed to cover uneasiness, and walked in front till they reached the road.

As they came level again he twitched the short sleeve of her shirt. "Why didn't you tell me months ago, when I started pestering you to marry me, about that clause in your father's will?"

"I wasn't aware of it then."

"Caswell seems to have been well informed for some time."

"Only four or five weeks. Roger, there isn't the least need for us to quarrel. We can go on being friends."

"Keep your friendship. I don't want to see you or live anywhere near you. I've heard too much about you."

He was behaving so strangely that she made no attempt to construe his meaning. She tried a smile, to which he returned a vindictive curl of the lips, and was about to turn towards Matt's store when Roger stopped, his expression fixed, and a weakness in her knees told her that Julian was at her back.

"Well, Crawford?" came the harsh enquiry.

Phil stepped to one side. "I'll go."

"No," exclaimed Roger. "You needn't bother to walk out so that the small boy may have his beating in private. Awfully sporting of you, but unnecessary. Go ahead, Mr. Caswell!"

"Are you mad, or just a fool? Do you realize that two cargo boats have been held up while you caroused at the Novada? Why didn't you return with Drew?"

"Because," replied Roger, in a deliberate, mincing tone which sent snakes along Phil's spine, "I fell among friends and enjoyed the change. I would have hung on there longer but I had to have more clothes. How do you like that?"

Tightly controlled, Julian said: "Astartes has been suggesting to you that you're underpaid and overworked. He's made you believe that your services are indispensable ——"

"He's told me other things, too!" Roger was almost shrill. "I know why you made Phil live in the plantation buildings. You're a fine one to preach celibacy, Mr. Mighty Caswell——"

"You're drunk"—Julian's voice was dangerously quiet— "or I'd twist your neck. Go sleep it off and come to my house later."

"So that you can fire me from behind an office desk? No, thanks. I'll fire myself right now. You can find someone else to take the kicks. I'm through."

Phil cried: "Roger, you can't! You don't know what you're saying."

But Julian cut in: "He knows all right. This isn't a sudden decision, is it, Crawford? You've had it under your hat a long time. If you walk out now the company will demand three months' salary and confiscate the year's bonus. You get that?"

"They can do what they damn well please," he shouted in childish anger. "I'm going to the Novada for two thousand a year—that's a salary as big as yours, you supercilious devil. . . ."

Phil heard the crack of a fist, saw the wild glare in

Roger's eyes before he toppled, and felt Julian's rough push at her back.

"Leave him," he said abruptly. "I'll call and ask Matt to take him home."

Slowly she clambered up the rutted slope to the plantation track. A clot had gathered in her throat and seemed to disperse and flood her with anguish. These days, life had nothing to offer but disillusion and pain. Had she obeyed Julian's first command to leave Valeira, Clin Dakers need not have died, and Roger would have finished his time content in the assurance of a fairly substantial bank balance and an affectionate reunion with his family. Above all, Julian would not now be embittered by her invasion of his privacy, nor hating her for the predicament into which Roger's resignation had plunged the plantation. As if fate had decided at this juncture to co-operate, next morning Julian sent over a letter which had come up with his mail. It was addressed to "Mrs. Julian Caswell", with the "Mrs." converted by a stroke of the blue pencil to "Mr." No doubt the post official had enjoyed what it deemed a typist's error. The plantation manager with a wife! Ho, ho!

Phil held in her fingers the lawyer's cheque for three hundred pounds, the key of release, and exile. Methodically, shutting her mind against grief, she made a list of her debts, and worked out how much would remain. At one-thirty, knowing Julian's custom of smoking a cigarette on his veranda after lunch, she walked over to the house.

But today he had no time for leisure. She came upon him grinding out a cigarette with his heel, his sun-helmet in his hand.

She held out the cheque. "It's come. I'd get Matt to change it, but for the name. I'm afraid it will have to be passed through your bank."

He gave the cheque a quick perusal and slipped it into his pocket. "Want it now?"

"Fairly soon. I owe Matt quite a bit . . . and you."

"You owe me nothing, and I'll settle with Matt," he answered flatly. "You'd better have fifty pounds cash and the rest put into an account. I'll see to it the minute I'm free."

She nodded thanks, expecting him to dismiss her with

96

some conventionality. But he stayed there, his gaze upon a rubbery weed at the base of the steps, his mind heaven knew where.

Her next words came rapidly: "Julian, until I go you must let me help. You must! It was my fault that Roger walked out, and I'd feel so much less badly about it if you'd let me do his job—the shipping part of it, anyway. I'm sure I could tackle it—I used to deputize for Nigel when he was sick. Please, Julian!"

Close as she was, he did not look at her. "The shipping is taken care of," he said, "and I can handle the clerical work myself, in the evenings. I've cabled Lagos offering Crawford's post to a man who approached me while I was there. If he accepts, he'll be here within a week, so Drew and I won't have to sweat off our hides for long."

"Oh." Deflated, she moved away. "Well, I'd like you to know that I'm cured of fighting for my own way. I'll do whatever you wish."

A pause. Then he said: "Don't reproach yourself over Crawford. The climate and conditions had more to do with cracking him up than your turning him down. You never encouraged him, did you?"

"We were friendly when you first came."

"How friendly?"

Uneasy under his probing, she said: "You know how it was. We were both young . . . and foolish."

"You kissed?" Mercilessly, he emphasized the implication she strove to avoid. "You're certainly making the rounds. There's no need to wince—you're fortunate to have got away with just kisses." He put on the helmet and dipped his hands into his breeches pockets. "Experience is ageing, isn't it? I expect you feel all of eighteen and a bit and completely jaded. Don't let it get you. In a year's time you'll be laughing at this. Goodbye."

Had she needed it, the brief exchange was further proof of his hostility. When they were together the whole atmosphere became loaded with it, and any pleasure she might have gained from his proximity was swamped in the urge to escape his bitter tongue.

There was nothing for her to do but waste the days till

the *Bassington* or some other ship with passenger accommodation put into the harbour.

CHAPTER XVI

PHIL was resting. All morning she had lifted the seedling shrubs and trees in her small garden and set them in old oil and paint tins, ready for planting out in Matt's weed-grown plot. A tricky business in this heat, but Manoela prophesied rain, and the roots had reached a convenient size for transplanting. Now, spent with heat and exertion, she lay half-clothed on her bed and watched a lizard which had retreated from the oppressive outdoors and fastened itself to the window-frame. It seemed a long, long time since she had last experienced a good spell of oblivion.

Manoela brought a tea-tray.

"Is it four already?" Phil asked languidly.

"Nearly four, missus. I bring tea early. Please, I want to go to the store."

"To buy more shoes, Manoela?"

"No, missus." The servant had lost a tooth and her smile was uncanny. "I am sick in the stomach. I buy medicine."

"Haven't you been taking the salts?"

"They no good, missus. My stomach want white pills."

"What sort of white pills?"

"Boy at the store—he know. I go now, missus."

Phil swung down her legs and drank her cup of tea. A faint coolness drifted over her bare skin and she thought how agreeable it would be to lie on a beach where the breeze was strong and the sea washed in icy foam about one's body. Soon she would be able to do that, but nothing was so pleasurable in practice as in anticipation. Perhaps pain also had its limits. She hoped so.

Automatically she shook out her mules and trod into them, but she made no further move till Manoela sped past the window, her headcloth flying and guttural vituperation streaming from her mouth. Phil opened the door.

"Manoela! Come here."

She approached, still panting, her shaking hands re-winding the scarf about her head.

"Tell me what you've been doing."

"Nothing, missus," A swallow and a gasp, "I run very fast. There was trouble this morning—the boy at the store and more boys. White master say he kill . . ."

Phil gathered that the drug leakage had been traced and forcible methods used to stop it. Natives who had expended much of their wages on dagga had been searched and their hoards confiscated. The whole waterfront was in an uproar, and Julian was in the thick of it.

She conquered a sudden sick trembling, reached up to a hook for her shorts and pulled them on. Manoela flopped forward into the room and crashed shut the door.

"They come! They will stab us!"

Phil dashed to the window. Yes, there were half a dozen natives in front of Julian's house, and squirming in their hold was Sam, the houseboy. They tied the boy, dragged him into the trees and ran back to the house. Did they intend to ransack the place and then set fire to it? What could she do against a bunch of maddened Africans? "Listen, Manoela. You, too, can use a knife. Crawl out and find Sam, and release him. Tell him to fetch the white master." Manoela moaned and dragged herself upright. Dully she peered at the deserted clearing, and without speaking she went to the door and crept out, doubled like a stalking chimpanzee. Phil buttoned her shirt and went back to the window. The stillness filled her with premonitory horror, so that she had to struggle with an impulse to scream in order to start some action. She had no gun, no weapon of any sort.

Presently her breath caught hard in her windpipe. The natives were appearing, one by one, sidling with almost imperceptible motion across Julian's veranda and dropping over the rail. She counted them. Eight altogether . . . no, nine. Why had the interval between the eighth and ninth stretched so long? Had the last one been entrusted with the task of igniting paraffin-drenched rags?

The naked brown backs had vanished. Phil ran out, vaulted her fence and raced over the grass and up to Julian's living-room. There she stopped dead, bewildered

by the normal atmosphere. Nothing unusual here. The bedroom door was locked, so that the main room must be the
scene of whatever harm had been hatched.

Phil came back to examine the desk, and on the floor
just below the knee-hole she saw a tiny ball of flame. A
seemingly innocuous globule of light at one end of a
waxed string whose other end was buried in an untidy little
paper packet. Simultaneously with a stab of shock her
slipper dropped on to the minute flame. A crude explosive.
There might be others!

Frantically she dragged out chairs and searched under
the cabinet and bookcase. Another of the fiendish things
concealed within a pile of magazines on a table, with the
string only two inches to go. A third on the floor by the
inner wall, this one even nearer to the deadline.

She dared not stay any longer. She wheeled, caught sight
of a frightening glow at the left of the door and flung herself towards the opening. With a thunderous crack the
wall split and cascaded.

A steamy drizzle was Julian's chief ally in getting the
natives back to their huts. The waterfront was quiet in the
early dusk. The sea, backing into a purple wall, was de-
creasingly visible through the grey veil of rain. Boat lights
appeared, a spatter of brassy stars suspended above the
waves.

Julian said: "This weather will keep them indoors; the
police should manage for the remainder of the night. Go
home and get some sleep, Drew. We may have another
heavy day tomorrow."

"If you're sure you don't need me any longer?" The
overseer's plain features looked inexpressibly weary.

"Absolutely. You've done well—I'll put it in my report."

"Thank you, sir. Good night."

Julian would have offered Drew a lift, but his car had
been parked behind the store for safety, and from this
point the man was half-way home. Julian strode swiftly
up the track, and as he climbed, Matt's burly figure
materialized, tented in oilskins.

"I've been hunting for you," the trader grunted. "Your

day's not ended yet, Julian. The devils have had a go at your house."

"D'you mean they've fired it?" came the swift demand. "Where's Phil?"

"Give me time, will you? Phil's girl, Manoela, came snivelling into my yard fifteen minutes ago. Seems that Phil watched a gang get rid of your boy and sent Manoela out to free him. The girl said she was combing the trees when she heard a loud bang. She ran back and saw the front wall of your house had collapsed. Manoela was so terrified that she hid in the forest and didn't budge till it began to rain. She went back to the cabin, but it was empty, so she came down here."

"What time did it happen?"

"A couple of hours ago—about four-thirty."

"No sign of Phil since then?"

"She's got the sense to hide, and anyway, she knows how to use a gun."

"She hasn't owned a gun since hers was lost," said Julian crisply. "Are you coming, Matt?"

He leapt the final yard or two of the ascent and ran. Within minutes Matt, his complexion a mottled red and his lungs bursting, was sprawled beside him in the car, as it rocketed up the trail to the clearing.

The car beams illuminated the log buildings, every one of them intact, and switched full on to the expanse of rubble which covered the veranda and half the living-room of the house.

Matt used an oath. "Explosive! Where did the beggars get it?"

"It might have been worse," snapped Julian. "But where the hell is Phil?"

He tripped over the prone form of Sam—poor Sam, his wrists and ankles raw from the tight grass-rope—and chased to the cabin. He lit the lamp and surveyed the dented bed, the tea-tray, a silk wrap over the back of a chair. Peremptory with anxiety, he called her name and was answered by an echo.

Outside he collided with Matt.

"No signs?" growled the trader. "She's probably close by, laughing at us."

"Unless she was unwise enough to show herself before they'd gone. She may be unconscious somewhere. Got a flashlight?"

"A small one."

"There are a couple in my desk. Wait. I'll fetch them."

He sprang over the boulders of wattle and daub, crossed the room to the desk in the corner and extracted the torches. To his touch the lamp felt whole, and he struck another match and set it to the wick. Couldn't have too much light in this murk. The torches went into his pockets and he grabbed the lamp by its copper base, and held it aloft, ready for the sprint back over the rain-soaked debris.

For a moment the lamp stayed poised; then it was lowered to a slab of plaster, and Julian sank to his haunches, his face as grey as the wreckage. From a mound of fragments protruded a tress of dusty hair.

The paralysis passed. He barked at Matt and began quickly and gently to uncover the bright head. Her cheek was cold and bruised; the pitifully thin silk shirt had given no protection to the slim shoulders. Thank God she was lying on her front. Julian could have smashed a fist into Matt's swearing mouth as the trader assisted him. Instead, he went on removing chunk after chunk till he could push fingers under her and feel the moth-wing beat of her heart.

Shakily, Matt said: "She's tough. I'll get some brandy ready."

"And then go up to the mission and bring back the doctor. Tell Sam to boil water—plenty of it."

Carefully he turned her and moved her farther into the room. She was ashen to the lips, her eyelids dark, her lines sharp as death. He unlocked his bedroom and brought out his mattress and blankets. Too risky to lift her on to a bed. He loosened the waist of her shorts and the neck of her shirt, got her on to the mattress and covered her closely.

For want of anything more pungent, he doused a handkerchief with brandy and wiped her nostrils and mouth with it. From a wad of cotton wool he squeezed neat brandy over her teeth, and in a few minutes he got results: a wrenching shudder and a heart-freezing moan.

"Phil," he whispered, bending over her. "Phil."

Her lids flickered wide. After a lengthy stare at him she breathed, "They didn't . . . hurt you?"

It was the humblest moment in Julian's life. He shook his head and placed his lips to her forehead.

Sam brought coffee and a can of water, and Julian bathed her face and hands and arms. But when he raised her and held a cup to her lips she gasped and her nails drew blood from his forearm.

"Maybe you've damaged a rib," he said, hoping to God that might be all. "Don't talk. The doctor will be here soon to fix you up."

She lay back, her eyes closed again, a heavy sweat gathering at her temples.

"Will you . . . stay with me, Julian?"

"Of course," he said thickly. "Of course."

CHAPTER XVII

THE effects of the morphia were diminishing. The pearl-grey walls floated, performed a mad little dance and righted themselves. It was not so much a room as a prison, a large, airy cell with dawn filtering through the mana mat which screened the high window. The sheets were very white, the blanket mud-brown with a red stripe.

Someone got up from a chair and stood above her. A middle-aged, white-clad nurse with a tropic-weary smile.

"Awake? That's good. You don't look too bad, my dear."

"You're new . . . aren't you?" Phil managed.

"New? Gracious, no! I've been here off and on for fifteen years. Shall we have a little drink?"

Phil waited while the nurse opened a cupboard and liquids gurgled. The spout of a feeding-cup loomed before her nose and she tried to recoil.

"You mustn't mind this, child. It's only for a week or so, till we can give you two pillows. That's right. Drink it up." Patiently she held the cup while Phil sipped. "People often say queer things when they first come round. What made you think I'm new here?"

"I thought you'd be Sister Harrington."

"And who's Sister Harrington, for goodness' sake?"

The commonplace voice jarred Phil, and she was too tired to speak much. "The Valeira mission," she answered.

"Bless you, this isn't Valeira. You're on the coast now, at Goanda Hospital. I'm Nurse Briggs. Mr. Caswell brought you here on the niftiest stretcher you ever saw. He'd kept you under on the boat with injections. Which reminds me. He made me promise to tell him the minute you stirred. Had enough, dear? Good."

Her rubber-soled feet padded away over the stone floor and a door clicked. Phil indulged in some painful deep breathing. It was horrible to be alive and wish you weren't. Again the snap of a door and Julian came to the bedside. Odd, but she had never noticed before how high and bony was his nose, how straight and white the edges of his teeth. But he had never looked at her like this before.

"It's good to see you in a real bed with a nurse to attend you," he said softly. "How do you feel?"

"I . . . I can't move."

"You're frightened. Haven't they told you what's wrong?" He dropped a knee on the seat of the nurse's chair to lean nearer. "It's nothing dreadful after all. Two ribs fractured and multiple bruises. Sounds grim, doesn't it, but I'm so relieved I can even smile. Bones mend, especially in a girl of your age. As we came over in the boat I visualized every internal complication there is, but the doctor here assures me you're a hundred per cent whole. He showed me an X-ray photograph."

"How long will I have to stay here?"

"In three or four weeks, you'll be back in circulation."

Back where? She contrived a smile. "You must be worn out, Julian. Have you had any food?"

"They're getting me some breakfast. You'll be all right here. The doctor's a great chap and the nurse knows her job."

"You're returning to Valeira today?"

"I wouldn't, if you needed me. But your best medicine is rest." He hesitated. "You won't get it with me around. I make you unhappy."

She did not refute it.

"I'll come out again on the next boat," he added, "in a week or so—and bring you some books and clothes. We've a lot to talk about . . . some time."

But not now. He lifted the grass mat at the window and described to her the wide sweep of bare earth down to the river, the palms, and a huge, ancient baobab with buttressed roots.

"This is the mouth of the Goanda river," he said. "There's nothing here but a native village and these buildings, but the hospital is quite famous, and a good many people come for treatment. Dr. Grenfell has devoted his life to tropical sickness." And so on.

All very interesting and laudable, but Phil was too low in mind and body to care about anything beyond the fact that soon she would be alone and suffering torments that no doctor could assuage.

The nurse knocked before entering. She came to the other side of the bed with a spurious verve which Phil later came to admire.

"I bet you didn't expect to see her looking so bright, Mr. Caswell. That bruise on her cheekbone will soon wear off, and next time you come we'll have her sitting up."

"I hope so, but don't let her persuade you to give her pillows before she's ready for them."

"You can trust me. There's a meal waiting for you in the doctor's dining-room—next to the lounge where you were before." She stepped back and smoothed the colourless hair that was worn in a roll round her cap. "The doctor wishes Miss Crane to have complete quiet till he comes to see her, so perhaps you'll say goodbye now."

Phil tried to meet Julian's eyes, but they were averted towards the nurse. She heard him murmur something and felt the pressure of his hand on hers. His stride receded. Then the nurse made her take more liquid from the repulsive spout, after which she slept.

On her sixth day Phil graduated to two pillows. On the tenth she was given a back-rest and allowed to brush her own hair. She was sitting up, wearing a faded pink dressing-jacket of the nurse's, when Julian came in with Dr. Grenfell. He smiled at her with a warmth in his eyes that set her humming. Careful, she told herself, you've still got a bandage round your ribs.

At last the doctor nodded and went out. Julian hooked forward a chair with his foot, but she patted the bed cover, and with a tight smile he lowered himself to her side.

"You're a bit of a fraud," he said, "much too well to be in bed. Has it been rotten?"

"Ghastly, but this makes up for it. Tell me about Valeira."

"Things have happened since you left. After a fortnight at the Novada Crawford came and asked to be taken back, but I refused, and got him shipped home right away. The man I told you about, from Lagos, arrived a few days ago and is shaping nicely."

"Where is he living?"

"With Drew, but we're building another bungalow on Daker's old site. Soon I shall be ready to expand the oil palm acreage, so I've written to London for a third overseer. They take a couple of months to engage and despatch anyone."

With a fingernail she traced the red stripe on the blanket. "Is your house repaired?"

"Practically." He paused. "I gave your box of goods to the nurse."

"You've stripped the cabin?"

"No," he said non-committally. "But I told Matt that you wouldn't be coming back and to take whatever belongs to him. When the sea is less choppy he's coming over to see you."

Phil's teeth had clamped. If only she had let him sit in the chair with two or three yards between them, instead of inviting him so close that she was aware of his slightest muscle-twitch and could smell the smoke on his breath.

"You were sparkling when I came in," he said, "and in a few minutes you've gone dreary. I'm not good for you, Phil."

With the courage of desperation, she asked: "Are you trying to convince me or yourself? Weren't you doing your damnedest to make me hate you before the wall of your house knocked me out, and aren't you reverting to the same tactics in gentler form? You don't have to be gentle with me, Julian. I can take it."

"I'm not sure you can," he said calmly, "but if you could hate me it would simplify the problem considerably. I'm not going to discuss it with you till you're on two feet and can pack a punch again, but meanwhile it wouldn't be a bad idea for you to weigh it up from my viewpoint, remembering that I'm thirty-six and still have four years of my contract to go."

Phil was silenced. He was making it unendurably clear that whatever hope had sprung within her from his assumption of responsibility on her behalf could have no permanent fulfilment.

"I'm not the Roger Crawford breed," he went on reasonably. "I shall work through my contract and perhaps renew."

"So from now on," she said, her chin up, "we're enemies. It's a relief to know where we stand." That evening Julian had dinner with the doctor, and later used the studio couch in the lounge as a bed. At daybreak he came in to wish Phil goodbye.

She had awakened in the dark and lain steeped in an agony of fresh disillusionment. The early daylight possessed a quality of sadness that hurt deep in her breast. She threw back the clothes, carefully lowered her feet to the floor and stood up. Her knees sagged, but with the support of the small table she reached the high window and shifted the mana mat on its string, so that more light came in. She was just tall enough to see out. She did not hear the door open.

"Phil! What are you doing?"

Strange, but she was scarcely moved by Julian's sudden appearance. She didn't care about the washed-out cotton nightgown and her tumbled hair. She leaned with her hands flat against the cold wall behind her.

"I thought you'd gone."

A couple of strides brought him near. "Get back to bed, there's a good girl. You knew I wouldn't go without seeing you. Come on, now."

"Don't touch me!"

"All right!"—angrily. "But get back to bed."

Her breathing was playing tricks and queer sensations were attacking her legs, but the wall remained a solid and assuring support.

"What I have to say will come easier if I stand, Julian. I . . . I'd rather you didn't come again. We haven't anything to discuss. Nothing's changed. When I can travel I'll go to the Cape and see the lawyer. Promise me you won't come again."

"I'll promise nothing, you crazy little fool," he said harshly, and the next minute she was lying on the bed, with Julian holding her shoulders and staring into her grief-dark eyes.

And then he kissed her. Not with the brutal force of that other kiss; nor tenderly, with compassion and understanding. It was a kiss so hard to analyse that hours afterwards, when Julian was back on Valeira and Phil was sitting on the dim balcony, picking over a cold lunch, she was no nearer a solution.

CHAPTER XVIII

AS soon as Phil was allowed up all day she had her meals at the house with the doctor and Nurse Briggs. Never did she hear them address each other except as "Doctor" and "Nurse," yet the bond between them was intimate and durable. How intimate she learned by degrees.

When she discovered that the woman actually lived at the house it did not strike Phil as peculiar. Rather, she congratulated them in her mind on an utterly selfless relationship, typifying a great nobility of spirit.

There came an evening when she wandered back to her room at the end of the main building rather later than usual, and sat in the dark balcony smoking a cigarette. The only lights were those in the house she had just left and the eternally red brazier near the river. Through the open windows of the hospital issued the murmur of natives and Katie's musically strident injunctions. Between times, Phil caught the zing of mosquitoes.

She saw the doctor's houseboy extinguish the veranda lamp. One by one the other lights died till only one was left, that in Nurse Brigg's bedroom. Phil thought it was the woman's bedroom because it had a french window which the nurse always used in preference to the front door. Dr. Grenfell never went in that way.

Now the french door opened and Nurse Briggs, in a dressing-gown, stood framed in the rectangle of light. Pityingly, Phil watched the no-longer-youthful movements as the mousey hair was unpinned and shaken out. How drab and futile her existence must often seem, yet there was no escaping it. She had stayed here too long.

Then Phil's heart gave a jump, for two figures were pasted where one had been. The doctor was there, his stoop grotesque in silhouette, his hand on the nurse's arm. They went inside, and the screen was drawn. Phil was trembling and heartsick. Instinctively she knew all about those two over there, their struggles and needs. If their nobility had slipped in this particular it was only because they were human, like everyone else. Everyone but Julian.

Towards the end of her fourth week Matt came round the bend of the river from the sea in a rowing-boat. The coaster in which he had crossed from the island lay at anchor in the river mouth.

"I reckon this is the wrong way round," he complained. "You could stand the sea better than I do, lovey."

"Oh, Matt!" she squeezed his arm. "If only I could come over!"

"If you're pining for us," he demanded in astonishment, "why don't you?"

She shook her head. "Julian wouldn't have it. I hope you brought your own drink. We use it here by the thimbleful for medicinal purposes."

"I was afraid of that," Matt grunted as he stepped over the low balcony wall.

Phil laughed. "It's like home to hear you again. Before you sit down take a look at my room. Enchanting, isn't it?"

Matt's thick nose wrinkled. "They trying to make a nun out of you?"

"It's just a small ward. Open the packets, Matt. I'm dying to see what you've brought."

He seemed to have concentrated on food and drink,

though books and cigarettes had been remembered.

"Julian chose the books," he said.

"He sent no . . . message?"

"Nothing special. He's busy with this new fellow, Davenport. Julian's due for his annual three weeks' leave, but he can't be away that long. He's talking of spending some days in Lagos."

"Oh." She made a sudden wild decision to transfer herself to Lagos and as quickly cancelled it. "I hope he'll put in here on the way."

Matt tasted his neat whisky and gazed speculatively into the glass. "I wouldn't bank anything on Julian if I were you, Phil. He likes you—he suffered quite a bit when you got yourself smashed up to save his house—but that sort of suffering isn't enough to change a man. He does his best for you, turns you over to a hospital and dips into his wad for your wants, but almost any man would do that. He's case-hardened. It would take the deuce of a blast to shake him."

"I know," she said quietly. "Except when he's angry he's entirely without emotion."

But in anger he could grip and leave bruises, and crush her mouth in a climax of self-scorn. Matt wasn't aware of that.

"Shall we have lunch here?" she asked, "or would you like to meet the doctor?"

"If it's all the same to you, lovey, I'll postpone a word with the doc till I'm ready to go. Medicos make me too conscious of my overworked liver." After lunch he snoozed, and when he awoke he had another drink to fortify himself for the interview with Dr. Grenfell. At the wooden landing-stage, an hour later, he patted the top of Phil's head in farewell and thrust something into her dress pocket.

"Give it to the doctor," he said, "to convince him I'm not the rogue I look." It was a cheque for a hundred pounds.

Watching the boat vanish between the mangroves, Phil felt her courage dwindle. Wherever she looked there were barriers; only here could she slip into a niche originally meant for a qualified self-sacrificing nurse. She would go on from day to day, existing on crumbs of gratitude, yet intensely aware of the pulsing, vivid life she might be living. Phil cleared the tea-cups and glasses from her balcony and emptied the ashtray. She flicked through a glossy-leaved magazine which Matt had brought. Perhaps it was coincidence that every other page pictured a man with Julian's distinctive features looking purposefully at a series of lovely women.

She went inside to arrange the books at the bottom of the wardrobe cupboard and presently her eyes began to sting and burn. She sat on the floor with her knees drawn up, wrenched by the difficult, aching sobs of hopelessness.

Saturday was "medicine day." From early morning, bush natives who had trudged from villages many miles inland lined up at the dispensary. Each one could recite a list of his own and his family's ailments, but had no money for the medicines doled out to him. The more grateful brought a few eggs, mostly addled by the sun, or a chicken or a stem of bananas. This Saturday Nurse Briggs was laid out by dysentery, and Phil stepped in to hand out bottles, pills and bandages for the doctor. The windows were wide and a boy outside kept the mat fans slung across the room working frantically, but the reek of rank wounds was inescapable. Several times she rushed to the back door of the dispensary to gulp in the hot, spice-laden breeze. Sweat coursed down the sides of her cheeks and gathered beneath her chin, her dress clung from shoulder to thigh, and a river ran from each armpit.

It was noon before all were dealt with and they could wash at the enamel bowl for the last time before lunch.

Wiping his hands, Dr. Grenfell said: "And now it is my duty to prescribe for you, young lady. Have a cool bath and a rest before you eat. You've been extraordinarily helpful this morning."

"I'm a queasy probationer," she replied ruefully.

He smiled in his distant, perfunctory manner, then looked at her more closely. "Probationer? Is that how you regard yourself? Could you settle here and take part in the work?"

"I'd like to, for a time, but I'd have to be quite free to

111

leave whenever I chose, or to go away and come back again."

"Naturally. You are nineteen?"

"Nearly."

"Very young. We cannot bind you, badly though Nurse Briggs requires help. Unfortunately, we have neither time nor facilities for training you properly, but there is a centre up the Coast where you can live and receive training, and earn a small salary besides. You are accustomed to the tropics, and I think you'd be happy there. If, on the other hand, you would prefer to remain here as general nursing assistant, we should be exceedingly grateful for your services."

Unattracted by either alternative, Phil thanked him politely.

"It is a serious step," he said. "Think it over long and well." Again that fleeting smile. "We will agree not to mention it for a further month. To the bath, Miss Crane, and an hour between your cool white sheets!"

Phil had no illusions about her own capacity for attending the sick. As Nurse Briggs stated one morning, after a child's burns had been dressed: "You'll never make a go of it if you keep on wincing at the sight of a wound, and tensing yourself when a child cries. If you can't forget the patient's pain, my dear, you'll be limp as a rag in no time."

True enough. Phil did end each day sapped of strength and the will to live, but it was a condition in which sleep came fairly easily, and for that benefit alone it was to be courted.

The moment the light was out, of course, she became wide awake and wallowed in a chasm of bewilderment and distress. Something would dart out from the prison of her mind—the mother she despised and could not recall; Nigel's antipathy to women; Clin Dakers with his hands on her throat—and she would turn into her pillow knowing it was Julian who prodded such memories into activity. Once she had admitted Julian she fell asleep.

CHAPTER XIX

EARLY one evening while Phil was bathing one of the native babies on the veranda, a shadow slanted across the table. Phil paled; her fingers curled over the edge of the table. "Hello, Julian. We weren't expecting you."

She called a native helper and instructed her to wrap the child and take her to her mother. Julian waited, frowning. "You shouldn't be working yet," he said tersely.

"Surely you wouldn't want me to be idle while Nurse Briggs has so much to do?" she said chidingly, as they moved along to her balcony. "Women are doing that sort of thing in all the hot countries of the world."

"I don't care," he bit out. "You're not to do it."

Wisely, she refrained from retort. In the balcony she indicated a chair. "I'll wash my hands and get you a drink."

"I'd prefer coffee," he said.

With a nod she went into her room. She lit the spirit stove and set the tiny tin saucepan to boil, washed and used a dab of powder. On a native basketwork tray she set two cups and saucers and a box of Scotch shortbread given her by Matt. The consuming ache to see Julian again had failed to culminate in delight at his nearness. Was his curtness merely the outcome of transient displeasure at the task in which he had surprised her? She would soon know.

She opened the door and he took the tray from her.

"Matt told me you were fit," he said. "No pains anywhere?"

Phil smiled. "Nothing pathological. Black or white coffee?"

She led him to talk about the plantation, and heard that the new overseer was consistently intelligent and conscientious, and the drug menace had fizzled out for a while. Julian had discovered that Astartes had sent down the load which caused the riot, and he had complained to the Portuguese authorities.

"A couple of officials came to take statements and I laid before them a bundle of facts. Rodrigo was cordially invited to attend a conference, and it goes without saying, he blandly denied all knowledge of the affair. He finished up tight as a tick, vowing that he loved me as a blood-brother." He grinned. "Somehow we both got our own way, so there should be peace for a period."

"It must be wonderful to taste conquest as often as you do."

He glanced at her sharply. "Everything you've gone through has been of your own choosing. No woman could live on Valeira for two years without being scarred, but at your age there's a chance of the scars fading." He leaned across the grass table. "Look here, Phil, this has to end. I'm on a week's holiday. I'll take you to Lagos and put you on a liner, and you can leave the dissolution of that bogus ceremony in my hands."

The sight of his brown paw alongside her own small fist roused in her a curious violence.

"It's in your hands," she cried. "Go ahead with it, but don't expect to ship me around as though I were a sack of meal. I'm sick of your insensitiveness. . . ."

Simultaneously they were on their feet.

"Shut up," he said. "The whole place will hear you."

"Let them, then they'll all know you for an overbearing brute." She was backing towards her bedroom door. "You may be king of the plantation, but here you're superfluous. I can do without your protection."

"Stop it, will you!" he said savagely. "The minute we get together sparks fly and you're the one who starts them. Doesn't that show how your nerves are cracking?"

"My nerves were sound enough till you got to work on them," she choked. "Go for your holiday, Julian. Find a woman in Lagos and laugh with her about the kid down in Goanda who fancies herself in love with you. . . ."

He was staring down at her with intensity. She gave a gasp of fright.

"Oh, no, no!" she muttered, and turned into the bed-room, thudding the door behind her.

When the doctor's houseboy knocked she ordered him away. He came back and she had to answer.

"You come to dinner, please, missus?"

"Not tonight," she jerked. "Tell the doctor I'm sorry, I have a headache."

Later Nurse Briggs appeared, bringing diluted tinned milk and some biscuits.

"Head no better, dear? I get them too . . . beasts. The doctor wondered if you'd been overdoing it, and Mr. Caswell said he thought you had."

"He's still here . . . Mr. Caswell?"

"Why, yes. He's staying till the end of the week."

It couldn't happen. Julian was joking, or testing her, or . . . her bones froze. Had he been aware all along that she loved him? Had he been warding off, with all the hardness in his nature, such a confession as she had made this evening?

"Where is he going to sleep?" she asked.

"At the Government rest-house, the other side of the village. I took you there once. Remember?"

Yes, Phil remembered. A square, one-room dwelling containing a few unimaginative pieces of Government furniture. The district officer slept there about three times a year, and by official order the place was always kept clean and aired.

Nurse Briggs said, "Think you'll sleep all right, or shall I beg a couple of tablets from the doctor?"

"Thanks so much, but . . . no."

"That's sensible of you. It's best to do without them if you can. Good night, my dear."

Phil was alone with her horror . . . and a gladness that she was not yet called upon to face the end.

Next morning she breakfasted as usual on the coffee and toast brought by the boy. She made her bed, tidied the room, and strode smartly along to the hospital entrance, sparing no glance for the house, and carried on with her round of the cots. About ten-thirty Nurse Briggs called her out to the veranda for a cup of tea. They chatted about the patients till the nurse had to go off and assist the doctor in the operating-room.

Phil walked along the veranda to her balcony . . . to find Julian sitting there.

"Good morning," he said pleasantly. "I saw you thread-

115

ing in this direction and thought I'd get here first. You're looking blooming, considering the sleepless night."

Momentarily startled, her lips parted to speak and then she met the quizzical light in his eyes, and her mouth compressed.

"I strolled about most of the dark hours myself," he admitted drily. "Come and sit down."

"I always change my shoes mid-morning," she said stiffly.

"Relax, and I'll fetch them for you."

Phil had no intention of continuing the scene begun yesterday. She remained outside on the path in the shade of a tree, and sat on the balcony wall to unlace the ward shoes lent her by Nurse Briggs. She let Julian draw them off and strap on her sandals because it was less trouble than arguing, but immediately he straightened she did so too.

"What about a trip up-river?" he said.

"No, thank you. I've work to do."

"You're let off while I'm here. I daresay we could rake up a picnic."

"No, thank you," she repeated.

"Afraid?" he jeered softly.

"No," she lied lightly. "I don't care to take a canoe ride with a strange man. If you felt normal you wouldn't invite me."

He smiled. "You're less cute than I thought. You can't see that by sending away the freighter this morning so that I've no alternative but to haunt Goanda for five or six days, I'm laying myself wide open."

"Not to me," she said huskily. "It was unkind of you to stay, Julian . . . horribly unkind."

"You left me no choice," he said shortly, adding with sarcasm: "You won't accuse me of neglect if I go for a cruise on my own? Unadulterated Goanda might curdle my brain."

Julian's presence at Goanda had a reverse effect to the one he had anticipated. Phil worked more desperately and passed the leisure hours alone in her room. She met him only at dinner or in front of an interested, dark-skinned audience. His moods, by turns both grim and taunting, were painful and puzzling; when his company was unavoidable she closed up, and got through with a conventional smile and platitudes.

The first three days he cleared off in a boat after a quick lunch, returning in time for a bath before dinner. The fourth day, while eating meal biscuit spread thinly with tinned butter, Phil tiptoed at her window to watch his preparations on the river bank. He was seated on a canvas chair about two hundred yards away, cleaning his rifle.

In a wave of sweat and dread, Phil recollected that in two more days she would be denied even the agonizing pleasure of surreptitious peeping. She dropped the unfinished biscuit on to a plate and dipped her face into a bowl of tepid water.

When she came out into the furnace blast Julian was gone, and so was the boat. How could he bear to travel the channel of the river in this lethal heat? It was worse than she had ever known on Valeira.

Dr. Grenfell, his silver head helmeted for the brief space between his house and the dispensary, called to her to follow him.

"You are distressed by this heat, Miss Crane?" he enquired when they were inside.

"It's certainly fierce," she said.

"So fierce that Nurse Briggs has had to lie down. I must dispense some medicines before the storm. Will you help?"

"Of course. The sky is clear. What makes you think there'll be a storm, Dr. Grenfell?"

"This stillness is the warning. Soon the sky will haze and a wind get up. Here, one sees no ominous accumulation of clouds, but they are there, beyond the trees. We'll waste no time. Some four-ounce and eight-ounce bottles, please."

A hospital boy carried the medicines to the nurse's office, and Phil emerged into the oven-hot veranda. The beds were being pushed back into the wards, and the storm shutters closed. The yard was deserted.

Subtly, the sky was changing, the steel-blue filming with a copper haze. From this distance the river was black glass, the tight-packed trees on the opposite bank cruelly inhospitable. Dr. Grenfell had said the river narrowed and be-

117

came more macabre as it twined inland. Julian could take care of himself—none better—but it was unsettling to think of him in a frail canoe on deep, squall-tossed waters. Maybe he had seen this storm approaching and turned back.

She went to the house and questioned the boy who squatted on the step. "Have you seen the white master from the island?"

"No, missus. Missus Brick she sleep. I sit here."

From which Phil supposed that his instructions were to prevent noise within the house while Nurse Briggs slept. Damn Julian. She hoped he'd get drenched and catch the snuffles; only a cold, not a chill. Sneezes and the miseries; enough to keep him off the river for the remainder of the week.

A sudden wind roared in from the treetops. Branches threshed, and the corrugated iron roofs of the small buildings creaked in preliminary protest. And now the thunder, full-throated and deceptively wooing; and horizontal shafts of flame that hurt the eyes. A dark pall was moving in, and large round drops smacked on her face and arms, but she could not bear to imprison herself in her room. The house would be more bearable.

Nurse Briggs, a tired greeting in her gesture, was sitting in the lounge. Phil declined tea, and paced from window to window, eyeing those huge single lumps of rain, her nerves a-quiver.

"Julian will be caught up the river," she said at last. "This is going to be a hefty storm."

"He'll have seen it brewing. He may beat the rain."

"He's stubborn enough to stay out in it."

"We ought to send a boy along with a fresh bath towel."

"I'll do it."

Grasping the excuse, she ran to the linen cupboard and dragged out a bath-sheet. Poking her head into the lounge, she said: "The boy seems to be missing. I'll take it over," and was out of the front door before the woman had time to raise an eyebrow.

The Government house was set exclusively at the end of the village, like a headman's. Beside it leaned a rotting flag-pole. Phil paused at the door, and after a minute she went in, blinking till her pupils adjusted themselves to the dimness.

Over the high back of a chair she draped the towel. She stood there, her breathing still uneven, taking in the room in all its sparse impersonality. If only Julian would show up.

"Well, well," he drawled from behind her. "Are you taking shelter or have you come to make tea?"

Phil swung round, saw his mocking glint and the powerful tanned shoulders, and chest left exposed by a singlet, and rightly concluded that he had never been on the river at all today. He had been resting within the mosquito net all the time. Her fears dissolved in fury.

She brought up her fist and he gripped it against him so that her fingers contracted and slackened nervelessly upon the vibrant warmth of his chest. The room was night-dark, stabbed by lightning, shuddering with thunder. The lean brown face above hers was diabolically self-assured. He twisted, kicked shut the door and dropped her wrist, freeing himself to haul her close to his arms.

She strained to his kiss, throat stretched, her hands pressing at his back as if she could never let him go. His mouth moved to her cheek and up to her temple, and she felt him crushing her shoulders and moving his hands over her, down to her waist. Julian's hands, strong and compelling; his heart striking into her breast.

It was raining, tumbling on the palm-thatch roof in an avalanche, but Phil didn't hear it. At last her body was alive, and singing.

CHAPTER XX

THE sun was past its zenith, but the bay still lay breathless in the shadow of Goanda headland. In the bowl of the bay palms swayed their green umbrellas. The only sound was the suck of the waves among the roots of the mangroves.

Phil, supine on the dried silt, felt the sun's heat on her thighs through the thick overhead branches, heard the lapping of the surf, and gazed up at a new, enthralling angle of Julian's jawbone. He was sitting beside her, exhaling an occasional arrow of smoke, and looking at the sea. His air was one of arrogant content.

"I've made him like that," Phil exulted within herself. "There's still a shell, but I'm inside with him, part of the man, part of his heart."

"I wonder what Matt and the others thought when the freighter went back without you?" she murmured.

"That there was a woman I couldn't tear myself away from."

She laughed. "They'd never believe it. They'll decide you've been sick and had to recover under the doctor's supervision."

"That's a half-truth, anyway. I shall have to shiver and wear a top-coat as I go aboard next Sunday."

A chill, like a touch of autumn, passed across Phil's face. "Any tea left in the flask?"

"About a cupful."

"Let's share it."

She sat up, emptied the sweetened, dark liquid into a cup and offered it.

"You first," he said, jabbing the remains of his cigarette into the sand.

When the cup was put away again he slipped back on crossed arms and she drew her feet under her and sat regarding him, all of youth and eagerness in her eyes.

"Are you happy, Julian?"

His mouth twitched. "There's nowhere else I'd rather be at this moment."

"Do you ever remember the plantation when you're with me?"

"Only to be glad I'm not there."

"Julian," she tried to keep the tenseness from her voice, "could you ever have sent me right away from you?"

"I don't know." His tones were steady, but he had closed his eyes. "I could have done it six months ago. If you'd agreed, I'd have had a shot at it last week."

"But not now?"

"I'm not a lunatic." Again the smile twitching at his mouth. "What are you trying to make me say . . . that I love you?"

"It would be rather . . . nice."

"All men say it, to all women, and for that reason it's an expression to be distrusted."

She took his hand between hers. "You haven't hesitated so long with other women, have you?"

"It never got me anywhere worth going. This feeling between you and me is very new. It's wiser to advance gently." His eyes opened, and though they scoffed at her, they also held tenderness. She was encouraged to brush her mouth over the hairs on the back of his hand.

"It doesn't matter, so long as you do," she said.

He laughed a little at the deliberate naïvety. "You'd twist a man's soul and pretend it grew that way."

"I used to be afraid yours *was* twisted," she told him soberly. "You were so bitter, so inhumanly intent upon your work."

"Don't take too much for granted, little one. A man of my age has changed as much as he's likely to. Remember that, when I disappoint you."

She was silent. He raised his head, reached and pulled her down with him. His breath came warmly across her lips.

"You're sweet," he said. "Try not to get hurt."

A plea impossible to obey, for is not anguish half of love?

The days and nights were passing so quickly. Days up the river or in the bay, when Julian sometimes told her of his wild boyhood in Cornwall or of other countries in which he had lived and planted. And hot, scented nights, which awakened an undreamed-of sensuality in Phil's nature.

She looked neither back nor far forward. But as his time with her narrowed she was seized with a desperation that showed itself in a reluctance to spend the briefest spell in the hospital. Doctor and nurse agreed that the jaunts with Julian were for her good; they were too busy to spare more than a word or two at dinner. Her conscience demurred, but not seriously.

Gaily she prepared the picnics and dressed in fresh linens. Her skin bloomed and her shoulders went back. She seemed to mature all at once with a new and exquisite fulness of love, and every sense was sharpened by the knowledge that Julian was keenly aware of her swift flowering.

He was as keyed up for her touch as she for his. She had never guessed so much power could be locked up in her body.

He could tease and jibe, reiterate that mortals were predominantly fickle and flick away sentimentality as though it was dust on his sleeve, but as far as it was in him to love anyone, he loved Phil. She felt it in every sinew, every racing drop of blood. *As far as it was in him to love anyone.*

Wasn't that the crux of her intimacy with him . . . an acceptance of his love as three-parts physical? She was too grateful for the miracle of his wanting her to demand more than he was willing, as yet, to yield.

On Friday he began throwing articles into his valise. "Shan't need this again," he said. Or: "Mustn't forget that. Matt doesn't stock my size." He hadn't much to pack, but she knew that he kept the valise open on a chair expressly for her sake. He had yet to learn that reminders only prolonged and intensified the pain of parting.

His last evening, after dinner, the doctor consulted him about the cheap gramophone in the lounge. Julian did his best with the poor, damp-corroded thing, and it was late when he and Phil entered the rest-house.

He lit the lamp and turned it low, shed his white jacket and emptied the pockets. She sat on a long, roughly-carved stool, and followed his movements, a cigarette greying between her fingers. The white jacket was carelessly folded and packed, a clean singlet, shirt and khaki drill shorts laid ready for the morning. From a drawer he took socks and a handkerchief, a couple of notebooks, some Portuguese money and an emergency flask of brandy, all of which he arrayed on the chest.

"All set," he said, and lowered himself to the stool beside her, stretching his legs in front of him.

His arm slid round her back. In the yellow half-light his face was sculptured in bronze, its angles sharp with shadows. He relieved Phil of the cigarette and trod it out on the floor. Then he bent his head and gave her a swift, hard kiss.

"I know what you're wishing, Phil—I'm wishing it, too. I'm not going to enjoy tomorrow any more than you are,

122

but we were both aware it would have to come."

"I haven't groused, have I?"

"My sweet, you've shown remarkable restraint. I've seen the question in your eyes a dozen times and been thankful for whatever it was that kept you from voicing it. Any other woman would have cried and clung."

"You'd loathe that," she said with surprising evenness, "and, in any case, your plans would remain unchanged by tears and pleading. But some time soon you will let me come to Valeira, won't you?"

"I hope it will be possible." He pressed her shoulder. "I'd feel a hell of a lot safer with you here, though, in the care of Dr. Grenfell. That chap at Valeira mission is hopelessly fuddled most of the time. And apart from health, there's still the obstacle of your being the only woman on the plantation. What with this new man, Davenport, and, in a few weeks, an untried cadet from England—I can see the Roger Crawford business starting all over again."

If only she could have said: "Who'd dare to try on anything with the manager's wife?" But some syllables were impossible of articulation.

"You'll come next week-end?" she asked instead.

He nodded. "On Friday evening till Sunday. Now that we're organized over there I should be able to get away most week-ends. For the present we shall have to be satisfied with that."

Not a bit of use arguing. When Julian made known a decision it was already part of his future mode of living. Suddenly she craved the pleasure of spurning him.

"What if I grow tired of Goanda, and move up towards Lagos?"

"Don't you dare!" He sprang up and carried her with him, bunching the scant flesh of her arms so that she winced with physical pain; his eyes were sparkling oddly. "If you did, I'd come after you and make you wish you hadn't."

"Sweet torture," she whispered, and laid her lips to his throat.

At dawn the boy brought coffee and Julian's breakfast. Phil, still in pyjamas and her hair cloudy, felt none of the voluptuous drowsiness of other mornings. She sat opposite to him, holding the tepid coffee and sipping, the lump near her larynx as harsh and round as if she had swallowed a peach-stone.

When he was ready to go the boy was told to carry the valise down to the waiting dinghy. Julian picked up his helmet and turned upon her a small controlled smile.

"So long, little one. Keep the hut dusted."

A quick kiss and he was gone. Phil's breath shivered in her lungs, and a terrible thought took possession: this was as bad as—worse than—Nigel's death.

A day or two had to elapse before she could think of Julian without a tempest of longing. The fear and uncertainty sidled in, niggling frets that robbed her of appetite and will. It wasn't important that he had avoided the trouble of explaining their marriage to Dr. Grenfell, but he might have asked where she kept her wedding ring. He might have remarked casually, "Handy our being married already, wasn't it?" and made her life joyous and beautiful.

Since the day of the storm he had referred neither to the marriage nor to its annulment. He was well enough acquainted with her mentality to have at least an inkling of her inbred desire for security; why otherwise would she have hung on in Valeira after Nigel died? Had he purposely held off the subject; did he consider it less dangerous to postpone it? He had everything pigeonholed, every reaction of hers forestalled. She could be sure that not one fact of their relationship had escaped him. In a way, that certainty was comforting. If his love for her did not include the devouring quality of Phil's for him, it went sufficiently deep to keep him concerned on her behalf.

Friday evening came. She dressed in white linen and ran to the bend of the river, straining her ears for the slap of water against a paddle. Quite soon the sound came, and she stood poised and taut, hidden from human eyes by the trees. She saw him seated in the boat and watched for his sudden smile. It came.

He bade the boy pull in and, when he had stepped on to the grass, gave the boat a shove along to the landing-stage.

They were alone . . . and wordless. He was staring at her steadily with a bright flame in his eyes. His hand came up

124

to rake familiarly through the banner of coppery hair, and to hold her head while he kissed her lips with the ferocity of a week's hunger. He bent and kissed the blue vein inside her wrist; he kissed the tender angle within her elbow, and came back to her mouth with possessive intensity.

"It's been so long," he said.

Phil, heart and eyes brimming, moved her cheek against the close-shaven chin. How completely groundless and foolish had been her doubts.

CHAPTER XXI

DR. GRENFELL said: "Well, young lady, I suppose it's pointless harking back to the conversation we had some time ago? Caswell's weekly descent upon us appears to have developed into a habit. I'm not deceived into believing he comes merely to help me start a farm colony for the natives. I'm exceedingly grateful to him, of course. He has the perfect brain for colonizing and a genuine interest in native problems. Still, I think I'm right in stating that he comes more to see you than to teach farming to the Africans?"

Phil didn't even blush. "I think you're right, too, Dr. Grenfell. I shall not go up the Coast and train as a nurse, after all."

"I guessed that, but I mention it because Charles Metcalfe, who is chief medico at the Levalle Institute of Tropical Hygiene, is on his way to see me. You'll meet him and hear about his work."

Phil's chief concern was that Dr. Metcalfe should arrive between week-ends. It would be too bad if the man clashed with Julian.

"I'm looking forward to it," she answered politely, visualizing a second silvery head bent in conference with Dr. Grenfell's.

In age and appearance Charles Metcalfe was an agreeable surprise. As he also had the decency to sail into Goanda on a Monday afternoon, Phil was disposed not to resent him.

He was above average height and slim. His features,

smooth and aquiline, had the pallid tinge of all indoor workers in the tropics, but his eyes, a soft dark brown, held an infinity of kindness and good humour. Though he could not have been more than a year or two over thirty, the flat black hair had receded in two arcs above his brow, endowing him with a scholarly air which he detested. Phil liked him at sight, and after three days' contact decided that he was one of the nicest men she had ever known. Charles was so utterly normal, and, she was sure, predictable. You'd know where you were with such a man.

So that the doctor might be free for technical talks, Charles spent hours in the hospital and dispensary. He played a neat game of tennis on hurriedly-cropped grass, and paddled a fast canoe up-river, but he was happiest on the veranda, sitting with a weak whisky at his side and some other person near by. His nature was neither solitary nor introspective.

He admired the doctor and Nurse Briggs and found relaxation and entertainment in Phil. Quite a rich little community, he thought. No passengers here.

He would have liked to stay longer and delve more thoroughly into the phenomenon of the good-looking, spirited girl tucked away in this festering clearing in the coastal forest.

The yacht upon whose deck he had slept on the trip down to Goanda had, immediately upon disembarking him, proceeded on its voyage. To get back to his Institute, Charles would have to travel inland—sixty miles up the river to the jungle highway, where he could pick up a jeep which his assistant was sending.

"And then back to the test tube and fluoroscope," he said to Phil. "I've been on leave a month and it seems like two years."

"I hope we'll meet again," she said frankly.

"So do I." He shook her hand and gave her the quiet smile which she was coming to know. "Don't forget us if you tire of Goanda. We can't get enough assistants, and we wouldn't expect more than six hours' light work out of you daily. Goodbye . . . Phil."

"Goodbye, Charles."

It was strange for the loaded canoe to disappear inland

instead of towards the sea. Phil wandered back to her room to finish her lunch and read a chapter of the novel he had passed on to her. By lunchtime next day, when she finished the book, Charles Metcalfe's imprint had faded. He meant hardly more than the tax collector who had called last month for the removal of his appendix. In fact, she omitted to tell Julian that they had had a visitor.

Julian was becoming more and more immersed in the plantation. With three keen overseers he was expanding the acreage of the cleared and newly-planted land by many square miles.

"We're half-way up the mountain-side and at one point have touched the mission grounds," he said.

"Will you encircle the mission?"

"Not for some time. I'm waiting for it to close down."

"Are there signs?"

"The old chap's dope-crazy, and Sister Harrington has had to pack up. The climate's got her."

"Poor thing," she said with pity. "She chose a frightful mode of living."

"Yes." He spoke slowly, as if weighing up whether to leave it there. Offhandedly he tacked on: "I went up to fetch her to the boat. I hadn't seen her for many months and the change in her sickened me. She was a yellow skeleton."

Phil made a sound of horror and compassion.

Julian went on: "I found out that she had worked in the tropics for eleven years without a break. She hasn't had Nurse Briggs' consolation." He grinned faintly at her startled expression, and amended, "Not in recent years, anyway."

"How did you know about Nurse Briggs and the doctor?"

"My sweet child," he teased, "they're a man and a woman, and equatorial nights are twelve hours long all the year round. Maybe neither would choose the other from a crowd, but"—a shrug—"why deny yourself what's there for the taking?"

She looked at him queerly—they were at the bay again —and scooped a palmful of grey sand. "So that's the masculine attitude," she said in flat tones.

"If you have the sanity and common sense of a doctor," he agreed. "But other mortals confuse the issue by insisting that the woman have bright streaks in her hair and hazel eyes and a voice that's husky and slurs the consonants."

Phil was won over. She did not pause to reflect that Julian's sanity and common sense were probably equal to those of the most cold-blooded surgeon.

Presently she said: "It must be a refreshing sight—row upon row of tiny oil-palms on the mountain slopes. Couldn't I come, Julian—just for a week?"

"You'd only want to stay on," he replied, without expression.

"Would that matter so very much—now?"

"I've explained why I won't have you on the island." His head turned abruptly seawards. "The set-up has changed. Matt has a new log house near mine in the clearing, and the overseers occupy the three bungalows on the cliff."

"All right," she managed after a moment. "Tell me more about the trees."

He nipped her bare knee. "The Valeira soil is the richest I've ever struck. Did I tell you we've started a tropical orchard for our own needs: pineapples, pawpaws, avocados, mangoes, and a few others? When the windbreaks are high enough to give shade I shall plant oranges and lemons."

"It takes years for fruit trees to bear."

"We ought to get a showing three years from now."

Three years from now. Phil was tempted to ask: "Shall I still be here, Julian, wading through the days and coming alive on Friday evening? Is that what you're offering me?"

Such an arrangement as theirs couldn't hold together for so long. From the viewpoint of a man who had forced himself to a celibate existence in hot places it must be convenient to say little, to have a woman of his own thirty miles away across the water. At present he was giving her two days a week, but as the plantation widened might not his time with her shrink to one day, or even less? Grimly ironical came the picture of Julian sparing her an hour or two once a fortnight in the interests of his health and peace of mind. She shivered, and groped for his hand. It was there, as warm and compelling as his mouth in the curve of her neck.

Oddly, her doubts were strongest when Julian was close. Perhaps it was only in his aura that she could be positively, tinglingly awake, both to ecstasy and its potential dwindling to a trickle of bitter pleasure. She thought, if it ever ends let it break off clean; anything else would be long-drawn death.

There happened a week-end when Julian neither appeared at the river mouth nor sent a message. Two days of stark agony, followed by five more of desperate, nerve-shaking hope. On Friday she was pitifully cautious. No clean dress; no chasing down to the river bend.

At tea on the hospital veranda, Nurse Briggs talked wearily, in her slightly common voice, about cutting out some overalls from the never-failing bale of white cotton, and getting the village women to hem new sheets. Phil could not listen. Her tongue had the appalling taste of anxiety and too many cigarettes.

She looked at her watch. If he was coming he had just about reached the bend; in five minutes he would jump on to the landing-stage. She couldn't go out; not, anyway, till his voice sounded. If the minutes ticked silently by till dusk, she would have saved herself the shattering experience of last Friday.

Then, somehow, she was out on the beaten earth path, scanning the fifty yards of cleared bank with the stage in the middle. And when the boat pushed from the trees and veered she ran, her heart hot in her throat. She was actually on the planks, extending two hands when he landed.

"I missed you at the bend," he said.

"After last week I was scared. Oh, Julian!"

He softened. "Sorry about that. I picked up a germ and was on my back for three days. Matt had a touch of it, too. Have you kept well?"

Phil nodded. She had no rights where he was concerned; she could not demand to know if he were ill. At that moment she would have liked to lean her weight against him, and weep.

CHAPTER XXII

THE sewing party had collected at the foot of the baobab tree. They sat between the great roots and leaned their backs on them. Their skirts, voluminous from waist to ankle, spread over the dust so that the materials they sewed should be kept spotless. Today, all had bodices, or at least a wide band of coloured cotton tight under the armpits; none would have ventured so near the hospital half-clad.

Phil, having just had a bath in her bedroom, was luxuriously drinking a cup of tea on her balcony wrapped in a print house-gown she had recently made for herself. She heard the babble and the chugging machine, and took quiet delight in the colourful group.

She became aware of a boy patiently awaiting her attention on the other side of the balcony wall. He thrust at her a letter.

"From white master, please."

With a bump of the heart Phil recognized the writing. Swiftly she tore the flap and extracted the pencilled note.

Don't be alarmed, my sweet. I have to go to Lagos, and have stopped here to let you know. If it's convenient, come to the bay for half an hour. The boy will bring you.

If it's convenient!

Phil said, "Wait!" and hastened into her room to slough the wrap and drag on a dress.

The boy loped ahead to the bend of the river. He had apparently learned well his instructions, for a white dinghy, much too grand and clean to belong to a freighter, was pulled well under the trees out of sight of a passing canoe. Deftly he poled away from the reeds and set the boat speeding towards the headland.

The river opened, and between the leaning trees Phil glimpsed a yacht, pale and sleek as those which had passed close to Valeira from Lisbon. Sea chipped at the dinghy's side, a tide so strong that the boy grunted with the effort of rounding the headland and pulling up through the waves to the silt bar where Julian bent, ready to lift Phil to a foothold among the mangrove roots.

He said: "The sea's risen since I sent the note, but I'm glad you made it. Watch your feet—it's slimy as hell."

He half carried her along the reef and over the bar to a spot they both knew, which was shut in by bush.

"You didn't mind my not coming in the boat to fetch you?" he asked, after they'd kissed. "If I'd been seen it would have meant tedious explanations. I have to be away again before dark."

"In that?" Phil indicated the yacht.

"Yes, chipper, isn't she? The property of one of the company directors. I told you a couple of weeks ago that a man was due to call on us at the island. He isn't coming, after all. By the time he reached Nigeria his wife had had enough. She's gone home by liner, but he, having travelled so far, would like a talk with me."

"So he sent the yacht. How long will you be gone, Julian?"

"About five days. I shall return in a coaster, and try to drop off here on my way back, possibly next Tuesday. Don't reckon on it, though. Nothing's dependable in these waters. But in any event I'll make the crossing as usual the following Friday."

She stood with her shoulder against his chest, surveying the superb craft which, even at anchor, rode the waves sweetly, with grace.

"She's fitted up like a roadhouse," he said. "Ten cabins, a lounge, a bar and a billiards room. Tennis and dancing on deck."

"Let me go aboard?" she pleaded.

"There isn't time. Besides," with a grin, "you might wheedle the captain to take you along."

She clutched the sleeves of his jacket and searched his eyes. "Couldn't it be done, Julian? Lagos isn't the island. You . . . did take me there once."

The reference was an error. She sensed it instantly in the way he stiffened, the deliberate intake of breath before he answered:

131

"This is hardly the moment to start a private debate. I'm beginning to wish I'd merely had a message delivered to you and sailed on. Don't!" as she trembled. "What a way to behave just now! I have to leave you in a few minutes."

His tone sobered and chilled her. She moved from the circle of his arms.

"I'm sorry. I've always been a little inconvenient in my desires, haven't I? You think I ought to be grateful for the chance of waiting for you to come to me at Goanda. Well, gratitude grows stale, and emotions tend to go ragged when they're overworked. You're selfish, Julian."

"I admit it," he said through his teeth. "And now will you be quiet and save your accusations till I get back!"

She loved and hated him. Recklessly, she demanded, "What will you do . . . serve me with a notice of annulment?"

Roughly, he jerked her round. "It's a bit late for that. Divorce is the word, but I'm not discussing it in anger or in haste."

"Of course not. You never did anything without drawing up a blueprint first. I'm aware that it's rotten and womanish to hurl this kind of thing at you when you're on the point of leaving, but I can't help it. If you wanted to you could take me with you to Lagos." She felt pain drawing tight in her throat. "You won't take me because the yacht will be met and you'd have to explain me as your wife . . . or something else."

His tanned cheekbones had darkened. In a cold and furious voice he said: "How right you are. Is it brutal of me to remind you that the sun has gone down and I'm expected to return to the yacht?"

As she turned he took the lead and grasped her hand with bone-cracking cruelty, hauling her after him between the shadowy mangroves, forcing her to move faster and faster over the slippery, mud-plastered roots. Once she floundered down into the silt and he had to crouch and drag her free. His eyes came close, a stony blue, and she wished he had left her to sink right under.

He got into the boat with her and barked at the boy to move fast. Big seas carried them into the river and the boy's rhythmic movements did the rest. Trees closed in, the branches chittering with homing birds. Phil sat and looked at the evil mouths in the bank between the buttressed boles, caverns hollowed by storm waters and latticed with vine. Liana flowers, red as the heart's blood, starred the dark foliage as though pasted there.

They were at the bend.

"I'll go with you through the trees," said Julian.

The path was narrow and night things were flying. As they approached near enough to see the lights of the hospital through the branches he stopped and examined the white blur of her face.

"I guess we've come to the end of the first phase," he said. "I hoped it would last longer, but you're too young and temperamental. I don't mean that viciously—it's simply a fact that we can't ignore. We were happy enough last weekend and if we're sensible we'll be happy again, though perhaps not in quite the same way. Maybe it's as well that I can't stay this evening. There's nothing like time for giving a quarrel its true perspective."

He was still remote and unbending, but she had to place her hand on his lapels and raise her head. "I've been a beast," she whispered. "You'll come next week?"

"Not till Friday. I'm not risking another ten-minute skirmish on the way back from Lagos."

He held her and kissed her, but without tenderness. In the hard mouth she felt his hurt and anger, his wish to have done with women for a while. She let him go and went back to the house.

The print wrap lay where she had let it fall earlier this evening, near the foot of her bed. About the room still hung the faint perfume of toilet soap from her bath. Expensive sandalwood soap, which Julian had brought her. Somehow it reduced the scene with Julian to an unvarnished fact. In his own words a phase had ended. Tonight, Phil felt peculiarly dry of emotion. Julian was on the high seas, the yacht creating a wondrous cool breeze of its own. Had he loved her, she would be there with him.

CHAPTER XXIII

FOR some weeks Matt had not been feeling too good. His digestion was haywire and he was awakened early each morning by a backache so severe that he had to get up and sit in a straight-backed chair. No joke, at his age, to stumble out of bed in the dark and sit like a mummy waiting for the pressure to lift.

Julian had become anxious and persistent. "You go to Goanda, Matt. Grenfell will put you right. Use the afternoon coaster on Friday." Later, when the arrangement was complete, Julian had said: "If Phil asks, tell her how I'm fixed. I'll go over next week-end."

Matt was only half deceived. One didn't need an outsize brain to calculate that a considerable number of the journeys Julian had made during the last five months had had Goanda as their destination; nor was the reason obscure. He considered Phil a young idiot, but he was not sorry for her. She'd got what she wanted, or an important part of it.

No, Matt was not sorry for her . . . not till the Friday evening when the boat pulled in to the Goanda landing-stage, and he was met by a slim, unhappy girl whose face was so pale and sick with disappointment that he knew she had been straining every hope that the boat would bring Julian, who hadn't come last week, or the week before.

"Well, Phil," he said, laying a thick red hand on her arm. "The old place hasn't changed much. Beats me how you stick it."

"It does me, when I stop to weigh it up. I'm glad you found time to come over, Matt."

"Necessity, lovey. I want the doc to go over my points."

"Have you been ill?"

"Not ill, just seedy. The heat, I shouldn't wonder. It's had a go at you, too, hasn't it?"

"This place is shut-in and steamy, like a hothouse; you tend to grow pale and leggy. Will you come straight to the house, Matt? Supper's just about ready."

The brittle lightness of her tone depressed Matt more

than if she had flicked away a tear and asked at once about Julian. He was not a man given to deep and smouldering passions—his nature was bedrock and tolerant—but looking at the stains beneath Phil's eyes as they both came into the bright lamplight of the doctor's lounge, he felt a grumbling anger against Julian. This was no way to treat the kid. She'd begged for it—no doubt about that—but Matt had thought better of Julian.

It was arranged at supper that he have his examination the following morning.

"You have lived too long in the tropics, my friend," Grenfell told him across the table. "A doctor knows the tricks, but even he may slip up. You careless men continually amaze me by your own good luck in avoiding most evils, and your tenacity. Don't worry about your health, Mr. Bryson. It is your will that is at fault."

"Why, damn it!" Matt ejaculated; he remembered the women and continued with less vehemence. "No one ever accused me of spinelessness before."

"Nor am I doing so now. But there is nothing more deadening to the human will than year upon year of excessive, malicious heat. If you were to move to a temperate climate you would experience immediate benefits: a lowering of blood-pressure, a stronger heart action, a clearer brain, and so on. I repeat this advice to every planter and trader who comes here, but it would be a sad day for West Africa if they followed it." He smiled in his perfunctory way. "Have some stewed pineapple, Mr. Bryson; cooking dispels the acid to a large extent."

Matt could imagine no dish less tempting than stewed pineapple. Nor did he wish to linger any later than tomorrow afternoon at Goanda. He excused himself rather hastily and went outside.

Down on the path he stood swearing to himself. What a filthy, cursed mess! Here was Phil incarcerated with a couple of talking corpses, burning herself out with a wrenching, hopeless love. Julian knew about it, of course; nothing naïve or blind about Julian. He might be fond of Phil, but it just wasn't in him to give her what she craved to make her happy.

For the life of him he could not see how Phil was to

avoid the final and bitterest heartache unless she cut loose right away, denying herself further contact with Julian. And how, in the name of a sacred monkey, did one accomplish such an end? The curry had brought Matt out in a sweat; his thoughts made him cold.

As Phil came quietly beside him he yanked out a handkerchief and wiped his neck and face.

"You get hot nights here, lovey."

"I don't mind them." Then, coolly, "Any message from Julian, Matt?"

"He's busy—just back from ten days in Lagos. He had to meet one of the company's directors there, but it turned out to be two directors and the daughter of one of them. All four returned in the yacht and they're staying at Julian's house."

"The daughter too?"

"Yes. Fine-looking girl and a good dresser—about twenty-five."

A pause. "Has he mentioned anything recently about coming here?"

"He did say he'll try next week-end. The visitors are supposed to shove off the middle of next week, but she's a headstrong woman and attracted to Julian."

"And . . . he?"

"It's hard to tell, but you can be certain he's aware he could marry a directorship in the plantation any time he likes."

In a minute or so Phil said flatly: "Julian enjoys playing host. Matt," a tremor ran through her, "I'm thinking of leaving here in a week or two. You might pass the information along to Julian."

"Where are you going?"

"To England."

"You'll keep in touch with us, Phil?"

"I'll try."

Matt left it there. He felt more exhausted than after a night of guzzling and poker.

Next morning, in Dr. Grenfell's surgery, he answered many queries and stripped himself for prodding and sounding. He compared his gross torso with the spare frame of the doctor and shied away from making a similar comparison between his own and the doctor's bank balances. With truculence he assured himself that that was the way of the world. Blast it, he wasn't going to turn sanctimonious in his old age.

To his relief the doctor shed his stethoscope and folded away the old-fashioned blood-pressure contraption.

"You're too fat," was the verdict, "and your body needs a cleansing diet. I don't have to tell you that you drink too much whisky and not enough water. You know your excesses better than I do. But let me say this: your heart is degenerating, your arteries stiffening and your breathing is much too shallow. Without observing you for a while and taking tests, I can give no diagnosis regarding your internal organs, but judging by your general condition, I'd be faintly accurate in stating . . ."

Feigning a wholly spurious interest in the doctor's monologue, Matt struggled up and put on his shirt. Having learned that, accidents apart, death was still a few years off, he had lost concern over his aches and indigestion. All he wanted now was to get away from the atmosphere of iodoform and tragedy.

He wrote a cheque, ate an appalling dry fish sandwich and prepared to leave. He said goodbye to Phil at the landing-stage.

"Why don't you look around for a bit of adventure?" he stated tritely. "Plenty of excitement about for a girl like you."

"I've had enough. A quiet life for me from now on."

On the way out to the freighter Matt asserted to himself that Phil was taking it hard because she was young, but she also had the elasticity of youth. Under the shivering northern skies her experiences in the tropics would assume a dream-like unreality. In time she would settle to a career, and maybe fling herself headlong into a more normal love affair. He'd be damned grateful to get aboard and soak up a real drink.

Phil waited till Sunday evening after supper before telling Dr. Grenfell and Nurse Briggs of her decision to leave Goanda. Neither asked for explanations, doubtless because they had long ago realized that her sojourn here was a thing of convenience, to be utilized by them while it lasted.

"What do I do—take the mail boat?" she asked.

The doctor nodded. "It's due here next Saturday with mail and supplies. You could go back in it to Port Andrew and from there you'd have to book another passage to Lagos. The coastal service from Port Andrew is excellent."

Saturday. That would allow Julian his chance, though she knew inside her that he would not come. Carefully she made piles of his belongings. The portable gramophone and records, his hundred or so books; the Coolette he had brought so that she could have a cool drink at night; the cabinet of playing-cards and chessmen.

Her own things fitted easily into the little wooden box, for she had given away to various patients her sketching materials and the clay models. Her year's allowance was half gone and her ticket to England would make a hole in the rest, but at the hospital she had become accustomed to dull and frugal fare. The financial side of it left her unmoved. Nor did she ponder what she would do in the strangeness of London. When the heart is an open wound the head has to work alone. Emotionally, Phil was vanquished.

Friday evening passed. A peculiar hush hung over the clearing, like the stillness before a squall. Phil missed the rustling among the palm fans, the whispering of the reeds and elephant grass. She sat in her room and wrote a note.

I am going to England. Later I shall make my home at the Cape. When you are ready to take legal proceedings, please get in touch with my lawyer; you have his address. Thank you for everything. Goodbye.

Lest it should fall into other hands she neither addressed nor signed the letter, but sealed it in an envelope which she slipped into the gramophone.

Far into the night she sat in the balcony. The darkness teemed with tiny life. The brazier continued to glow, the river to sparkle in patches where stars dipped closest. Lazy smoke plumed from the village, where fires were kept going to frighten away wild things and evil spirits.

And there, in the centre of the beaten earth expanse between hospital and river, spread the gigantic and ancient baobab tree, symbol of the timelessness and immutability of Africa.

A scrawny cock was crowing when Phil sought her last few hours' rest in the austere little bedroom.

CHAPTER XXIV

A JUTE and rubber magnate had once built himself a stucco eighteen-room mansion overlooking the ocean and about three miles from Port Andrew. Soon afterwards the poor man had gone the way of many another in the tropics, and the house had begun rapidly to follow his example, when Dr. Levalle, on the lookout for just such a bargain, happened along and bought the place for a modest couple of thousand. A further and considerably larger expenditure converted the pretentious place into the Levalle Institute for Tropical Hygiene.

When Levalle succumbed to one of the plagues he was aiming to combat it seemed as if his Institute would have to close down. Then Charles Metcalfe, who had just completed two years as a medical officer in Sierra Leone, came along and accepted the principalship, and the experiments were carried on from where Levalle had left off.

The fly in the amber of Charles' content was Madame Levalle. He admired her alien beauty and at times she disturbed him physically, but her callousness, her malice and vanity repelled him, so that when the shining burgundy limousine snaked up the drive, as it did this morning, it was an effort to smile and congratulate her on still another superb costume.

Today she wore blue silk, high and loose at the neck and moulded to the mature loveliness of her small figure. She was Charles' own age, or perhaps a little older. She gave him a tiny, red-tipped hand, holding it high as though expecting him to kiss her fingers. Charles didn't, but he smiled falsely as if he would have liked to. The woman could make so much trouble if she chose.

Sonya Levalle sank gracefully into one of the capacious canvas chairs on the terrace.

"Coffee, please, Charles. Stay with me. I wish to speak to you."

He ordered coffee from a white-coated boy, and took the other chair near the table.

"About the Institute, Madame?"

She frowned, a drawing together of perfectly arched black brows above dark, watchful eyes. People said Sonya had Hindu blood, that ten years ago Levalle, middle-aged and curiously unpractised in the ways of women, had rescued her from a Pondicherry gutter and been flattered by her youth and unusual looks into marrying her. Certainly her hair was blue-black silk and her complexion ashen as a Malay's, but her features were finer, more pointed and greedy than the gentle Indian contour. She said she was French.

"Do not call me Madame, Charles, especially when we are alone. No, it is not about the Institute. I am giving a dinner party and I want you to be there. Next Thursday."

"That's charming of you. Thanks." He loathed Sonya's parties, which were merely a series of picture frames for Sonya. He could see from her expression—an expert curving of the mouth and the tilt to the chin—that she was recalling to them both her last dinner party, when he had kissed her. She was like a sleek cat, still purring over last week's cream.

"Here's the coffee," he said. "Will you pour?"

She gave him his cup and lit a cigarette at his lighter. Her forefinger stroked his knuckle.

"You have fine hands, Charles . . . sensitive, tender. If I did not know that you also have passion, I would say that you are wholly the good physician. It is a pity that you English are so reserved. There is no getting into your mind. I wonder how you satisfy your women?"

He was saved from uttering some inanity by the roar of a Port Andrew taxi on the drive below. He stood up and moved to the top of the wide steps.

At his side, Sonya murmured: "A girl needing a job. You will turn her down, Charles."

But he was hurrying down the steps, extending his hands. "Phil! I never anticipated for a moment that you'd ever bother to find us. I'll dismiss the taxi. You run up there, out of the sun."

The girl did not run, Sonya noticed. She was thin, composed and tired—very tired. English, or at the most Colonial. Her green linen dress was neat, but travel-weary, and hair with reddish tints escaped from under the double-felt hat. Sonya did not like red or blonde hair.

Charles reached the terrace again almost on Phil's heels, and made the introduction.

Sonya nodded regally. "You have come to live in Port Andrew, Miss . . . er . . . Crane?"

"No," Phil said quietly. "This is a visit on my way to Lagos."

Charles indicated a chair. "I'll send for more coffee. Will you join us, Sonya?"

"Thank you, no. I have business to do in town." She had nothing to fear from this child; she was almost plain. "*Au revoir*, Charles."

He went with her to the car because he knew there would be hell to pay if he omitted the courtesy, and came back to find Phil sitting as he had left her. She was white, her knees were drawn up and her hands clasped upon them. The change in her was incredible. Her voice retained the husky sweetness, but it was dead.

"I've come to beg a favour," she said.

"Have some coffee first. Black?"

"Do I look so jaded? I spent the night on a mail boat—in a hammock above a cage of monkeys. We were stuck outside Port Andrew."

"What a pity. We'd have found a bed for you somewhere."

"Would you? That's why I am here." She stirred the coffee and drank a little. "From the boat this morning I went to the shipping office and bought a ticket for Lagos, but the coaster doesn't sail till tomorrow. There's no hotel, of course, and the club takes men only. The shipping clerk was a little upstage, gave me to understand that women don't travel alone in West Africa, and I'd better think up the name of a friend pretty quick."

"So you did. We'll fix you up. I'm only sorry it's not for more than one night." He sat back in the same position from which he had viewed Sonya. "Meeting some-one in Lagos?"

"Only a third boat. I'm going to England."

"But you've no people there?"

"I've no people anywhere. When one decides to cut away from the tropics one has to pick on a place to go."

Charles said: "If you're in need of an anchor for a time why not use us? Nothing's so bad when you've work to do and a friend to call on."

"If I accepted your kindness it could only be for a period, which would hardly be fair to you."

"Why shouldn't we both give it a month's trial? Don't answer yet. As soon as you feel rested, I'll take you round and you shall say whether you'd rather sleep here tonight in what used to be a nurse's room, or in the spare room of a nice woman I know in town."

He digressed about the garden and the coastline and the sociable crowd at the club. When a faint colour had crept up under her skin he led the way to the laboratory where four young men were working, and into his office, and on to the records office, where Phil met two wives of labora-tory assistants, Mrs. Kevin and Mrs. Coombs.

"Kevin and his wife are due for a long vacation," Charles said when they had emerged once more into the corridor. "If you could slip into her place we'd all be grateful. The records aren't complicated, but they're terri-bly important; as soon as they lag we're in the cart."

They mounted wide stone stairs to the upper floor. The two dormitories occupied the whole of one side of the main corridor. On the other were bedrooms and bathrooms.

"We call this side the boarding-house," said Charles. "The Coombs and the Kevins have the two largest rooms, the next is officially mine, though I seldom sleep here, and those at the end were originally reserved for nurses. They're empty now, so you can select which you like."

But he opened first the door of the room which he was sure would attract her most. It had a huge, semi-circular window that opened to a roofed balcony which command-ed a magnificent vista of white-capped sea, remote white houses with red roofs, and a dark green sweep of forest. From a seat near the ornamental iron staircase one looked twenty feet down at the garden and close enough to touch grew a flower-laden frangipani.

Charles was saying: "The male nurses—we have only three—sleep in a separate building. We all eat in the dining-room or on the terrace, and there's a jeep belonging to the Institute which will run you into town. If you feel you can stay, and I hope you will, I'd like to assure you that you'll have no contact with sickness. Nearly all our patients are seen by appointment, and few remain over-night; and anyway, you'd see nothing of them. I'm offering you a clerical post among a bunch of grand people."

"You're extraordinarily kind, Charles."

He crossed to the door. "Lie down for an hour. I'll have some food brought up to you. We can send for your things later if you make up your mind to throw in with us."

He snicked the door behind him and went down to his office. Abstractedly he thumbed through a report, and then he gave it up and dropped his jaws into his hands, his eyes following the slack movements of a garden boy outside.

No doubt about it, the girl must be persuaded to live at the Institute and put in a regular six hours a day. She must be made to throw off the numbness and laugh herself back to prettiness and vitality. He wondered what could possibly have happened to her in such a spot as Goanda. A man, of course, a trader or a district official. Why was it that the nicest girls inevitably fell for swine? He recollected her wide eyes and laughing mouth, her eagerness and high spirits. The man had done that to her, as well.

At two o'clock Phil knocked at his door.

"I'd like to do that job," she said hesitantly. "But no salary—no strings."

"Good. Go along and get matey in the records department. You're one of us."

Not quite, though. Sonya was still to be won over. Charles sighed to himself. When Phil's footsteps had receded he lifted the telephone and dialled, hoping that this was one of the days when the apparatus jibbed. But no. The unmistakable grunt of a houseboy.

"Is Madame there?" he enquired.

She was. "This is unusual, Charles. I was about to take my *siesta*."

"Forgive me. Would you prefer me to ring later?"

"Certainly not. What is it, *chéri*?"

"Our talk this morning was interrupted. How soon can we continue it?" Damned hypocrite, he named himself.

"This evening, *mon cher*. I go to dinner with the General, but he is very respectable. He brings me home at ten. You will come for a nightcap?"

"If I may. I won't keep you longer now, Sonya. Goodbye."

As he replaced the telephone, Charles shrugged with distaste. It was all very sordid, but he did get a sort of wry kick from it, and kisses with Sonya were not an extortionate price for Phil's presence and the chance of making her whole again. Somehow, he didn't think Sonya would mind if he went no further than kissing; she'd regard it as flattering evidence of worthier desires. Sonya was after marriage . . . with an Englishman; preferably Charles, who was good-looking and received by the upper hundred in Port Andrew. Her ambitions were so obvious that he made the mistake of believing them fairly harmless.

CHAPTER XXV

PHIL'S duties were easy and pleasant. Within a few days Mrs. Kevin departed with her husband for North Africa, and Phil found herself partnering Mrs. Coombs in the records office, and dealing alone with the library.

The books, three parts technical and medical and the rest an assortment of fiction and biography, lined a square room on the ground floor. Charles had passed over to Phil the care of the library because there is nothing so effective as a roomful of reading-matter to transport a person into a different world.

He would have liked to hear her step lighten and the smile come back into her voice. Occasionally he took her for a drive through the coast road away from the town, and stopped to smell and watch the sea. She was quiet and uncommunicative, and Charles congratulated himself. This was the first stage of recovery.

A week of rain set in; sudden clashing storms petering down to several hours of torrent, then sulphurous sunshine followed by hot mists. Sometimes Phil was overcome by loneliness and terror. This African world was so dense, so violent, the jungle so hostile and suffocating. She could not stand it another day, another hour. One of her worst moments came on a Saturday morning, when most of the others had driven hopefully into town to the polo.

She was on the beach fighting for courage when a storm broke. In seconds, as she moved without haste through the trees, her shirt and shorts were soaked and, by the time she reached the Institute, her hair dripped like strings of seaweed and the rest of her shed a pool into the hall. Upstairs, she met Charles coming from one of the dormitories.

"Good God!" he exclaimed, and swung wide a bathroom door, pushing her inside in front of him.

"Get out of your clothes and wrap in a towel," he said professionally. "Have the bath as hot as you can bear it and dry thoroughly. Be quick."

Ten minutes later, wearing a second large towel, she went to her bedroom and found there a glass of hot milk and a couple of tablets. She had swallowed both and was dressed when Charles knocked.

He looked her over critically, the drying curling hair about the small face, her pale lips. She was trembling.

"You took those tablets?" he asked quickly.

"Yes. I haven't a fever."

"What is it, then?"

"Hurrying, and the milk. I feel rather dizzy."

Charles stared, and a sense of shock spread through his system. Her head bent and she nodded like a sad, defeated child.

"Yes," she said. "I'm going to have a baby."

"Oh, my dear," he murmured, as though her hurt were his.

Gently he pressed her down into a chair, and sat near by on the arm of another. "Can you speak about it?"

She took a long, shivering breath. "I suspected it before

I left Goanda. I'm sure now. I'm getting used to the idea."

"But, Phil, what about the man?"

"He . . . we were married, but had agreed to a divorce. I shall be all right. I have an allowance."

Charles put aside the personal blow. She was heart-breakingly young. "He has a right to know about this."

"No. He'd hate it. He didn't want a wife—he'd loathe to be burdened with a family."

"That's hardly the point. Let me get in touch with him for you, Phil. It's fair to give him his chance."

"You don't know him. Besides, I don't want him that way."

He stood up.

"Well, thanks for telling me, Phil. It won't harm you to go on as you are for the present, so long as you keep healthy."

For the first time since he had come in she met his eyes. "It's between you and me, Charles?"

He smiled. "Absolutely, and for the next month or two I'm your doctor. My first prescription is dinner with me tonight at the club."

"My wardrobe wouldn't run to it."

"Very well. Tea, and perhaps some dancing till sun-downer time. You can wear anything for that. Game?"

She smiled slightly and inclined her head.

The rain finished at about noon, so Charles drove her into town early enough for a tour of the shops.

Port Andrew was a white and green town with avenues leading down to the wide Marine Drive where the blocks of offices were situated. Charles lived at the other end of one of these avenues, but he did not take Phil to the bungalow he shared with an education officer. After buying a few things they went straight to the club and had tea, after which they joined the dancers on the terrace.

Phil had last danced to a band in Cape Town when she was sixteen. Not that the three young men who now provided ·rhythm could be termed a band; a gramophone record would have yielded more harmony. But their presence in an alcove shut off by palmettoes gave an illusion of sophistication.

Men and women included Phil in their glances. They raised enquiring brows, and the men winked. In a port of this size everyone knew everyone else. Phil thought, if it weren't so hot I'd settle here; they wouldn't snub me with Charles as my ally.

And Charles thought what a damned nuisance it would be if Sonya heard rumours. It had been simple until this morning, but now he had a whale-size problem on his hands. Phil mustn't be hurt any more. Perhaps he'd better see Sonya this evening; introduce an offhand reference to this little jaunt. How he detested the subterfuge and lying. If only Levalle had left the trusteeship in the sole hands of the lawyer instead of besottedly including his wife.

As the feeling of resigned bitterness wore off, Phil experienced odd moments of fearful anticipation. She would stand still in the middle of her room and contemplate the miracle which was in creation inside her body. The knowledge that she possessed something of Julian that he could never take away helped to assuage the dreadful ache of loss. The loneliness was temporary. This time next year she would be whole and free, guardian of small dependent flesh and blood. She would never be lonely or aimless again.

There were other moments, of course, which lengthened unendurably into the dark hours, when the grief which was never absent rose to a sweating, wrenching agony.

The week-ends, once the offices had been locked at noon on Saturday, stretched long and somnolent. The two bachelor assistants invariably spent the whole time with friends in town, and the Coombs were either out, too, or in their room. Phil always felt as if she had the vast building and grounds to herself.

On Sundays a houseboy climbed the iron staircase and brought her meals to the balcony. She dozed through the heat of the day, read a little and frequently ended up at a card table with the Coombs.

This Sunday she had managed a bathe—not in the sea, for Port Andrew had no sweet lagoon with palms leaning over it—but at the private pool used by the Government officials and their wives. Charles had taken her there and given her a light lunch afterwards, and now she was back on her balcony, perspiring again, but fresher for the sensation of having freed her limbs and talked with jolly people.

She heard the slam of a car door. Not the jeep's; she couldn't have missed its clatter up the drive. The Coombs must be entertaining today. She adjusted her cushion and attempted to slide into the narcotic mood of her novel.

A step on the iron stairs. The boy was early with tea today. She glanced over the edge of her book, saw the rising head of Sonya Levalle and felt the shrinking of distaste and apprehension.

Sonya, dark, observant and vicious with jealousy, recognized the expression of consternation and veiled astonishment.

"You are surprised to see me, Miss Crane?"

"Well, naturally, but do sit down."

Sonya threw off the scarf and smoothed the black silk hair. Her rings scintillated. "You have the airiest room in the building, Miss Crane."

"Yes. I'm very forunate."

"This was my husband's room when we lived here. Although he had passed much of his life in India, he was unhappy in the heat. I insisted that he have this room. Charles has told you about my husband?"

"A little. I'm sure he was a great man."

"A great scientist and a gentleman. My father, who was an officer of the French Army at Pondicherry, had tremendous affection for Armand. My mother, I regret to say, did not live to meet my husband. She died in Paris when I was young. My grandparents did not approve of my father taking me to India, but how thankful I am that he did."

It streamed out like a rehearsed passage in a play. Sonya had recited it so often that she believed it herself.

"You have had an exciting life, Madame," said Phil.

"My life—for myself—is only just beginning," came the sharp retort. "For ten years I dedicated myself to Armand Levalle and his work. Next time I will marry purely for love."

Phil was willing to place the kindest construction on Sonya's purpose in marrying Levalle. As she hadn't the least desire to discuss tender emotions with the woman she got up and peered over the rail for the houseboy. She knew that Sonya was watching her movements and making comparisons with her own undeniable charms, but just then Madame Levalle meant very little to Phil.

"How long had you known Charles before you came here?" Sonya asked.

"I was living at Goanda. He came as a guest to the hospital there for three days."

"That was all?"

Phil nodded. "He told me there was a job here, if I cared to take it."

"He told you that?"

"Only in fun," Phil retracted swiftly.

Sonya had risen and crossed to the wall. Her face was a tight sallow mask. "Why did you come here, Miss Crane?"

"You know why."

"I know the excuse you fabricated in order to gain Charles' sympathy and push in under the same roof with him. You are not rich. You would not work at the Institute without pay unless it suited some plan in your mind."

Phil hated the woman's nearness, her heavy perfume and the cruel dark eyes with tell-tale yellow in the whites.

"No, I'm not rich. I stayed so that Mrs. Kevin could take a holiday."

The cool tones tinged with contempt were followed by an electric silence. Sonya's nostrils had widened.

"It is best that we understand each other," she said. "You will please be ready to go when Mrs. Kevin returns to her duties, in a fortnight."

"Very well. Will you wait and have some tea?"

But Sonya was already descending from the balcony by the way she had come.

CHAPTER XXVI

DURING the next week Charles was abnormally busy. Besides an unprecedented demand for serums from doctors and hospitals inland, the Institute dealt with a

149

record number of patients. At any other time he would have welcomed the influx, for upon this year's statistics depended his chances of Government assistance and throwing off the yoke of Sonya's trusteeship.

Before Phil's arrival he had handled Levalle's widow warily and with restraint. True, he had kissed her, but when a woman of Sonya's temperament and experience manoeuvred a man into a certain situation the only get-out was an embrace. Now he saw himself hurtling at speed towards a relationship more perilous than any he had hitherto shared with a woman, and unfortunately he was disliking her more at every moment.

On Monday morning Phil had come to his office and told him of Sonya's visit, and he had inwardly seethed.

"You must take no notice," he said. "I'm Principal of the Institute, not Sonya. When Mrs. Kevin returns we'll fix you up with light work in the lab." From beneath half-lowered lids he examined her. "How long is it—five months to go?"

"About that." She hesitated, searching for words. "You've been so kind, Charles. I wouldn't want to cause a bother for you. I have to go to England some time; it might as well be soon."

He nodded gravely. "In a few weeks this climate will be no good to you. You'll need cooler air and fresh food. Phil, you've got to tell me how I can get in touch with your husband." She whitened, and leaning over the desk he went on rapidly: "You think that because I haven't badgered you I've accepted your refusal to let him know how you're placed. But I can't accept it, Phil. It goes against a man's nature to stand by and allow a woman to take such a major event in her life alone, and unhappy. He must have loved you or he wouldn't have married you."

"He married me because I needed my father's legacy. Otherwise I'd have been penniless until I'm twenty-one."

With sudden vehemence he said: "He loved you at the time I visited Goanda. Every pulse in your body assured you of it."

"Please, Charles." Her eyes had filmed and gone dark. Her voice shook. "I deceived myself. Please believe that and say no more about it."

"But, my dear girl, how can I keep silent, knowing you still care for him? You realize that I could write to Dr. Grenfell and ask for details?"

"You won't do that," she said huskily. "If I thought you might I'd go away tomorrow."

Charles felt helpless. He pushed to his feet, came round to where she sat and looked down at the crown of her head.

"Phil, have you considered it from his angle? As you reminded me before, I don't know the man . . . but *you* do. Convince me that he's a complete swine and I'll never speak of him again."

The face she raised was sharp with agony. "A man isn't a swine because he can't love a woman the way she wants him to. Apart from anything else, what he offered wasn't enough. What would I gain by dragging him in at this stage? I'd still have to go alone to England, and the divorce would only be deferred. It's common sense to avoid a double dose of punishment if you can."

All that week and over the week-end the matter lay like a dormant spectre at the back of his mind. On Wednesday the Kevins were expected back, and that morning Mrs. Coombs tapped on Charles' office door.

Her bright round cheeks were dimpled. "Can you spare me a minute, Dr. Metcalfe? It isn't business."

"Go ahead, Mrs. Coombs."

"Well, Friday is Mrs. Kevin's birthday."

"Oh." Charles anticipated what was coming. "You'd like to fix up the usual birthday dinner at the club?"

"Yes. What I'm not sure about is—do we invite Madame Levalle? She came to your party last year, but she hasn't attended one of ours."

Charles pondered. "Would you like me to sound her?"

"Will you?" she asked, delighted. "You see, with an equal number of men and women we could make a real highspot of it. The Kevins and the Coombs, Boyd and Phil Crane, Dick Merrow knows a girl who'll come, and then there's you and Madame Levalle. Five men and five women. We'd be the envy of Port Andrew!"

He smiled: "I'll ring her at lunch-time."

Mrs. Coombs withdrew and Charles was left with revived uncertainties. No danger of Sonya refusing to adorn

Mrs. Kevin's party, for she enjoyed queening it over the staff and playing hostess to his host. But would she stir up more unpleasantness? How he wished he could see some blue beyond the thunderheads.

When, over afternoon tea, Mrs. Coombs told her of the proposed party for Mrs. Kevin, Phil would have preferred to back out. Charles happened to catch her glance and inclined his head, so she accepted, thinking that the event would also serve as her own farewell.

The guests at the dinner party were eleven instead of the planned ten. It seemed that Sonya's General had formed the habit of dining with her on Fridays, and rather than wound him by breaking the sequence, she had brought him along. Before the evening was through Phil had guessed that the woman was playing him off against Charles.

It was a well-managed party, but it went on too long. Tropical parties are like that, for there is nothing less inviting than a net-shrouded bed on a hot, sticky night. Most of the men had drunk freely and unwisely, and Mrs. Kevin and Dick Merrow's girl-friend were almost paralysed. Only Charles, Sonya and Phil remained unwaveringly sober.

Sonya danced but once, with the General. For the rest she sat in a corner of the club salon, a jewelled box on her lap, from which now and then her tiny fingers extracted a rust-coloured leaf which she slipped between her lips and chewed. When she spoke her breath came in moist, sickly scented gusts. In her lovely features lurked sullen dissatisfaction, which Charles' presence at her right hand did nothing to diminish.

At two o'clock he said, "Would you like me to take you home, Sonya?"

"I would, but not yet. The General is drunk; he, too, must be escorted to his house."

"We might all have gone together. If you're in no hurry I'll take Phil and come back for you."

"Miss Crane?" Sonya bent across him in order to view more closely Phil's wan face with smudges under the eyes. "Miss Crane is the youngest here. She can leave with the others."

Charles was standing. "Age has nothing to do with tiredness. Phil needs her bed."

With displeasure, Sonya retorted: "It is ridiculous, the way you fuss over a child of nineteen. I am not blind, Charles. I saw you shield her from the draught at the door and pour away her second cocktail. If she is tired, let Boyd or Merrow take her. You are not a chauffeur."

"Neither is fit to drive," he answered abruptly. "Are you ready, Phil?"

As she got to her feet, Sonya did the same. The dark eyes, half-veiled, roamed with deliberation over the tawny head and slim shoulders.

"I'll hang on," Phil said hastily. "Please don't trouble, Charles."

"Get your coat," was his reply, "I'll meet you on the front terrace in five minutes."

"Good night, Miss Crane," drawled Sonya.

Phil murmured an answer and moved off.

"Was that necessary?" Charles said quietly. "Haven't you any sympathy at all with your own sex, Sonya?"

"Sympathy?" She shrugged. "Why should that girl be given sympathy? If the heat upsets her, there are other places, less hot. The Institute is not a haven for love-lorn adolescents, Charles."

"What do you mean by that?"

"She hopes you will keep her here because she is in love with you."

"Listen, Sonya," he said steadily, "Phil's the victim of a disastrous love-affair. She's going to England to get over it. By giving her work to do we've helped her, and I, personally, shall go on helping her till she sails."

After a pause she said in a softer voice, "She has nothing to do with you and me, Charles?"

"Nothing at all."

She smiled. "You forgive me for the little *crise de nerfs*?"

"Of course," he assured her, a trifle wearily.

"I feared she might come between us. You will send her away soon?"

Phil's unhappiness roused not the smallest compassion in Sonya; her self-absorption was complete.

She fingered his lapel and whispered: "Drive the girl to the Institute, but do not be long, *cheri*. You and I will see the General to his house, and after that we shall be alone for a precious hour before dawn. You wish that?"

Fortunately, he got away with a smile and a pat on her fingers. The music had ended and the dancers were dispersing. The throng, predominantly male, oozed on to the terrace, and Charles had to push his way to where Phil, like a forlorn bird, leaned against a pillar. Without speaking, he took a firm hold of her elbow and led her to the car. They were out on the coast road, speeding between tall trees on one side and scrub and sea on the other, before he looked in her direction.

"Warm enough?" he enquired. "Lucky that tomorrow's Saturday. You have my permission to lie late."

"Thank you." She sounded cold and frightened.

For a wild half-minute he imagined himself taking her to England, seeing the business through, and eventually marrying her. If it were as simple as that!

He had an impulse to stop the car and draw her into his arms and tell her that he loved her and would never abandon her. It was that damned sentimentality of his, the insidious softness which had put him off becomng a general practitioner. Coming down from Sierra Leone he had forsworn sentimentality. Bugs were to be his future, and marriage, if it came, would be with a hard-headed nurse who could look after herself amid heat and disease. And here was Phil reopening all the old longings and turning them into regrets.

He angled into the Institute drive. "Did you bring the key to the balcony door?"

She took it from her bag. "I'd rather use that way."

He braked. Suspecting her desire to go in alone, he said, "I'll sit here till you've switched on. Good night, Phil."

She crossed the grass to the iron steps and mounted them. He saw her head as she stood at the glass door of her room, and then she disappeared into a black rectangle. A light blossomed, and she came back to pull curtains and close the screen.

Charles lit a cigarette and reversed. And now for the repetitive farce with Sonya. A farce, because neither of them ever lost their head. For all the sultry promise of her body, Sonya was cold and hard as iron.

CHAPTER XXVII

PHIL'S enquiries at the shipping office elicited the news that passenger accommodation from Lagos to England was limited. Tentatively she booked a berth three weeks ahead and begged to be advised of a possible cancellation on an earlier boat. She had driven the box-car into town to pick up some supplies which Charles had heard were awaiting collection in one of the wharves, so it was with a sense of relief in having a job to do that she left the shipping office and made for the Customs Road.

Her instructions were to hand over the advice note and sit tight till the stuff was packed into the car. She chose a patch of shade in front of the sheds and called a uniformed native to take the white slip to a Eurasian foreman.

She became conscious of being scrutinized. A small man wearing the inescapable khaki drill and a grubby topi stood in the full glare of the sun, inspecting the wording on the wagon. Aware that she noticed him, he approached and tipped his helmet.

"Excuse me, miss," in tones which she believed to be Lancastrian. "I see you're from the Institute of Tropical Hygiene. I've been trying to find a taxi to take me there."

She smiled. "When my load is aboard I shall be driving back. Maybe you'd like to come along?"

"I certainly would. Can I tickle up these blighters for you?"

His tickling up had effect. The precious cargo of apparatus and chemicals was stowed and he got in beside her.

"Clem Pringle's the name," he said, as she started the engine. "Adventurer, of no fixed abode."

She had met others like him in West Africa; men who had come out on short contact and either gone partially native or been nailed here by easy money. Their usual epitaph was a mountain of empty whisky bottles. She wondered if he had absorbed a germ into his system, though the patients mostly appeared worried and thin.

"I had treatment from Dr. Metcalfe in Freetown," he answered her silent questions, "and I thought, seeing I'm here, it was time to show some gratitude. I trade for animals and sell 'em to zoos. I've come to buy a white rhino from a chap in Port Andrew, but I've got a lot of surplus snakes and monkeys. Think Dr. Metcalfe could do with 'em?"

"Our zoo is fairly full."

"Pity to tip 'em into the sea," he said.

They were following a burgundy car which glittered in the sunshine.

"That's a lordly turn-out," he commented. "Who is she?"

"Madame Levalle, widow of the Doctor Levalle who started the Institute."

After that Phil ignored her garrulous companion, for she was sure that Sonya, having recognized jeep and driver, had purposely slowed. From the opposite direction ambled a mule team so Phil had to crawl and inhale oil fumes from the heated engine and swelter with the heat of the sun through the thin metal roof.

The mules clopped past and the road was clear. Phil pulled out. She was nearly level with Sonya and preparing to smile in passing when the saloon car leapt ahead. Dazed with heat and restricted breathing, Phil must have jarred the wheel. Her bumper grazed Sonya's rear mudguard.

"Bitch!" ejaculated Mr. Pringle.

Phil set her teeth and went on driving. Sonya's car sped out of sight, and when they reached the Institute it was parked outside the main entrance. Phil halted the box-car just behind it.

She was about to ask Mr. Pringle to take a seat in the hall when Charles, followed by Sonya, emerged from his office.

"Are you all right, Phil?" he queried at once.

"I told you she was not hurt," Sonya said tartly. "Her wretched driving has badly scratched my car. I am amazed that you should allow her to drive the jeep, Charles."

"I haven't yet got at what happened," he returned. "Take your time, Phil."

His perturbed frown cooled Phil's anger. Sonya did not know that she was sailing in three weeks or she would not have fabricated the incident. None of it mattered.

"It was my fault," she began.

"The hell it was!" burst out the little north-countryman. "I was beside the young lady. The red car was meandering about, asking for a dent. We tried to pass and she shot forward. The poor driver, Madame, was you!"

"Is this man a friend of yours, Miss Crane?" Sonya asked, dangerously polite.

"Only for this last half-hour," he inserted vigorously. "I came to see Dr. Metcalfe. The name's Pringle, Doctor."

Charles had his hand on Phil's arm. "I remember you, Pringle. Glad you called. Mind waiting?" To Phil he said quietly: "Go into the office. I'm so sorry about this, my dear. No, Sonya," as she stepped to the doorway, "I must ask you, too, to wait elsewhere."

"Be careful, Charles," she breathed, the dark eyes flaming. "Perhaps I have guessed more about Miss Crane than you think."

"In that case you will understand my anxiety." And he went in and closed the door.

Phil drank the bitter liquid he mixed for her and pressed a hand to her forehead. She gave a ghostly little laugh.

"I felt so well when I set out this morning. I bought my ticket to England and collected your goods. I offered Mr. Pringle a lift and we were going smoothly till Madame Levalle came from an avenue on to the Marine Drive. She saw me on her tail and slowed. There were some mules in front—they may have straggled and forced her almost to a stop. You know what it's like in the wagon in the sunshine —pretty overpowering unless you're moving fast. I . . . well, I—"

"I don't want an explanation, Phil. I can't help feeling a bit sick that this has occurred, but only for your sake." He sighed deeply. "As far as I'm concerned she can take over the Institute and run it herself. I'm through."

"Oh, no, Charles. You can't relinquish it now. I'll live somewhere else for my last three weeks. Make it up with Sonya. Tell her I'm leaving."

"She realizes that I despise her. I've fought to throw off her trusteeship and, with luck, this year should see the end

157

of it, but I'm lingering no longer to find out. I've had enough."

He accompanied her into the hall. Sonya was gone, but Pringle stood up with an expectant smile, and happily shook the hand Charles extended.

"You said I was to look you up if my travels brought me this way, Doctor."

"Two years since then," Charles reminded him. "Come out on the terrace for a drink and tell me what you've been doing with yourself."

Phil passed through the corridor to the kitchen, and bade two boys unload the box-car and carry the packages very carefully into the master's office. When the transfer was completed, she decided to go and rest, but instead of using the main stairs she went out the back way to stroll round to her private entrance.

With her foot on the lower iron step, Phil paused. Between the limbs of the frangipani she could glimpse the glistening nose of Sonya's car. The woman must still be hanging around somewhere. Poor Charles: he was not to evade his showdown. Slowly and thoughtfully, she trod the ornamental stairs, and at the top she paused again, while her heart jerked and righted itself. Sonya was straightening from a deck-chair on the balcony; behind her the french door was wide open, and Phil knew that her few possessions had been subjected to a brazen search.

She stayed holding the curving rail, fury so violent in her breast that her voice came thin and cracked.

"Did you happen upon what you were looking for, Madame Levalle?"

"No, but it is of no consequence." Sonya's sculptured smile had a devilish cast. "I was seeking confirmation that you are much less innocent than you appear, Miss Crane, but you are convicted by your own flush of shame. You will pack and leave this place at once."

"I'll do nothing of the sort. Go and make your demands of Dr. Metcalfe."

"You pride yourself on his protection, but nevertheless you will have to obey me. This is not a home for unmarried mothers."

Sonya's triumphant bearing had prepared Phil for the

epithet, but her knuckles tightened over the rail and a nerve stabbed hard in her throat. If her colour faded, her shoulders remained squared and her chin tilted.

A sudden rage brought Sonya very near. "You have done your best to entangle Charles. You preyed on him with your soft eyes and voice, you fawned for his pity. You have been hoping that he will marry you soon . . . very soon."

Phil was incapable of speech and fascinated by the quick, viperish movements of the other's mouth. Filled with a loathing so profound that involuntarily she recoiled from contamination, she yet could not lift her feet from the stone floor.

"You deny nothing!" Sonya spat at her. "In France we have a name for a woman like you—it is not a nice name. You would ruin a man's career for your own selfish ends, you would take pleasure where you find it and trap Charles into bearing the consequences—"

Phil, forced against the rail, had closed her eyes to shut out the fiendish features. The tirade ceased. She gave a little dry sob and groped blindly for the staircase. She heard Sonya's exclamation, felt a thrust at her waist, and fell. She screamed, and bumped headlong to the foot of the steps.

Sonya twisted and ran back through the bedroom to the upper corridor. Swiftly she descended to the hall and out to the deserted terrace. Cursing the wagon, she swung her car over the flower-beds and raced out to the Marine Drive.

It was Charles who lifted Phil and carried her to the bed in his surgery, and it was he who, some hours later, brushed the tendrils from her clammy forehead as she returned to consciousness.

With infinite gentleness he told her, "You'll soon recover, Phil . . . but you've lost the baby."

CHAPTER XXVIII

IN this life we are called upon to bear only what we can; which means, of course, that each blow should toughen and condition us for the next. Phil might pardonably have wondered why her refusal to leave Valeira a long time ago should have resulted in so much pain and loss; she might have carped at an ungenerous fate and been excused an occasional bout of weeping.

But this final experience had pierced too deep to be assuaged by tears. She emerged from it gallantly, but seamed with a bitterness that no amount of kindness from Charles could disperse. Nothing would ever hurt her again.

She accepted the offer of a spare room in the house of a Government official in town, and agreed to help Charles at the Institute three days a week. The passage to England was cancelled; when she decided to leave West Africa her destination would be the Cape.

Sonya had fled from Port Andrew. Her General hung on for a time, looking pathetically lost, and then he sold his furniture and sailed away, presumably to retire in Bath or Bournemouth.

For the present, Charles was content to sit back and watch Phil make what she would of the circumstances. When she was dining elsewhere he often slipped along for a talk with Jan Bridges, Phil's hostess, who admitted that though she liked Phil, there was no getting near her. Jan was plain and fair and forthright.

"You can't judge today's crop of young things by my generation, Charles. At twenty we kicked around the West End of London and considered ourselves frightful nuts. If we hardened we became cynics and saw no good in anything. Phil's isn't that sort of hardness. I'd rather call it a frank repudiation of sentimentality."

Jan had been told that Phil had "had a few knocks," but not the precise nature of the knocks.

"Phil's not like other girls," he said. "No one can help her much and she sets her own standards. The best part of her is buttoned up."

Jan shrugged. "That's true of most of us in this ruddy Hades. I'd hate to think some of my friends hadn't a better side than the one they show the world. What's the odds if Phil won't take men at their own conceited valuation? She's to be congratulated on having learned it so young."

"So long as she doesn't remain embittered over it," he agreed.

Phil could not have lived in a more agreeable and less demanding household. Much of the time Jan's husband was away on tour, and Jan was one of those women who are happiest in a crowd. So when Phil was at home she either had the house to herself or melted into a throng of perspiring guests. There were no awkward intervals with an older, inquisitive woman.

But one evening she came in to find Charles taking a lone drink in Jan's lounge. He had been away for three days, paying a routine visit to a hospital.

"I got in this evening to find my house-mate giving a poker-party," he explained, "so I walked round to see Jan. She seems to be out."

"You might have joined the game," she suggested, taking a cigarette from the crystal box on the table.

"I'm not a poker addict." He slid forward another chair and struck a match for her. "You're home early tonight."

"Sometimes I get a bit tired of the bunch—they're so raw." She stretched her legs in front of her and crossed her ankles. "It's strange how alike people are when lots of them get together. The half-dozen women go in for shredding reputations, and the men haven't an idea between them beyond drinking and gambling—and the girls they can't have. You'd think the tropics would breathe character into people."

"That's a quaint notion; the reverse is the fact. You're comparing Port Andrew with primitive spots on the coast where a man's personality isn't watered by convention and pleasure-seeking. I was afraid you'd soon weary of this place."

"It's the people, not the place. Or probably it's me." Unexpectedly she added, "Did you keep the appointment with Dr. Levalle's executor the other day?"

"Yes—I thought you'd forgotten. He gave me good news. Sonya's backed out of the trusteeship; she's returning to India. Next week I have a conference with the Health Department on the question of finance and extensions to the Institute."

"I'm glad. You've worked enough for it."

He placed an ashtray on the arm of the divan and said mildly: "They're showing a film at the club pavilion to-morrow evening. Could you bear to sit it out with me?"

"I promised to meet the others for dinner." She squashed out her cigarette and looked at him. "I'll put them off if you like."

"I do like," he said casually and, after a pause, he went on to describe the trip through swamp which he had just made.

Charles was not the type to take things for granted; nor was he in any sense a fool. He was well aware that it would be a long, long time before Phil could respond even slightly to another man, and he was also sufficiently acquainted with her sensitiveness to realize that his very knowledge of and sympathy in her trouble constituted a barrier to easy intimacy. But Charles had never taken any step in a hurry.

For that week-end the club had arranged many festivities and tournaments. The events at sea were prevented by heavy storms that transformed the waves into tumbling mountains and hemmed in the coasters close to harbour, but the intervals were plenty long enough for squash and tennis matches, a swimming gala at the pool, and polo. Jan Bridges, the indefatigable expert in parties of all kinds, particularly the card-playing variety, organized bridge and whist drives.

Charles attended most of the revels. In the comparative cool of early evening he partnered Phil in the tennis doubles, and on Saturday he drove her out to the races. On Sunday, both were of the party which picnicked at a native village down the coast and bartered tins of sweet corn and tablets of soap for metal pots and painted gourds.

He brought her home to Jan's house in good time to bath and dress for the special dinner at the club.

"I'll come for you at a quarter to eight," he said. "Get in half an hour's rest, if you can."

She smiled and nodded. Charles was always insisting on the necessity for rest.

Jan who was expecting some people for cocktails, used the bath first. Before Phil wallowed in tepid foam she arranged trays of savouries and bottles and glasses, and then, Jan, sheathed in silver tissue, took over.

"Go ahead and titivate, child. You did say Charles was coming for you?"

"At seven forty-five."

"In that case you won't mind if we clear off as soon as we've had drinks. I assured the club chef that I'd be on hand from seven-thirty."

Phil had reached her bedroom clad in a bathrobe when Jan's guests arrived. She heard them laughing and talking on the veranda in tones which anticipated hours of excitement. She herself felt no increase of temperature. Perhaps the club would be crammed, the dinner more appetizing than usual, the band augmented and livelier, but what else would distinguish this night from any other during the last six weeks? The same faces, the same feverish atmosphere.

Phil got into her dress, a new white one, low-cut and smooth over shoulders and hips. She tidied her hair, rubbed on a hint of rouge and lipstick, and stood back for a dispassionate view of her figure.

Charles was late, and she began hanging away the skirt she had worn earlier, and tucking soiled underwear into her linen-basket ready for the laundry boy. She came into the lounge and dropped her wrap on to a chair. The lamp was low, and the doors, wide to the night, admitted a myriad small sounds and the warm scent of luxuriant growth. She lit a cigarette and glanced at the clock. After eight. Maybe Charles had been called upon to doctor someone; his friends often preferred his advice to that of the practising medico.

Half-way through the cigarette his car drew up outside. Phil pressed the butt into an ashtray and swept up her wrap. He came up the path and leapt the steps. She was about to say: "Don't apologize, Charles. I haven't minded waiting." Then the pulled corners of his mouth, the way his eyes rested briefly upon her and swiftly lowered, drove conventionalities from her thoughts.

"A tragedy somewhere?" she asked at once.

"No." He stood before her. "It's . . . Phil, I've had a visitor."

"What sort of a visitor?" But she knew already.

"Julian Caswell. You've got to see him, my dear."

Her only sign of emotion was a catch in her breathing. "How did . . . he come here?"

"Through your lawyer in Cape Town. You gave the Institute as your address and he went there first. Everyone was down here at the club, but Johannes told him where I live. He demands to see you, Phil."

She moistened her lips. "He hasn't the right to demand anything. Where is he now?"

"Still at my house, alone. At first he insisted on coming here with me, but I made him realize that it would be hardly fair to confront you without warning. I promised to take you back."

The youth had gone out of her. She was an unflinching, bitter woman. "I never want to see him again. Drive me to the club, Charles, and then go home and send him away."

He put out a hand as though to take one of hers, but she avoided it.

"I'd spare you this if I could, Phil, but there's no way out for you. He hasn't sailed all the way from Valeira through electric storms and battering seas to be put off by a few words from me. He's here to see you and nothing will stand in his way. Hadn't you better get it over?"

"All he wishes me to know can be said through an attorney. I won't see him." In sudden fear, she whispered, "Charles, you haven't . . ."

"Of course not. That's between you and him. I certainly think he ought to know, but only you can tell him."

"I don't want his pity. I don't want anything from him."

Charles paused. Caswell had come too soon. She had not had time to live down the tragedy.

"I'm on your side, Phil, but I can't see how you're going to evade meeting him. It's bound to be painful, but you can make it final."

Her head lifted. Her jaw went taut. "You mean well, Charles, but you haven't the least idea what you're suggesting. Nothing . . . *nothing* would induce me to go to your house tonight for an interview with Julian."

A small noise at the doorway made both swing round.

"If that's true," said Julian quietly, "it's as well that I decided to follow Dr. Metcalfe."

CHAPTER XXIX

SHE stood there, very straight and pale, her hands unconsciously clenched at her sides. He advanced into the room and stared down at her, his bearing so unchanged that her tension snapped and she twisted towards Charles.

"Please take me to the club."

"You're staying here with me," said Julian, "unless you prefer that we use my taxi and go elsewhere. I must ask you to leave us, Dr. Metcalfe."

"No, Charles." Again she gathered her wrap. "I'll go with you."

Sternly Julian barred her way. "You've a lot to explain and quite a bit to listen to. None of what we have to say can possibly interest Dr. Metcalfe. Let him go."

Charles said: "He's right, Phil. I'll come back later." Curiously withdrawn, he went out.

Till the sound of his car had died neither spoke. Julian slipped his cigarette-case from his pocket but didn't open it. He let it slide with a clatter to rest on the small table near his knee. Almost imperceptibly Phil had put the width of the room between them. She still held her green evening coat clasped tight against her waist, but she felt calmer now. She even allowed herself a glance at his tropical suit, a glance which sped up over his set brown face, and gave her a hard courage.

"Supposing you have the first word," he said abruptly.

"I shouldn't know what to do with it," she returned.

"You could start with your reason for walking out on me."

"I could—if you weren't aware of it already."

Half-savagely, he came back at her. "The quarrel that evening at the bay was too puerile to break up what had grown between us. It was filthy luck that I couldn't come over, but I sent Matt. He gave me your message that you were happy and understood what was keeping me on the island."

So Matt had played goblin. For the moment his purpose eluded Phil, but it was all in the past and hardly mattered.

"A director's daughter, wasn't it?" she asked coolly.

"Phil! Did he let you think that?" Julian covered a few paces and turned. His voice no longer rasped. "No, you wouldn't have believed it. There was more to it than passing jealousy."

"Maybe I didn't trust you."

"That's a damnable thing to say after the way I neglected the plantation two days of every week to be with you. Circumstances kept us apart for three week-ends and on the fourth you vanished." He had sat on the back of the divan, facing her, his head thrust forward. "This is my side of it: I was on the island with guests in the house. We had a burst of tolerably good weather and I couldn't get rid of them. At last they arranged to go—on the evening of the day you left Goanda. At dawn next morning I made the trip, to find neat piles of things I'd given you and half a dozen words of scribble that made no sense. From Grenfell I learned that your first stop was Port Andrew, so I came right on."

"Here . . . to Port Andrew?"

"What else would I do? I'd never heard of Metcalfe or the Institute. I enquired at the shipping offices, ascertained that you'd landed and bought a ticket for Lagos, and then made the discovery that the up-coast boat had sailed, probably with you on board. By then my anger was gone; I just wanted to find you."

She had moved to the other side of Jan's piano and was examining a photograph. Resolutely, she ignored his final sentence. "So you travelled on to Lagos."

"I did, and drew blank. I hadn't any doubt that you were lying when you gave your destination as England. Cape Town was far more likely. I tried everything—shipping, the airport, railways. I sounded everyone I knew, and had to conclude that you'd booked out under an assumed name. There was nothing to do but cable your lawyer in Cape Town and return to Valeira."

"That was nearly six months ago."

"Six months of hell," he said grimly. "You've plenty to answer for."

The green coat was at her feet. She leaned against the wall, regarding him coldly. "You seem to have overlooked an important aspect of our relationship. I was no less free than you were. A mistress isn't bound in the same way as a wife."

Dark blood rose under his tan. "From the second I saw you this evening I've been expecting that. You've hardened, convinced yourself I'm just a brute who took all he considered himself entitled to and tired of it." He straightened and came round to the front of the divan, and she saw signs of strain in his gesture. "Can't we sit down? Hurling pleasantries across a dozen feet of space won't get us far."

She sank into the nearest chair, a straight one with wooden arms upon which her fingers curled. Julian had the divan to himself.

"Have you ever wondered why I married you?" he asked.

"You'd tried every other means of banishing me from the island, and we agreed that as soon as my money came through I'd get out of your way."

"Didn't it strike you that I might instead have arranged a loan with your lawyer, without your knowledge, to cover the three years' allowance till you came of age?"

"I don't think so," she said slowly. "You were older, and in those days I was unsure of myself."

Tight-mouthed, he added: "And you felt yourself falling in love with me. You may not have suspected it, but you were, just as I was falling in love with you. I'm not protesting that I married you for love. I didn't—not consciously, anyway. My attitude was dog-in-the-mangerish: I hadn't much room in my life for a wife, but the idea of your marrying someone else was disturbing. After we'd gone through the ceremony I found myself thinking too much about you. I had to remind myself constantly that you were simply a child being helped over a spot. That was why I never let you forget the terms of our bargain. I didn't know I loved you till the night I came across you knocked out under the ruins of my house."

Phil said: "It wasn't love—only a climax of pity—and, well, gratitude. It smote you suddenly that to want to save your possessions I must have . . . cared a great deal."

"Put what construction on it you like, but it made me

happy—and terribly afraid." His voice went low and vibrant. "For God's sake, Phil. Need I go on?"

She was clinging to the chair with all her nerves. "No," she managed, "you needn't." She had to pause. "A few minutes ago you dismissed the row we had last time we met as of no consequence. . . ."

He was on his feet, bending over her, his familiar fragrance about her head. "I was a swine, attempting to pin down the best in two worlds. At Goanda you were as safe as anyone could be in the tropics, and I could keep on at the plantation. Can't you see how I was placed?"

She was suddenly blazing angry. With an exclamation she sprang upright and jerked away from the chair, and from Julian.

"I can see your selfishness, your deliberate obtuseness where my feelings were concerned! Your heart was in the plantation and I was an agreeable tonic to be taken at the week-ends. The fact that we'd been before a registrar placated your conscience, but you made sure that no one else heard about it."

"For your sake more than mine. Why the devil d'you suppose I'm here tonight?"

"Your ego was flicked. Previously, you've terminated your own affairs, but this time the woman was inconsiderate enough to leave you high and dry."

He gave a harsh little laugh. "You seem to have spent the last few months loathing me. Maybe I deserved it, once. Possibly, even when we were living together at Goanda, I had qualms as to whether it could last. I haven't any now." His hands shoved into his pockets. Crisply, he went on: "You're going back with me to Valeira. We'll start properly, as husband and wife, and give it every chance of succeeding. When my time is up I won't renew. We'll go to Kenya."

She laughed, but not as he had done. Her hands pressed over her eyes and the sobbing laughter shook her body and came from her throat in tearing gasps.

He grasped her shoulders. "Phil, my sweet!"

But she wrenched away. "It's funny . . . horribly funny . . . your saying that . . . now." The ghastly smile streamed with tears. "It's too late. I've been cured of loving you. I don't want you, Julian. You can revert to being the plantation boss with no strings . . . or you can marry the director's daughter. I don't want you!"

She fled from the lounge to her bedroom, snapped shut the door and snicked the catch. Presently, in the darkness, her shivering ceased. She hung her dress in the wardrobe, slipped into a wrap and lay down, dazed with weariness and an excess of emotion.

Charles had decided to linger on among the revellers at the club. The noise and the demand for conversation were a necessity in his present mood. He had eschewed his reserved table for two, and inserted a chair between Mrs. Kevin and young Boyd at a larger, more central, one. Near by, Jan Bridges scintillated among her group of friends. At forty, she must be nearly the oldest woman in the room, yet her sparkle was undeniable and attractive. The other women seemed content to be members of the pursued minority.

The music from the salon teased his nerves. The saccharin sweetness, all rhythm and no body, penetrated the clatter of dishes and gossip like a cloying liquid. The earlier diners were dancing in there, revolving like puppets, yet he felt an urge to join them.

Though he was only half-way through dinner when Jan's party trickled out he followed. He danced, and later merged with a gang who were throwing dice. The game palled and he edged round the dancers towards the vestibule. In the wide archway he stopped, for standing at the bar, his beige suit conspicuous among the white evening wear of the other men, stood Julian Caswell. Charles was impelled forward.

Without expression, Julian made room for him. "What will you have, Metcalfe?"

"Whisky and water."

To the barman Julian said, "Two more whiskys," and he drained the glass he was holding.

"Staying overnight?" asked Charles.

"Several nights, probably. I've booked a room here. Is it always like this on Sundays?"

"Generally it's dead, but we've been having tournaments in every sport you can think of and this is an all-round victory celebration."

The drinks were brought and Charles filled up his tumbler with water. Julian, he noticed, was swallowing his neat. To end a silence, he pointed out one or two local characters.

Julian shrugged. "The mixture as before. Polo players, poker fiends, playboys and heat-drugged women. Got a cigarette? I left mine at . . ." he let it tail off.

Charles placed a packet between the glasses. He looked round, spotted Jan and beckoned. Smilingly, she detached herself and came over.

"Jan," said Charles, "this is Mr. Caswell. He's a planter at Valeira island. . . . Meet Mrs. Bridges."

Julian nodded. "How d'you do? Have a drink?"

"Thanks. Grenadilla—if they can run to it—with a splash of gin. What do you plant Mr. Caswell?"

"Cacao and oil palms." He spoke with a trace of irritation, his brows a thick, dark line.

"I ought to be horsewhipped for commencing an acquaintanceship so tritely," Jan answered equably, "but you must make allowances. We're all a little high this evening. If you've nothing better to do, come over to dinner tomorrow and see us in our normal state."

"I didn't quite complete the introduction," Charles inserted hurriedly. "You see, Caswell, Phil is living with Mrs. Bridges. It was Jan's house you visited an hour or so ago."

"Really?" demanded Jan, delighted. "Are you a man from Phil's brief past?"

"She's my wife," he said, and called a passing waiter.

Jan muttered something inaudible. Aloud, with the breeziest of smiles, she said: "Well, I shall have to leave it to you whether you come to dinner. I hope you will."

He instructed the waiter to take a hundred Turkish and a bottle of whisky up to Room Fifteen, signed the chit and finished his drink.

"Will you excuse me? I have to get my bag from the boat before I can turn in. Good night."

They watched him stride out on to the terrace. Then Jan exhaled deeply.

"So he's one of the 'few knocks'."

"He's all of them," Charles sighed.

"You knew he existed?"

"Yes, but not much more. She's turned him down or he wouldn't be here. I expect she's gone to bed."

"He's in love with her."

"With a man of his type you can't be sure, but I hope he's in torment."

Jan lifted her glance to his face. "That's not like you, Charles. Even without complications, love can be torture." Studiously inconsequent, she fell back on flippancy. "Did you hear him order a bottle of whisky. D'you suppose he's going on a private bender?"

Charles envied her knack of assimilating startling news with equanimity. However he tried to obliterate Phil, she kept insinuating herself into his thoughts. As if he were in her room, a detached and silent observer, he could see her writhing and sweating in her bed, turning her pillow for the balm of cooler linen, fighting the nightmare of revived pain.

CHAPTER XXX

MONDAY was one of Phil's days at the Institute. She awoke with a clamped head and the unpleasant taste of hunger, but neither deterred her from dressing and spending the usual fifteen minutes over her toilet. From habit, the house-boy had placed her breakfast-tray on the veranda table, and she poured some coffee and lit a cigarette while waiting for the box-car.

The jeep, with its native driver, appeared on the road, and it was with a sense of release that Phil ran out to it. All the way down the avenue and along the Marine Drive she stared through the window at the gardens and the whitecrested sea. Odd, how greedily the mind fastens on externals in times of stress.

The day lulled with its ordinariness. Phil sterilized and measured, entered records and consulted files. During the afternoon a couple of former patients looked in and Charles called her out to the terrace to have tea with them.

Both had been cured of recurrent fevers yet neither had made haste to leave swamp country. In fact, their errand today was to beg certain serums for their medicine chests. They were going up-river for a spell with the intention of ultimately working towards the Cameroons to collect ivory. They were aware that this part of West Africa did not abound with elephants, but no matter. Ivory was only an excuse, anyway.

With Charles, Phil wished them luck. As she re-entered the building a clock struck five, and the remnants of this morning's confidence seeped away. She almost expected Charles' detaining hand, his quiet, "You know he's staying at the club, Phil?"

"I . . . thought he might."

"If you're still in love with him, don't let pride keep you apart."

"He hasn't altered," she said. "There's no piercing him."

Charles was not surprised. "But he came here meaning to take you back with him?"

"He's never yet shirked a responsibility. That's why he won't remain here long. There's the plantation."

"What if you have to meet him every day for a week?"

Her shoulders lifted. "I'm prepared for it. I've only to be as hard as he is." A treacherous tremor came into her voice as she added, "Will you drop me at Jan's house on your way home?"

To be tensed against shocks is not to obviate the chance of their happening. When Phil walked up Jan's path that evening she saw men and women gathered on the veranda for sundowners. Julian appeared, and in her tiredness he seemed disproportionately tall and broad, and his touch on her arm burned.

"Come indoors for your drink," he murmured. "It's less hot and noisy."

Already he was accepted by these people. They used his Christian name and winked as he appropriated the only eligible girl and pushed her in front of him into the lounge.

Phil took the cocktail he offered and tasted it. She said, "I like to have it in my bedroom."

"I don't blame you. This is the sort of hayride I escaped

from when I left Kenya. Down that one, and I'll get you something else to drink while you're dressing."

She sipped, looking past him. "When are you going, Julian?"

"To Valeira?" he queried politely. "As soon as you're ready."

"I told you last night——"

"I remember every syllable, but you were strung up and I was naturally on edge myself. Any time during these last months you could have found me at Valeira, but for all I knew you might have been at the other end of the earth."

"It would have been kinder had you stayed on the island and acquiesced to the divorce."

"Kinder to whom . . . Charles Metcalfe?" he enquired, still pleasant, but keen-eyed. "Tell me something. Why did you choose to acquaint him with our marriage—him and no one else?"

"It slipped out in the early days, when I was unhappy."

"You haven't been unhappy since then?"

"I was getting along nicely, till yesterday."

"When I turned up and jerked you back to essentials. Charles Metcalfe isn't an essential . . . is he?"

"Not in the way you mean—no man is, not even you."

He relieved her of the glass and rocked it between finger and thumb. All traces of his smile had gone. "You haven't lost all feeling for me—you're not the type. You're afraid to come back in case I hurt you again. There's one thing you don't realize, Phil. I'm in your hands. I'm beginning to appreciate just how you felt when everything sweet in your life depended on me."

Phil had started to say, "You can never go back . . ." when Jan came in from the veranda, her brow pleated with preoccupation.

"Oh, hello, you two. Phil, do you know what happened to that pocket chess set? Jack and Clive are going on tour and they want to borrow it."

"It's probably in one of the drawers." Phil searched and produced the red leather case.

"Thanks." Jan grinned at them. "Did I interrupt an argument?"

"Certainly not," he said.

Her head went critically to one side as she surveyed them: Phil pale and defensive, Julian aloof, his mouth, for some reason, sarcastic.

"Give me five minutes' notice if you decide to move in with us, Julian."

With a wicked smile Jan went out to rejoin her friends. Phil could not look at Julian. She felt his hate of his position, his savage aversion from Charles and Jan, who, in the midst of a curious audience, were knowledgeable and avid for signs and hints.

She said, "My bath will be ready at five-thirty. The water will be covered with insects."

And he answered, "Run along, then," so coldly that she was annoyed with herself for crediting him with non-existent emotions.

In her room, Phil swung back the net and sat on the edge of the bed. She was tired with heat and work, and empty but for an insupportable ache for all she had held and lost. She knew that, as she understood the meaning and necessities of love, she would never love anyone but Julian. Even in the abnormal life he had chosen for them—five days of strain and two days of joy—they had come close in many more ways than the physical. With his invasion and possession of her the years between them had dissolved. Even Julian had ceased to mention them.

During the past months she had thought of him as something that had hurt her in passing and moved on beyond her orbit. Now he had come back and she was struggling for the courage to turn away from love. No, from the semblance of love, for there is no reality in a love that is nearly one-sided and dragged all ways by secrets and withdrawals.

There came a tap at the door. Expecting the boy, she murmured a weary "Come in." The tray entered first, carried by Julian. He sat it down on the dressing-table.

"I've swiped some sandwiches and coffee for you. Later on the boy will tip out that water and replace it with fresh."

He knelt and drew off her sandals, brought a soaked sponge and, regardless of the polished floorboards, bathed her feet, dusting them after drying with bath powder. Her will felt drugged. His crisp hair dipped near her cheek and she closed her eyes against the faint scent of it. When he had finished he poured some coffee. Phil had loosened the top buttons at the front of her dress for coolness before he came in, and now, straight and white-faced, slim legs dangling like a child's, she caught the collar together in one hand and accepted the cup with the other. He kicked a stool close to her knees and lowered himself to it.

"That damned Institute is too much for you. From today, Metcalfe will have to do without you. Try one of those sandwiches. It's newly-baked bread, from the freighter. That sea-cook certainly knows his job."

Phil put down her cup and took a sandwich. Julian bit one, and smiled at her. "Not bad?"

"Quite good. But I shan't want any more. Take them out again when you go."

"We'll spend tomorrow together," he said, "just lazing and talking. The next day I'll have the freighter loaded, and we'll sail on Thursday. These people mean nothing to us, Phil. We shall never see them again. Why should we care what they learn about us now?"

He wasn't going to let humiliation bite too deep, thought Phil. . . . Oh, why couldn't she allow him one decent impulse?

"I'm not going with you, Julian."

"You are, my sweet. If you weren't so tired I'd show you why. Maybe tomorrow. Some more coffee?"

She shook her head. "Please take the tray."

He leaned forward and she went rigid, scarcely daring to breathe. His forehead pressed into the flesh below her shoulder, and for a minute recollection of the old heavenly weight of him in her arms in the darkness swamped her senses.

With both hands she pushed him. Her voice almost croaked. "It's no good. I couldn't bear to live with you again. It took too much out of me—everything."

"Not this time. I love you. I did before, but not like this." His elbows dug hard into her thighs as his hands curved to her waist. His mouth spoke only inches distant from her lips. "I want you, Phil."

Her brain groped. No depth of sorrow in him for the agony he had caused her. He'd said: "I love you. I want

175

you," arrogant in the assumption that the promise of renewed remorseless love-making would conquer.

"I'm finished," she said dully. "Go out and find some other woman."

He moved backwards, stood up and thrust aside the stool. He seemed to fill the room.

"All right," he said. "Maybe I will!"

With fatal quietness the door snicked behind him. After a few seconds Phil pushed over the catch and undressed. She scooped the scum of insects from the tin tub with her washbowl and stepped in. The tepid water rose over her hot skin with a slight, salutary shock.

She used a towel and drew her dressing-gown around her, knotting the girdle. While she was hanging up the dress she had taken off Jan knocked, and she had to unfasten the door.

"Heavens, child, aren't you dressed yet? We're all ready to shove off to the club."

As an excuse for turning her back, Phil picked up her brush and began to draw it over her hair. "I've had a long day, Jan, and I'm not hungry. I'll stay here and go to bed early."

"Julian's going with us—it's his treat."

"It makes no difference."

"It should. There are several here who'll make play for him, and there's nothing so potent as a cold wife to make a man easy meat." She came a little farther into the room. "This afternoon I had the impertinence to ask Julian how long you'd been married. A year isn't fair trial, Phil, particularly as you've spent practically half of it apart."

"Some mistakes are evident the minute they're made."

"And some look like mistakes when they're only growing pains or the pinch of readjustment. You're still living at six months ago, when you quarrelled, or whatever it was. This advice may sound crude, but to bring your feelings up to date you ought to share a room for a night . . . it would clear the air of toxins."

Pausing, brush-handle tight in her hand, Phil said: "Your reactions are masculine, Jan . . . they're Julian's. You're captured by the idea of a man neglecting his plantation to chase after an erring wife. But I happen to know that the plantation is so well organized that it can easily run without him for ten days. You see if he doesn't get restive by the end of the week—if he stays that long."

"Stubborn little ass, aren't you? D'you think he's blind to the fact that you're still in love with him?"

Phil twisted to look at her. "No, but I'm not so far gone as to let him stampede me back to Valeira." Bitterly, she added: "He's never known defeat or suffering. Through him, I've made the acquaintance of both, and neither his protestations nor your well-intentioned advice will persuade me to stick out my chin for more. I'm sorry this should happen in your house, Jan, but for my part you needn't invite him again."

Jan sighed. "You're being an awful fool, darling, but I suppose you haven't enough years and experience to turn this situation to solid account. I'd forgive a man almost anything rather than smash my marriage, but I've had seventeen years of it, and grown a good many roots." She shrugged good-humouredly. "Cynthia Catenham seems to be Julian's choice, probably because she's at the other end of the pole from you. Dark, sophisticated and twice married—her husband's hundreds of miles inland. You may have noticed at the swimming-pool that she strips well. Good night, duckie."

Phil waited until tranquillity had settled over the house before opening her door to the side veranda. The sudden night had fallen, the air and sky were still. Trees had blackened, and stars, huge and crystalline, seemed suspended between them. Later there would be a moon to create near-daylight, and towards dawn the mist would steal its brilliance and smother everything, leaving a steaming world to be faced in the morning.

Tonight, the smell, a heavy perfume mixed with the ever-present exhalations of rotting vegetation, sickened Phil. It reminded her of the greedy eroticism of Mrs. Catenham, and for a moment brought Sonya Levalle very clearly to mind. Jan was proud of sending out roots, but Phil feared them. Once she had had illusions, taut heartstrings and terrible yearnings. Now she desired only that which was denied her: peace.

IT was good to be rocketing along the narrow road which rose and passed the convent and sloped down to twine through a forest of palms and casuarinas, with here and there a giant mahogany tree. Good to know that Port Andrew was behind one for eight hours or so.

The day out had been Jan's suggestion. On Friday she had received a letter from her husband stating that he hoped to be home within a week, and to settle for a good long spell. Jan, stirred from her complacency, averred that she must have action or perish of impatience. She threw out an invitation to all who cared to bring their own food, and borrowed an open two-seater for herself and Phil.

They had begun with a bathe at the pool, eaten a cold breakfast at the pavilion and piled into the chain of cars. Four men went first, "just in case it might be expedient to use a rifle", and Jan followed, with half a dozen assorted vehicles stringing along after. They were making for the lake which lay in a hollow in the jungle.

Julian was driving the third or fourth car, Phil wasn't sure which. He had hired one of the new town taxis for the day, and selected Cynthia Catenham and two junior Government officials as passengers. Phil had answered his "Good morning" at the pool, and sat as far away from him as possible at breakfast. She had been prepared for him to come to the picnic, for wherever she happened to be spending her leisure hours during the past week Julian had managed somehow to make an appearance. Quite often he was accompanied by the dark Cynthia.

Phil had schooled her temperature and stiffly ignored the drumming of her heart, but her nerves needed rest which they didn't get. When he walked the aisle in the dining-oom at the club and paused at the table she might be sharing with Jan or Charles, she felt her nerves stretch like keyed-up wires while her tones went leaden. If he dropped in at Jan's for a sundowner or morning coffee, a throbbing set up in various parts of her body. Her only consolation was that it couldn't last; nine days had elapsed since he left the plantation.

"When Brad's been home a day or so I shall give a party," Jan was saying. "The poor old boy must have been paralysed with boredom, spending so long palavering with chiefs and whatnot. It's a brute of a life. I went with him till I caught fever."

"Malaria, Jan?"

"Yes, rather badly. We'd been away two months and were on the last lap, only about seventy miles from Port Andrew. We stayed a night with an agricultural man and, because he was short of quinine, left him all we had except a dozen tablets, which should have lasted us in the usual five-grain doses till we got home. Storms held us up at a rest-house, and our quinine was finished, but we didn't worry. As you know, the effects of quinine don't pile up—it's the daily intake that does the trick. I went down with fever and Brad hadn't a thing to give me. He sent boys in various directions and eventually one came back with a doctor, who pumped stuff into me till I could talk sensibly. Brad's never taken me with him since then." Conversationally, she tacked on. "Drag off this shroud and give me a cigarette, Phil."

After puffing a ball of smoke Jan grunted contentedly. "When Brad's about the place we don't bother the club very much."

"You won't want me there. I can always go back to the Institute, Jan."

"It isn't as though you were intrusive," she answered, a remark which left the matter open.

It took half an hour for all the cars to park and by that time several of the men were enjoying a dip in the lake. None of the women hankered for the experience, for the water was incredibly deep and pitted with sinister eddies. It was also reputed to shelter strange fish and water-snakes.

Julian sprawled on the farther edge of the check table-cloth which was spread over the rugs. From her seat at a table Phil had only to raise her glance a fraction to watch him dispose of tinned chicken and ham, vegetable salad, a section of pawpaw, soft cheese with rusks and a very tall glass of whisky and lemon. She wished Charles were there so that she, like the other women, could have exchanged banter with one of the grounded males. She was thankful when Julian lay back with his hands under his head and stared at the sky.

Someone started the gramophone; an intolerably sweet Chopin walz. The chatter went on. Julian sat up and reached for his jacket. He tapped both pockets and turned to where the coat had lain, scanning the rug.

"Looking for your cigarettes, darling?" laughed Cynthia from another table. "I lifted them on the way up. Don't you remember?"

She slid down to the rug beside him, the gold case in her hands. Smiling into his face she lodged two cigarettes between her lips and steadied them to his lighter.

"Take one, Julian."

He did, and held it. Phil was tense, her spine a rod. She thought, if he smokes it I shall know he's staying to finish an affair with Cynthia; he doesn't like her, but he'd do it to punish me. He's fiendishly cruel.

Without haste, Phil made heaps of the plates on her table, grouped the glasses and cutlery and wiped the sweat from her hands with a napkin. The others were sleepy; some had already closed their eyes and a man caused sniggers by a full-throated snore. No one commented when Phil skirted the clearing and sauntered down to the water's edge. By casual sideways steps she came to the path through the bush which surrounded the lake.

Now she was climbing earnestly, dragging herself up from rock to rock, clinging with feet and fingers to the age-old roots which knuckled over ledges and vanished underground, to merge again a few yards distant. She heard the bubble and splash of a tiny waterfall, and found a smooth rock near it upon which to rest. She was drenched with sweat. Her pink silk dress was plastered flat to her back and hips, and moisture itched down from her temples. The hair near her head was soaked, and her blood pounded. She flattened some young ferns, lay upon them in a blankness of solitude, and went to sleep.

Phil roused uneasily from a dream. She couldn't have slept long, for the grey light among the trees retained the faint radiance of daylight and her dress had not completely dried out.

"Phil! Phil!"

So it had not been a dream. He had pursued and was calling her, his voice imperious with anxiety. Did he think he might have driven her to suicide?

She saw him first, his white shoulders mounting towards her, his forearm corded as he gripped and took his weight. He stopped and looked up, and she was sure the blue had changed to black in his eyes.

"You might have answered!"

She pushed aside the wisps which had dried against her forehead. "I was asleep."

He accomplished the last few yards and dropped on to a corner of her fern bed.

"So you were asleep," he said with brittle conciseness. "This is a hell of a place to choose for an afternoon nap."

"It's free, and private . . . or it was."

"Suppose you'd got lost, or broken your neck in the descent."

"One neck less," she returned.

From her dress pocket she extracted a comb and mirror, and for the next few minutes proceeded to make use of them. Suddenly he seized the comb and flung it wide, into the thick growth alongside the waterfall.

"You're developing delightful habits through associating with Cynthia," she said. "May I powder my nose?"

"You know damn well I wouldn't touch that woman."

"Why not? She's safe—impossible to harm."

He grasped her hair and caught back her head. "That's about enough," he said, and kissed her with such force that the salt taste of blood ran on to her tongue from inside her lip.

Her nails curled viciously into the flesh of his shoulder, and in the momentary weakening of his hold she pulled away.

"Strong, aren't you?" She felt round her neck. "I thought you'd decided that was one way of closing my windpipe for good."

"So did I," he savagely agreed. "What's got into you? Why are you behaving like something subhuman? If it's a

181

new line of self-defence, you're wasting the effort."

"However I behaved you'd view it in the light most flattering to yourself. Your ego won't allow you to believe that all I want from you is my freedom."

"If you weren't in love with me, you could have it."

"The response I expected. You used not to be so obvious, Julian."

"If we're throwing brickbats again, you used to have infinite qualities of charm and tenderness." He snapped off a fern frond and raised it to his mouth.

"Don't," she said sharply.

"Don't what?"

"Bite that thing. We're near water."

He threw it down and gazed at her with concentration. "What do you care if I trap a fever? One neck less."

"Oh, for heaven's sake!" she cried. "You came to fetch me, so let's go."

"No." He grabbed her wrist. "At last we're really alone. There's no door to admit Clever Jan or Brother Charles. Before we leave here I'll compel you to admit you love me."

She was becoming frightened; a heaviness gathered in her chest. "And how will you set about it?" she challenged. "With another tainted kiss?"

Like a smouldering fire splashed with oil, he blazed. With a wrench of her wrist he had her on her back and was pinning her shoulders into the crushed leaves. She saw his jaw angular against the arching spears of the palms, heard the violent shuddering of his breath in his lungs before he pulled her into a furious, ruthless embrace.

Phil's arm lay across her eyes. Blurred senses were attempting to focus. She smelled the sap of pulped stems, and cigarette smoke. Her mouth felt bruised, her throat parched, and behind her eyes stabbed scorching pain. She wished she were dead.

Ten yards down on a rock sat Julian, one knee drawn up to support an elbow. It was the spiral from his cigarette that smarted in her nostrils. Mechanically she brushed the bits from her head and shook out her dress. Hearing her actions he turned and came up.

Neither looked at the other.

"I'll go first," he said. "Avoid the tufts of grass, if you can."

The journey to the path was as brief as he could make it and was contrived without contact. But before they faced the blatant stares of Jan and her friends he halted.

"Phil . . . I'm not going to beg you to forgive me till I can forgive myself."

"I asked for it," she said tonelessly.

"You did, but that doesn't let me out. Nothing of that kind ever happened to me before in my life."

"Well, now you've something new to paste in your scrapbook."

"Don't, Phil. It hurts now, but we'll live it down because we love each other. I'll resign from Valeira at once. We'll get out of the tropics—go to Kenya and start our own plantation. . . ."

"We!" She gave a hoarse little laugh. "If I needed a prod to make my decision, I've had it."

Gramophone music, a martial piece, burst shatteringly upon the air. Quickly Phil swerved from him, and entered the clearing.

CHAPTER XXXII

THE next week was a busy one for Jan. Almost every day the Eurasian dressmaker came to fit new dresses, or deliver some shirts she had copied for Brad. The house had to be cleaned from end to end and the portable bath brightened with the only paint on hand—a sage green. The "bathroom", a cubicle attached as an afterthought to the back of the house and never used by Jan or Phil, abounded with spiders and scorpions, but as Brad refused to bathe anywhere else it had to be decontaminated and whitewashed. Jan managed to buy a mirror to replace the tarnished square on the wall.

In the evenings Phil helped with the needlework. After

cocktails the crowd moved off to the club without Jan, and the two women passed quiet hours together and retired early. Even Charles, who liked to look in for an hour after dinner if there was a chance of finding Jan at home, gave the house a miss this week.

On Wednesday afternoon Phil had been standing by in the lab. for the results of a blood test, when Charles came over carrying a steel chair.

"Never stand when you needn't," he said. "I thought you'd learned that by now."

"It isn't for long." She knelt on the cold leather seat.

"I suppose you're aware you're looking like death?" he said.

"Blame the blue light. It's merciless. I don't know how you stand it for hours on end."

It was like Charles to come unequivocally to the point. "When did you last see Julian?"

"On Sunday. I . . . imagine he'll be sailing soon."

"Why should you?"

"The plantation. There'll be trouble if he neglects it much longer."

"He doesn't care."

"Of course he cares." Her glance shifted from the rack of test tubes on the desk in front of them to Charles' aquiline features. "His trees are his whole existence. Anything else is by the way."

"Except you. You're making a frightful blunder, Phil, embittering both of you for ever. Is it fair that he should suffer for something of which he's entirely ignorant? Where's your sense of justice?"

She shrugged. "Passed over to his camp, Charles?"

"I met him last night at the club. He's coming to my house for dinner tonight. At least, he didn't say no."

"That's . . . rotten of you." Her face was fine-drawn and shadowed.

"My dear, you're seeing caddishness where none exists. We shan't talk about you. Since the first night he hasn't once mentioned you to me. I invited him because he's a man who can't drink himself stupid or make do with another woman. He's too brutally alive." He could see that

184

she wasn't listening, and added with blunt emphasis, "You're heading for a breakdown."

Phil waited silently for the card of details, and when Boyd brought it she took it straight to the surgery and handed it to Kevin. From there she went to the rest-room and discarded her overall. She washed and made-up at the swing mirror which stood upon a white enamelled table.

It was no good. Her time at Port Andrew was tapering inevitably to its close. She would like to board a vessel this instant and make for the horizon, leaving the pain and destruction where they belonged.

Strangely, like an omen, a letter for Phil had appeared in the hall rack since lunch time. The overseas mail often came late in the day. She read the suave note from the Cape Town lawyer—no allusion to his betrayal of her whereabouts to Julian—and placed the cheque in her bag. She was equipped for a year of wandering.

Jan's husband reached town late on Thursday night. In her bedroom, Phil heard the car and the sudden reverberation of Jan's bedroom door. The two seemed to have fused in the corridor. Jan muttered several muffled and agonized endearments and, after an interval, the man laughed: "Jan, you idiot. I've made you filthy!"

Phil had been reading in a chair. She jumped up from it, cast off her wrap and slipped into bed. Her mind kept travelling back to those sounds outside her door and the intimate murmurs from the kitchen. They were forty and still in love. Their life together had honesty . . . and blessed security.

Setting out for the Institute the following morning she saw the mud-coated car still loaded with Brad's gear. He and Jan would have a wonderful day pitching out the rubbish and hiding away his tent and holdall.

That evening Jan was full of Saturday's party; a house party, for Brad loved to entertain in his own home. Charles, who had driven Phil from the Institute, popped in to shake hands with Brad and have a drink.

"Tomorrow at seven-thirty," Jan told him gaily, "in honour of my returned spouse."

"Tomorrow? I'd kept open Sunday for you. I've a guest tomorrow."

"Bring him along."

Charles hesitated, glad that Phil had gone to her bath. "It's Julian."

"Oh. He doesn't seem to dog our Phil any more. He only comes when she's out. I thought he hated your hide."

"Not exactly. He's interested in tropical medicine—and we've driven out to the Institute a couple of times."

"Well, be sure to break into the party some time tomorrow night, won't you, but bring Julian at your own risk."

Charles and Brad patted each other's shoulders, and Jan laughed from pure happiness. Charles strode back to his car, the frown of self-accusation and worry settling back even before he had switched on the ignition.

He kept thinking, if that bitch Sonya had never met Phil . . . It was through me they met, my fault that Sonya grew jealous. I could have appeased her—if I hadn't been half in love with Phil. I gained from the woman's disappearance, but what about Phil? What has she ever got out of anything but a filthy deal?

After breakfast on Saturday, Jan and Phil went shopping. Brad started out with them, but the sight of other men directing their cars towards the polo ground was too much for him.

Jan said, "Put us down at the shops and go. If we're tired we'll cadge a lift."

"No, dear, I'll do the cadging." And Brad virtuously got out of the car. A minute later he stepped into another, and had the audacity to wave as he sped past his wife.

Jan grinned. "He's had the best out of this old bus, the humbug."

When, eventually, the car wheezed them back home, a light lunch was ready and Brad was waiting. It puzzled him how anyone could spend more than five minutes in Port Andrew's shopping centre.

From mid-afternoon the dinner occupied Jan. The cookboy had been known to wade through three courses without mishap, but for tonight she had planned five, and she meant to have them, perfectly cooked and perfectly served. *Hors d'oeuvres* were easy; they came from tins. Fish was tricky, especially the sauce, but the savoury and roast

186

presented the most ticklish tasks. The oven was small and eccentric.

By six, all but the last-minute preparations had been achieved. Because the boys were busy, Jan and Phil used the bath cubicle and returned to their rooms to dress.

The heat of the kitchen had withered Phil's energies; the bath brought out the usual sweat. Alarmingly spent, she sank into her wicker chair. Shakily, she stretched over and lit the lamp, and then put on her stockings. The dampness of her skin made it difficult to pull on her dress, and when at last it was smooth and fastened she felt sick with the struggle. To rub on rouge and lipstick was an ordeal.

"Brad's poured you a drink," Jan said, when Phil came into the lounge. "A strong one, like mine. Soak it up."

The whisky did help; it stopped the trembling and put a smile on her lips. She admired Jan's emerald and white gown, and told Brad that he should always wear an evening suit—it made him so handsome.

People began to arrive, and the women to exclaim over the flowers. Talk and laughter and blankets of smoke. Phil kept hoping that the next car would bring Charles, but at a quarter to eight they drifted in to dinner, and she realized with a dull shock that he wasn't coming.

She couldn't eat. Her table companions conversed with her and jested, and her answers, in a light, strengthless voice, appeared to satisfy. The meal hung on interminably. Toasts were the excuse to drink more, and yet more. This was going to become one of those orgies that guests recall with relish. A party wasn't a party unless you got cockeyed and flirted with someone's wife. And they took some getting cockeyed, these seasoned drinkers of the Coast.

In the general move, Phil went outside. The veranda filled and couples wandered down into the garden. From the open gateway, she looked up the avenue to the line of cars.

Another car tacked on the motley crocodile and a man got out. Tall enough for Julian, but lacking his width of shoulder. Would she ever get over the stupidity of longing for all men to be Julian?

She recognized Charles and hurried to meet him. Oddly, he slowed.

"We've had dinner," she said. "I was afraid you wouldn't come at all."

He had halted and bent his head towards her. In strained tones he asked: "Afraid? Why?"

"The drink and the noise. You make me forget them."

There was a pause.

"Phil," he said, "I came to see you, not for the party. Come and sit in the car."

She let him take her arm. "I don't like your voice, Charles." Panic surged into her own. "Is it Julian? He's hurt?"

"No . . . yes. Not physically."

He tucked in her dress and slammed the door. When he was beside her, a hand on the wheel, she saw him more clearly. He looked hard and drawn, as if he had just told a patient he had six months to live. Somehow she held back, waiting.

"I don't know if I planned it or not," he said, "but it was bound to happen if Julian and I saw much of each other. We've met every night this week."

"Yes?"

"I did tell you he was having dinner with me on Wednesday? Well, he came again this evening. At first I intended to make you a third. I suppose I cherished vague notions of throwing down a glove between you and leaving you to fight it out. Jan's party vetoed that, but I'd already invited Julian."

"Please go on."

"My house-partner is away for the week-end, so there were just the two of us. I had you on my mind so much that it seemed he must know . . . because, of course, you were even more tangibly in his thoughts."

"But, Charles . . ."

"That's the sort of person you are, Phil." He smiled at her. "We had a meal, and carried our drinks into my work-room to observe some cultures. After a while he became interested in an elevation of the Institute which hangs on the wall. I pointed out the dormitories, and then found myself saying: 'That end room was Phil's. We've removed the iron staircase since she fell from the balcony.'"

Her throat made a clicking sound, but nothing more.

Charles ended: "Julian said queerly, 'She fell the whole length from the upper floor?' Well . . . the wall was down and I plunged. I had to do it, Phil. I said, 'Yes, that's how she lost the baby.'"

"Oh, Charles!—in a dead little whisper.

She felt his arm about her and rested against his shoulder. He held her till the numbness lessened and she trembled with the renewed impact of pain, Julian's pain.

"How could you do that to him, Charles?"

He suppressed a spurt of triumph. "I was right. You'd told him nothing because you'd convinced yourself that he wasn't conditioned for suffering, that he couldn't stand the anguish of knowing."

"But the shock! What did he do?"

"Looked shot away for a bit, then he drained his drink and said good night. I came straight here."

"Will he have gone to the club?"

"I suppose so. Where else could he be alone, but in his room?"

"I can't bear to think of what he's enduring. Charles, I must go to him."

"Yes, my dear," he said at once. "You must."

The notes of a flute came thin and plaintive through the window. Charles shut them out with the roar of his engine, and they drove the couple of blocks to the club.

"I won't come in with you, Phil. Would you like me to wait?"

"No." As she tried to smile a nerve jerked at the corner of her mouth. "I'll see you tomorrow."

"I hope so. I'm sure this is for the best, my dear."

She left him and hastened along the drive and up the steps. There were fewer familiar faces in the lounge, for most of her acquaintances were at Jan's. A few men lolled at the bar and one of them called to her to come and have a drink. She shook her head and entered the small reception office. She consulted the key-board for the number of Julian's room. Fifteen; with a brass key on the hook below the number. Did that mean Julian had not yet returned?

Swiftly she lifted the key and backed out. She passed the bar, travelled the passage to the stairs at a casual pace, and quickened till she reaced the upper landing. Another endless corridor. Yes, this was the room. She tapped, heard nothing, and fitted the key into the lock.

She stole in and shut the door, pausing with one hand over her hammering heart to stare at the small tongue of light in the lamp. Perhaps it was a club custom to leave a glimmer in each bedroom. Such a bare, impersonal apartment; a netted bed and teak wardrobe and chest, a table near the window with two hard chairs pushed up, a grass mat and a rattan lounger. Half an inch of Julian's valise, the one into which she had shed tears while helping to pack, peeped from under the hem of the bedcover.

Feeling her knees weaken, she crossed and sat at the shadowy end of the lounger. Where could Julian be if not here or dulling his wounds with drink at the bar? Supposing he stayed out all night. Supposing a thousand things. A throttled sob forced from her throat.

His step, when it came, was spiritless. As she had done half an hour ago, he shut the door and leaned back on it for a moment. His face terrified her into stillness. Instinctively, she knew that he had walked fast and far, and found no relief. Before she could move he was at the chest, getting out a bottle and a glass. He hadn't seen her. The glass filled and he set it down on the table without tasting it. He dragged out one of the dining-chairs and dropped into it.

His fist slipped over the table and his forehead went down upon his sleeve. For a second she remained steely with the control she had imposed upon herself. Then she was on her feet at his side, extending a hand to touch him.

"Julian."

He looked up at her and drew a long, sharp breath as if he had been stabbed. She was conscious only of his haggardness and the blind darkness of his eyes.

She swayed nearer. He turned his face into her breast and contracted his arms like a vice about her.

Presently he stirred. "Phil . . ."

She stroked his hair. "Not yet, darling," she said softly. "There's plenty of time."

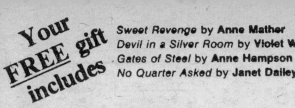